The Reckoning

Also by Jack Bodine
in Large Print:

Beginner's Luck: The Pecos Kid

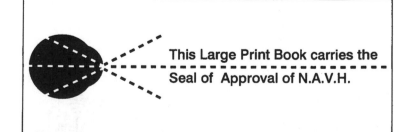

The Reckoning: The Pecos Kid

Book #2

Jack Bodine

Thorndike Press • Waterville, Maine

Published in 2002 by arrangement with Lowenstein Associates, Inc.

Thorndike Press Large Print Western Series.

The tree indicium is a trademark of Thorndike Press.

The text of this Large Print edition is unabridged. Other aspects of the book may vary from the original edition.

Cover design by Thorndike Press Staff.

Set in 16 pt. Plantin by Rick Gundberg.

Printed in the United States on permanent paper.

Library of Congress Cataloging-in-Publication Data

Bodine, Jack.
   The reckoning / Jack Bodine.
     p. cm. — (The Pecos kid)
   ISBN 0-7862-3828-3 (lg. print : hc : alk. paper)
   1. Braddock, Duane (Fictitious character) — Fiction.
  2. Large type books. I. Title.
  PS3552.O366 R43 2002
  813'.54—dc21   2001058200

The Reckoning

Big Al Thornton sat at a desk in his West Texas ranch house. He studied bills, letters of credit, miscellaneous legal documents, and saw somebody was suing him over a well. Sometimes he thought that the Bar T was running him, instead of him running it.

He was sixty, with thick graying hair, a square solid jaw, and blue eyes. He lit a cigar and looked out the window at a vast sprawl of rangeland, with weird spires and glyphs in the hazy distance. Cattle wearing his brand grazed as far as he could see, but sometimes he'd trade it all for the days when he'd been a cowboy, with no sleepless nights due to unpaid bills, sick cattle, marauding Indians, drunken ramrods, rebellious men, and that goddamned well.

Myrtle, his wife, entered the office, wearing a gray dress with a white apron. She was twenty years younger than he, a former schoolmarm. "There's a cowboy that just showed up, looking for a job. He's got that wary look, as if the posse'll arrive at any moment, but other than that — seems a decent lad. His name's Duane Braddock."

Branding season had just commenced, and Big Al tended to trust his wife's intuition. "Send him in."

His eyes fell on her hips as they passed through the door. Some women, when they get older, spread out like mattresses on legs, but Myrtle had retained a remarkable portion of what had drawn him to her in the first place, and caused him to renounce the freedom of the bunkhouse.

He tended to embellish bunkhouse life with a certain false glow. In fact, it had been arduous physical labor from dawn to dusk, and he'd lived with the usual odd lot of drunkards, gamblers, whore-masters, decent cowboys, and men on the dodge in filthy, broken-down bunkhouses. There was a knock on the door.

"Come in!" Big Al said.

A medium-height cowboy with black hair and long sideburns appeared at the entrance to the office. He wore black jeans, a purple shirt, and red bandanna, carrying a black hat with a silver concho hatband, and a gun slung low and tied down, gunfighter style.

"Have a seat," Big Al said. "How old are you?"

"Eighteen."

Thornton measured his broad shoulders, healthy arms, long legs. "Tell me about yerself."

"I worked at a ranch in Titus County — the Circle Y, before coming here."

"You from Titus County?"

"No."

Duane didn't offer more information, and Big Al could understand why Myrtle thought the cowboy was wanted in another jurisdiction. He looked ready to jump on his horse and ride away, but Big Al had been on the dodge himself a few times, and could understand the feeling. Besides, it was bad manners to ask too many questions about a man's past. "I need another cowboy, so you showed up at the right time. Give me a day's work fer a day's pay, and we'll git along fine. The bunkhouse is behind the barn, and the foreman's name's McGrath. Tell him yer hired."

Big Al returned to the papers on his desk as the interview came to an end. The newly hired cowboy arose from the chair and walked softly out of the office. In the parlor, he noted the Apache blanket hanging above the fireplace mantel. It reminded him of the monastery in the Guadalupe Mountains, where he'd been raised. Duane Braddock had been brought there at the age of one year, after his parents died under mysterious circumstances. He'd grown up studying, praying, and singing Gregorian Chants. Two months ago he'd been expelled, after fighting with another acolyte. Now he was a regular cowboy, planning to get married next Sunday.

Sometimes he thought that events were moving too quickly. His bride-to-be lived in nearby Shelby, where she was looking for work, too. They'd met in Titusville, where she'd been singing at the Round-Up Saloon, and he was drifting through, just out of the monastery. Now he was hopelessly in love with her, and it appeared that she felt the same way about him. It was a love match made in heaven, he believed, and he was anxious to see her again.

Duane walked toward Thunderbolt, his black stallion tied to the hitching rail in front of the main house. "Looks like we've got jobs," Duane said, as he climbed into the saddle. He rode toward the corral, thinking of his bride-to-be, and how happy she'd be when she found out that he had a job. She worried constantly about money, and there were certain other problems: she was thirty-one years old, and the difference in their ages, which had seemed insignificant at first, was becoming a widening gap. She could go from joy to despair within moments, and had a habit of throwing objects, often at him. But he considered her amazingly beautiful, and that was the glue that held them together.

As he neared the barn, he noticed a cowboy in a white hat riding toward him. There was something odd about him, and then, as he drew closer, Duane realized that the cowboy was a young woman in man's clothes. Duane wondered if his eyes were playing tricks on him; he'd never seen a woman dressed like a cowboy before, sitting tall in her saddle. She smiled as she passed, and he wasn't sure of how to respond. He turned around for another look, and noticed her rump bouncing up and down in the saddle. Suddenly she glanced backward at him, their eyes met, and both turned quickly toward their original directions.

Do they have female cowboys at the Bar T? Duane wondered. How come she dresses like that?

Inside the barn, sixteen-year-old Phyllis Thornton brushed Suzie down carefully, looking for sores, insect bites, and burrs. The barn was cool, its timbers creaking in the wind, and Big Al's daughter wondered who the stranger was, for she seldom saw men her own age at the ranch. There'd been something haunted in his eyes.

Phyllis frequently found herself thinking about males. She was becoming old, while most of her friends were married, some with children of their own. But the only men she saw were her father's cowboys, either too ancient, not particularly appealing, or afraid of the boss's daughter. She'd probably have to settle for one of the supposedly "nice" sons of another rancher, or become an old maid.

She strolled toward the main house like a cowboy in her high-heeled boots with pointy toes. She had a pert nose, robust breasts, and straight black hair cut just beneath her ears. She entered the house, and made her way down the hall to her father's office.

He was bent over his desk, working at ranch business, and she felt sorry for him, knowing he'd rather be on a horse than sweating over columns of numbers. She stood in the doorway, cheeks bronzed with the sun, hat and gloves in her hand. "The ramrod says he'll need at least two more weeks," she said. "The herd has scattered farther than he'd thought."

Big Al frowned. "Every time I ask him, it's another two weeks. Did he say anythin' about injuns?"

"They've seen Comanches, but no trouble so far. By the way, I just noticed a stranger on the way to the corral. Have you hired him, or is he a horse thief?"

Big Al's memory wasn't clear, but then he remembered. "Yes — Braddock. He's not a horse thief, far as I know."

"I'd say that he just got out of jail."

"I don't care where he came from — long as he does his job. Now run along and see if your mother needs any help."

He heard her boots recede down the hallway, then returned to his documents and ledgers. If any lowdown son of a bitch ever lays a hand on her, he'd better be ready to die.

Stale tobacco smoke permeated the bunkhouse, discarded animal bones littered the floor, and drawings of semiclad females in provocative poses were nailed to the walls. Duane found an empty bunk against the back wall, and heard a faint gnawing sound, as if tiny teeth were chewing the timbers of the building.

He unrolled his blanket, and inside were another pair of jeans, a few shirts, and extra cartridges for his Colt. He rolled a cigarette, sat on the edge of his bunk, and continued to hear tiny creatures sharpening their teeth on the dirty old shack.

Duane felt dispirited by its rundown ambiance, and fondly recalled the monastery in the clouds. The monks, priests, and orphan boys had cleaned it constantly, and the air had smelled of incense mixed with ponderosa pines. But Duane had become increasingly curious about the outside world, and then one of the other boys had insulted him in an especially painful way. Duane punched him, leading to the all-out fight that had got him expelled by the old abbot. That catastrophe occurred about two months ago, and since then he'd been in numerous fistfights and shootouts. He didn't like to be pushed around, and was unable to turn the other cheek to the bullies and outlaws of the world.

He heard the scurry of feet, then an enormous rat crawled out from underneath a bunk. The monster twitched his tail nervously as he chewed a lump of something on the floor, and failed to see the shadow of death above him. Duane drew his Colt, thumbed back the hammer, and pulled the trigger. The bunkhouse echoed with the shot, his hand kicked in the air, and smoke billowed around him. The rat lay dead, the top of his head blown off, blood splattered along the splintered floorboard.

"What the hell's goin' on in thar!" A spindly old man with a white beard appeared, carrying a double-barreled shotgun.

"Just killed the biggest rat I ever saw," Duane replied.

The old man drew closer, and his ragged brown cowboy hat had the front brim pinned to the crown. "We got more rats than we know what to do with. Next time we go to town, we got to find us a cat." The old man focused his rheumy eyes on Duane. "Don't reckon I ever seed you afore. Who the hell are you?"

"Duane Braddock. I just got hired."

"I'm Seamus McSweeny, the cook. Welcome to the Bar T. Hungry?"

Duane grinned. "I could use a meal around now."

"Well, come on to the kitchen. I'll give you some stew, and I've got biscuits left over from dinner."

"I saw a woman dressed like a man a few minutes ago. Does she work here too?"

McSweeny looked askance at Duane. "Hell no — that's Miss Phyllis, the boss's daughter."

"Why does she wear men's clothes?"

"You ever try to ride a horse in a dress?"

The kitchen was a stove, some cupboards, and a washbasin in a small offshoot of the main bunkhouse. Duane knew that the new man would be the butt of everybody's jokes, but was prepared for the worst. "What's the ramrod like?" he asked.

"Not a bad feller when he's sober. We work hard, but it's a good spread, and we're proud of her."

"Is Phyllis married?"

McSweeny winked. "You a-gittin' ideas?"

"She's awfully pretty."

"You better forget about her, 'cause her daddy don't want her to marry the likes of us. He was a cowboy onc't hisself, and knows what he's pertecting her from."

"He doesn't have to worry about me," Duane said. "I've got my own woman back in Shelby, and we're getting married as soon as we find a preacher."

"I've been married a few times," Seamus McSweeny allowed. "Never was so unhappy in all my days. Nag, nag, nag all the damn time, and if'n it ain't one thing, it's another. I don't know whar they larn it from, but I'd druther fight a Comanche than a woman, because a Comanche might kill you, but at least it's quick and clean."

Duane Braddock's bride-to-be, tall, blond Vanessa Fontaine, studied her face in the mirror. In a few moments she'd meet the citizens of Shelby, who were considering her for the position of schoolmarm, and she wanted to look perfect. The town had never had a

16

schoolmarm before, as mothers alternated in the position, but none had sufficient time, and teaching had been erratic. Now Vanessa had to convince them to hire her, provide room and board, and pay a small salary.

She marveled at the current twist of her chaotic life. Somehow, against common sense, she'd fallen in love with a man thirteen years younger than she, who had no money, and she'd actually run away with him into the nether reaches of Texas!

What have I done? she sometimes asked herself. Somehow, Duane Braddock made her feel alive for the first time since her former fiancé was killed at Gettysburg. She'd vowed to be faithful to Beauregard's memory forever, but now, eight years later, she was marrying Duane Braddock.

She couldn't explain it to herself, and had given up trying. She'd come to crave him desperately, as he appeared to crave her. Sometimes she thought she'd gone mad. They spent most of their time in bed, but she couldn't resist him, and he couldn't resist her. God only knows how it'll turn out, she mused.

Their plan was for both to work, and save money for a ranch. But he'd earn practically nothing as a cowboy, and she'd be paid even less as schoolmarm, provided the local townspeople hired her, and she wasn't sure that she could manage a roomful of unruly children, never mind impart knowledge to them.

Vanessa had led a pampered life until the final year of the war. A former Charleston belle, all her wealth and most members of her family had been wiped out by Sherman's march to the sea, and Reconstruction was too harsh a pill for her to swallow. She had no money and no friends among the carpetbaggers and scalawags who'd taken over the government, so she'd drifted West, and earned her living singing old Confederate Army songs in saloons where war veterans congregated. A large number had fled to Texas, and she'd followed them all the way to Duane Braddock at the Round-Up Saloon in Titusville. And now she was marrying him, although they barely knew each other.

There was a knock on the door. "Come in."

Mrs. Gertrude Gibson, wife of the man who owned the general store and house where Vanessa was residing, stood in the doorway. A jolly woman with fluffy white hair, wearing glasses and a long navy blue dress, she said: "We're ready to see you, dear. Follow me, please."

Vanessa felt as if she were going before a firing squad, as she followed Mrs. Gibson through the small unpainted house, a far cry from the opulent old family plantation. They passed a series of small rooms and narrow corridors, finally arriving in the main room of the general store, where eight people had gathered among canned goods, bolts of cloth, bridles, ranch hardware, and bags of beans. Mrs. Gibson introduced Vanessa to Mrs. Phipps, the blacksmith's wife; Mrs. Longwell, the blacksmith's assistant's wife; Mrs. Boylan, wife of a jack-of-all-trades, and finally, last but not least: the baldheaded, sleepy-eyed Parson J. Whittaker Jones.

"Shelby's got eight children," declared Mr. Gibson, the stout, florid-faced only merchant in town. "We've often talked 'bout advertisin' fer a schoolmarm, but we din't 'spect someone to come here at her own expense, and then maybe git turned down. We want the best fer our children, not a schoolmarm who can barely read and write herself. Would you mind telling us *your* qualifications, Miss Fontaine?"

Vanessa stood in the best available lighting, her back to the window, sunlight surrounding her head with a halo of gold. She'd expected the question, and rehearsed her lines in advance.

"I may not be the best candidate," she began modestly, "but I know much more than merely how to read and write. I was educated at Miss Dalton's School in Charleston, and have read many of the world's great classics. I've also performed research on a variety of subjects, and wrote essays reporting my findings. My professors were among the best available in the South, and my piano instructor had been a friend of Franz Liszt."

Mrs. Phipps wrinkled her long skinny nose. "Who?"

Parson Jones replied nasally, "Didn't he run off with somebody's wife?"

"I was referring," said Vanessa, "to his professional competence."

The parson's coal-black eyes glittered with barely concealed fanaticism. "Your background is most impressive, Miss Fontaine, but there's another matter to which we must attend. As you know, a schoolmarm is expected to set a high example of morality to the children. Here I'm afraid that I must be frank with you. We're aware that you've come to town with a . . . certain young man with whom you aren't married — is that correct?"

"We intend to get married as soon as we locate a parson, and it seems as though I've just found him. My fiancé will be here on Saturday night, and perhaps you can do the honors Sunday morning?"

The parson smiled, for he knew that a financial contribution was headed his way. "I'd be honored, my dear," he said with an obsequious bow. Vanessa looked each of them in the eye, as though she were onstage at the Round-Up Saloon. "I've had a thorough education, and I remember well the lessons that my own teachers used. I can promise you a hardworking, honest effort to educate your children."

Mr. Gibson smiled. "Well, I guess it's time for us to vote. We'll have to ask you to return to your room, Miss Fontaine."

Before Vanessa could leave, they heard a commotion on the street. Mr. Gibson yanked a pistol out of his belt, and rushed to the window. Parson Jones took down a double-barreled shotgun. Massed hoofbeats came to their ears, as if a large number of riders had come to town, possibly a Comanche war party, or a roving band of outlaws. Mr. Gibson opened the front door and peered down the street. A smile creased his face, as he declared: "It's the army!"

Everyone rushed outside, and stood on the dirt sidewalk in front of the store. Dust-covered blue uniforms approached, yellow bandannas fluttering in the breeze. A tall brawny officer rode in front, beside a private carrying a guidon flag of the Fourth Cavalry.

"Sure is good to see them boys," said Mrs. Phipps.

"Fer a moment, I thought they was injuns," added Mrs. Longwell nervously.

"Hope there ain't no trouble," offered Mrs. Boylan.

The detachment drew closer, and Vanessa could see the blond mustache of the officer. He sat erectly in his saddle, and raised his glove in the air. "Detachment — halt!"

The soldiers stopped in the middle of the street, and the officer climbed down from his saddle. He was six-feet-four, and wore his wide-brimmed cavalry hat slanted low over his eyes. "I'm Lieutenant Dawes. We were wondering if you've had any problems with Indians lately."

"Are they on the warpath again?" Mr. Gibson asked.

"Do they ever go off the warpath?" Lieutenant Dawes replied dryly. "We've been ordered to set up an outpost here, until further notice. Hope that won't be an inconvenience."

"This territory won't be safe," Gibson said, "until we kill all the injuns."

"If my men cause any difficulties, I hope you'll let me know." Lieutenant Dawes remounted, wheeled his horse, and led the detachment out of town.

"Nothing I'd druther see than the cavalry," Gibson announced, as he headed back to the general store. "Hope they stay permanent, so's we don't have to worry no more about them goddamned Comanches."

Vanessa stood near the door, and observed the lieutenant's perfect riding posture, elbows close to his sides. He looks like a West Pointer, she mused. I wonder if he was one the bluecoat bastards who burned old Dixie down?

The cowboys filed into the bunkhouse, groaning, cursing, grumbling, and burping. One of them asked, "What's fer supper tonight, cookie?"

"Same as last night," retorted the man in the kitchen.

Another voice joined the conversation. "I'm so goddamned sick of beef, I'm ready to kill somebody."

Duane sat on his bunk, trying to evaluate what kind of men they were, and how dangerous. One burly fellow with light brown hair stopped at the next bunk. "Who the hell're you?"

"Just got hired today. Where's the ramrod?"

"In his cabin out back."

Duane strolled to the door, and tried to look rough, but they appeared skeptical of his very existence, and he figured there'd be a rattler in his bunk when he returned.

Long shadows crossed the backyard as the sun sank toward red-toothed horizons ablaze with flame. At least nobody tried to shoot me in the back *yet*, Duane thought, trying to be optimistic. He crossed to the rear of the bunkhouse, and came to a small cabin adorned with the sun-bleached skull of a steer. Duane knocked on the door.

"Who's 'ere?"

"Big Al hired me this morning."

Duane heard a curse, and then the door was opened by a mean-looking man approximately Duane's height, but with a flowing brown mustache and a substantial gut. "What's yer name?"

"Duane Braddock."

"Where'd you work afore?"

"The Lazy Y, near Titusville."

McGrath had the jowls of a bulldog, and suspicious eyes. "Seems I heard of a Braddock once."

Duane spat casually at the ground. "There was an outlaw named Joe Braddock awhile back, but he was no kin of mine."

"Got hung, I believe."

"That's what I heard. Do you know where?"

"Cain't say that I do." McGrath looked at him disapprovingly. "It's brandin' time, and we work hard here. I'll expect you to keep up."

"I'll do my best, sir."

Duane touched his forefinger to the brim of his hat, as the door slammed in his face. In the distance, the half-moon floated in the sky like a Viking ship, the heavenly sea ablaze with stars. Duane thought he'd walk to settle himself down. He'd just met someone who'd heard of his father, and wondered how to wheedle more information.

Duane had come to the Pecos Country with one principal purpose: to find out what happened to his parents. According to records in the monastery office, Duane's father had been hunted down and killed by unnamed lawmen, while his mother died shortly thereafter of a strange disease. They hadn't got married, and evidently she was a dance hall girl, probably a prostitute. Duane was humiliated by his illicit parentage, and it had caused the fight that got him thrown out of the monastery.

His thumbs hooked in the front pockets of his jeans, a cigarette hung from the corner of his mouth, and his hat perched on the back of his head. He strolled in the moonlight, wondering if his father had been a cattle rustler, or a back shooter. All Duane could remember was a black mustache, the aroma of tobacco and whiskey, and a certain bluff devil-may-care attitude toward the world.

He'd suckled at his mother's breast for a year, then she was gone. He didn't even know her name. He often wondered what she was like, and how much of himself was hers alone. Whenever he thought of her, he had vague recollections of warmth, comfort, delicious perfume, and blond curls. But what can a one-year-old remember, and how much was wishful thinking? Duane intended to track down news of her, too.

If lost parents weren't enough to occupy a man's mind, Duane also had his bride-to-be in town, subject to possible temptations. They'd lived together nearly a month, and he'd seen her in the wan dawn light like a tall farm girl with an impossibly long neck. Her nose had a strange bend that he hadn't been aware of when they'd first clawed at each other's clothes, and she was terribly cranky at times. Sometimes, in harsh light, she looked awfully old.

He'd discovered that his great golden goddess was merely a person, yet he couldn't forget her Mona Lisa smile, the eyes that drilled into his soul, the crown of golden hair, regal bearing, he could go on and on, remembering her advantages, not to mention her assets, nobility, courage under pressure, wit, cosmopolitan charm, etc. His heart swelled with love, and he couldn't wait for Saturday night, when he'd writhe in her arms, and to hell with the rest of the world.

He heard something, and stopped cold in his tracks. Vanessa Fontaine vanished, his hand lowered toward his Colt, he spit the cigarette out of his mouth and stepped on the red dot. The faint sound of footsteps came to him, he hauled iron, and thumbed back the hammer.

A woman stepped into a shaft of moonlight, hands clasped behind her back, head bowed in thought. Duane stood like a statue as she strolled closer. "Miss Thornton?"

She looked up suddenly, yanked the Remington out of her belt, eyes widening with surprise.

"I saw you walking," he said with a grin, "and thought I should announce myself, so you wouldn't think I was a Comanche."

He couldn't help noticing her mouth, which reminded him of a rosebud, compared to the relatively thin-lipped Vanessa Fontaine. He also checked her bosom development, much more substantial than that of his soon-to-be wife.

She recovered quickly, and the rosebud became a smile. "You're the new cowboy that my father just hired today."

"Duane Braddock," he replied, removing his hat politely. "I saw you this afternoon, and at first thought you were a man."

"I was returning from an errand for my father, and had ridden a fairly long distance."

"Weren't you afraid of Indians?"

"You can't stop living because of the Indians. I remember seeing you this afternoon, too, and thought you were an owl hoot. Are you?"

"Not as far as I know. How long have you lived here?"

"Just about all my life. What are you from?"

"Long distance from here."

They gazed at each other in the moonlight, and he realized that she was a fresh ripe fruit waiting to be plucked, but he was engaged to Vanessa Fontaine.

He heard her say, "If you're not afraid to work, you'll get along all right. My father and mother started with a little shack, and built up the Bar T from there. We're not owned by Eastern or British investors."

"I like to work hard," Duane said with a grin. "Builds up the muscles."

Their eyes shimmered in the darkness, and a coyote howled mournfully in a far-off cave. Duane felt drawn to her, then remembered Big Al.

"Got to get up early tomorrow. Nice meeting you, Miss Thornton."

"Call me Phyllis, and I enjoyed talking with you, too, Duane. Good luck."

She headed back to the main house, leaving Duane shrouded in shadows. Duane had little experience with women, but was impressed by her womanly glow. He experienced lecherous thoughts, as he headed toward the bunkhouse. A man has to stay on course, otherwise he becomes a fool, chasing every skirt in sight. I will never be unfaithful to Vanessa Fontaine, not even in my mind.

Clayton Dawes climbed down from his horse in front of the moon-dappled general store. Lights shone through the window, carving his sturdy profile as he threw his reins over the hitching rail. Then he adjusted the service revolver on his hip, and opened the front door.

Next to the iron stove, a group of men sat at a round table, playing cards. Coins adorned the top of the table, with a bottle of white lightning. "Evening, Lieutenant," said Mr. Phipps, who looked like a praying mantis playing poker.

Lieutenant Dawes nodded as he made his way to the counter, where Mr. Gibson sat, reading an old Austin newspaper. "What can I do fer you?"

"My men'll start drifting in here later, and choirboys don't generally join the army. If they give you any trouble, just call my name. You can expect to sell a lot of whiskey, though, and by the way, could you pour me a glass?"

"Hope your boys don't shoot the place up, like the last bunch from the Fourth Cavalry what passed this way."

"Can't promise you that," Lieutenant Dawes replied, as he placed a coin on the counter. "They're a wild bunch of boys."

Gibson filled a tumbler half full of whiskey. "Injuns've got everybody in this town scared to death. We pay taxes just like everybody else, and seems to me we're entitled to army protection."

"The decisions are made in Washington, and I'm just the junior officer who gets the dirty jobs." Lieutenant Dawes scratched his bronzed cheek, and added casually, "Thought I saw a new face today — tall blond woman, late twenties. Who's she?"

Gibson chortled roguishly. "You've got an eye for a pretty face, Lieutenant — I can see that. She's Miss Vanessa Fontaine, our schoolmarm — gittin' married on Sunday."

"Who's the lucky man?"

"Duane Braddock, a cowboy. Do you think General Sheridan would read a letter if I sent it to him?"

"You'll have a better chance if you send it to your congressman."

"That scalawag bastard?"

Gibson rejoined the poker game, while Lieutenant Dawes leaned his elbow on the counter. Twenty-eight years old, a West Point graduate, he feared that he'd be a first lieutenant for the rest of his life, because promotions in the frontier army were practically nonexistent, and an officer was considered lucky if he could merely hold onto his commission. If that wasn't enough, he could end up with a Comanche arrow in his gullet. Sometimes he thought of resigning his commission, and becoming an engineer, but what if he couldn't find a job? His father was a retired general, and wouldn't support an unemployed son indefinitely. Lieutenant Dawes liked the army, but felt strangely unfulfilled. It'd be a lot easier if I had a wife to keep me company, he mused, as he sipped white lightning.

Duane approached the bunkhouse, and all the lights were out, the other cowboys already in bed. Tomorrow he'd begin his first day of work, but found himself thinking about Phyllis Thornton instead. If I weren't getting married, I sure could get interested in Miss Thornton. She's around my age, and we understand each other.

He entered the dark, silent bunkhouse, and moved toward his bunk, passing wheezes and snores, plus odors of whiskey, feet, and armpits mixing with remnants of supper. Finally he arrived at his bunk, and was about to remove his boots, when he remembered that there probably was a rattlesnake beneath his blanket, because he was the new man in the bunkhouse.

He took a corner of the fabric, pulled back suddenly, and revealed not a rattlesnake, but a dead rat lying on the mattress. Duane froze, as full implications struck. He knew that he should throw the rat out the door, and go to sleep like a good cowboy. He was aware that the rat wasn't personal, and they'd do it to any new cowboy. He debated with himself over what to do. If he punched one of them, he could be fired before his first full day began, but sometimes a man had to make clear at the outset that he wouldn't tolerate rudeness.

He smiled bitterly in the darkness, because he knew that they'd never stop putting rats in his bunk, or spiders in his food, until he drew the line. "Who's the son of a bitch who did this!" he demanded.

Nobody moved, but Duane knew that they were all awake, waiting for his reaction. His anger stoked hotter, because they were ignoring him.

"He's afraid to show his face," Duane continued, "because he's a coward, in addition to being a son of a bitch!"

"Go to sleep," somebody growled from the far side of the bunkhouse.

"I'll make the coward *eat* this rat!" Duane screamed, as he began to lose control.

A snore came from a few bunks away. The bunkhouse became placid again. Duane wanted to battle for his reputation, but no one would accommodate him. His face grew red with embarrassment, he heard a giggle, then a guffaw.

"If I ever find out who you are," Duane said, "you'll regret the day you ever set eyes on me."

He picked up the rat by the tail, carried it outside, and threw it onto the sage. Then he washed his hands and face in the basin, and dried himself with the common towel that stank of sweat and cattle. He tried to calm himself, but his blood was up. At least I let them know that I'm not tolerating any more of their stupid pranks.

He reentered the bunkhouse and walked down the aisle to his blanket. His plan was to roll it up and sleep on another straw mattress, but as he drew closer, he saw something dark and ominous lying where the previous rat had been. It was, of course, another rat, and Duane thought the top of his head would blow off.

He knew that he should throw the rat out the door, and go to bed. They couldn't have an endless supply of rats, but it seemed a disgusting insult, and he had a thin hide. "I wouldn't think much of a man," he said in a deadly voice, "who's afraid to show his face. He must be a sneaky little back shooter, and his mother was probably a polecat. Or maybe he's just a rat himself, hiding beneath his blankets."

"Yer makin' a big thing out've nawthin'," complained a voice in the darkness. "We all got to work tomorrow."

Duane spun toward the direction of the voice. "Nobody's sleeping until the turd who did this steps forward. Was it you?"

"It was me," said a new voice.

Duane peered toward the front of the bunkhouse, where somebody was rolling out of bed. Duane moved toward him and saw a tall, slim cowboy with curly red hair and a prominent nose.

"You the one who put the rat on my bed?"

"So what if I was?"

Duane threw the dead furry creature at him, but the redhead ducked, and the rat slammed into the wall. Duane moved closer to the redhead, who stepped into the middle of the aisle.

Somebody said, "Take it easy, boys. Fer Chrissakes, it was only a couple of rats."

Duane knew that he'd just heard the voice of reason, but if he backed down now, he'd get rats in his bed for the rest of his life. Duane's tormentor was several inches taller than he, with a longer reach, and perhaps ten pounds more, or in other words, a string bean weak around the middle. Duane had participated in many schoolyard brawls at the monastery and had continued that tradition since coming into the secular world. His spiritual advisor, Brother Paolo, had been a pugilist prior to taking his vows, and had taught Duane basic offense and defense. If your opponent had longer arms, you go inside, work his body, and the uppercut might be useful, not to mention the head butt if things really got nasty.

The cowboys crowded around the two men circling each other in the darkness. The redhead couldn't get whipped by the newest hand, and the newest hand couldn't back down to prudent living. Somebody lit the lamp, and Duane was forced to take a second look at his adversary.

The redhead wore long dirty white underwear, his feet encased in cowboy boots, and due to some strange atavistic instinct, he'd put on his cowboy hat. He appeared comical, his back flap half unbuttoned, and the cowboys couldn't suppress their laughter. The redhead looked down at himself, and blushed like a girl. The mood changed suddenly from violence to cowboy mirth. Duane stared at his adversary, who looked ridiculous. Somehow, Duane became amused.

"A man needs his sleep," somebody growled. "We've got a hard day tomorrow."

The lamp was blown out. Duane and the redhead stared at each other in the darkness, but Duane wasn't quite so mad anymore. "If I ever find another rat in my bed," he said, "I'll beat the piss out of you."

"Anytime," replied the redhead.

The cowboys meandered back to their bunks. Duane lifted his blanket from the ratty mattress and threw it onto another empty one against the back wall. Then he pulled off his boots, fluffed up a pillow made from his extra clothes, lay down, and prayed silently.

Dear Lord, please don't let me do anything stupid tomorrow, because Vanessa and I need this job.

Vanessa sat on a rickety wooden chair and looked out the window at the soldiers' campfires glowing at the edge of town. At least I've got a roof over my head, and a job, she thought. I'll teach children to read and write if it kills me.

Figures moved around the campfires, and she heard a soldier plunking a guitar. It was an old melody from the Blue Ridge Mountains, or the great Smokies, but it could also be an Irish tune, or even an Italian one, for the frontier army got the rejects from everywhere, and according to what people had told Vanessa, the officers even worse than the men.

She recalled the lieutenant who'd conferred so confidently with Mr. Gibson earlier in the day. Somehow, through a process she didn't quite understand, he'd become leader of the detachment. What makes one man rise and another fall? she wondered. Is it a quality that can be taught, or must you be born with it?

She thought of her husband-to-be, who was a decent boy, but there are some things that you don't learn until you're thirty. Sometimes she felt more like Duane's mother than his bride-to-be. She and Duane had no money, and she could end up as Shelby's schoolmarm for the rest of her life.

She didn't require a plantation, only a little home with a steady income. I wonder how much a lieutenant earns? Then she smiled at the odd turn of her mind. You're scheduled to marry one man, and you're thinking about another?

CHAPTER 2

The chuck wagon dangled pots, pans, and utensils as it rolled over the grassy plain, the sun a pan of silver in the sky. The Bar T crew was headed for the northern range, where they'd live in the open like Indians, eating meat off the hoof, lying down on the bare ground at night, and hoping no rattlers would crawl beneath the covers with them.

Duane rode at the back of the formation, feeling earth emanations seep into his bones. The infinity of the range surged around him, reminding him of mild ecstasies he'd experienced in the monastery in the clouds. He spent most of his life studying in the scriptorium, and sometimes wondered if he'd wasted his time. He could detail the logical proofs of God's existence, according to Saint Thomas Aquinas, but it seemed sterile and abstract compared to the actual wide open frontier world.

"Howdy," said a voice to his left.

Duane snapped out of his contemplative mood, and saw Don Jordan, one of the Bar T cowboys. He was around Duane's height, a few pounds heavier, with medium brown hair beneath his smudged white cowboy hat. Duane wondered if another cowboy prank was in the making, such as a dead rat in his afternoon stew. "Howdy," he said suspiciously.

"I was hired two weeks ago, and was the tenderfoot until you showed up. All I've got to say is: Thank God you're here. I didn't think I could take much more."

Duane evaluated Jordan, and the first thing that struck him was the northern accent, since most Texas cowboys were from the South, and ninety percent had been in the Confederate Army. "Where are you from?" he asked, curiosity overcoming good manners.

"Massachusetts."

"I'm surprised you haven't been shot by now."

"I mind my business, do my work, and keep my mouth shut. Besides, I know it's not easy to give up your way of life, just because somebody in Washington says so. You can't put this country back together by punishing the former leaders of the Confederacy."

"Don't like politics," Duane declared. "But slavery was a sin, and even the Pope said so."

"You're a Catholic?"

"I was raised in a Franciscan orphanage."

"My family was Methodist, but I don't go to church anymore. Isn't this land magnificent?"

Duane gazed at clumps of grama grass, myriad varieties of cactus, and mesquite trees all the way to the horizon. The sky was brilliant blue, and the sun rolled steadily upward toward the peak of heaven.

"What brings you all the way from Massachusetts?"

"I didn't want to work in an office, or go to sea. How about you?"

"I want to learn the cattle business."

"It doesn't seem very complicated. You brand them, make sure they get enough to eat, and then drive them to market. Have you seen Miss Phyllis yet?"

"I guess every cowboy in the bunkhouse wants to get his hands on her."

"She'll probably marry some rich rancher's son one of these days, and merge their holdings in more ways than one."

"He'll be a lucky man, whoever he is."

"Miss Phyllis is the prettiest girl in these parts, but there isn't much to choose from, unfortunately. I thought of marrying somebody back home, and bringing her out here, but Boston girls are accustomed to plumbing,

41

servants, and city conveniences. They think that Southerners, particularly Texans, are barbarians. And then, of course, they wouldn't want their hair to adorn the lodgepole of some Comanche's tent."

Duane had many questions, but held them in abeyance for another time. Bad manners to probe too deeply in the beginning, because so many cowboys were wanted by men with badges, and even Duane had certain facts that he hoped to conceal.

The ramrod's booming voice called to them from the front of the formation. "Where's that tenderfoot? Somebody git him the hell up hyar!"

Duane nudged Thunderbolt's flanks, and the horse quickened his pace. Duane rode around the cowboys, and wondered what the assignment would be, as he angled toward McGrath. "Yes, sir?"

"What you say yer name was?"

"Braddock."

"Take the point with Ross, here. If either of you sees injuns, ride back and tell me how many, where they're headin', what they're wearin', and if any of 'em's got rifles."

Ross had short legs, rounded shoulders, and large ears. "What if they shoot first?"

"We'll be right there to help out. Now get movin', and keep yer eyes peeled."

Ross spurred his grulla, and the animal burst into a trot. Duane nudged Thunderbolt, and side by side, the two cowboys rode at moderate speed across the open range, their horses kicking clods of dirt. Duane leaned toward Thunderbolt's flowing black mane, to present less resistance to the wind. Ross said nothing, his mouth set in a grim, hard-bitten line. He was in his late twenties, and his face looked like hand-tooled leather.

The windstream felt good against Duane's cheeks, and he liked the speed. Thunderbolt had plenty of bottom, and Duane felt the animal's strength surge beneath him. They approached Ferguson, a snake-eyed cowboy with a cigarette dangling out the corner of his mouth, riding the point. Ross and Duane slowed down as they came alongside. "See any injuns?" Ross asked.

"If I did, you would've knowed it."

Ferguson drew the rein of his sorrel and aimed him back toward the cloud of dust following in the distance. Duane took his position alongside Ross, and since Duane was a tenderfoot, that meant he couldn't initiate conversation. He kept waiting for Ross to speak, but that knight of the range kept his lips shut.

Duane scanned surrounding terrain for Indians. He'd observed Apaches at the monas-

43

tery, when they'd stopped by the well on their travels. The monks prudently kept their distance, but on one occasion, Duane had seen what looked like a red scalp hanging from a warrior's belt. It was their land, but was everybody else supposed to pack up and go home?

Ross bit off a plug of tobacco, but didn't offer any to Duane. "Where you from, kid?"

"Guadalupe Mountains."

"What the hell's in the Guadalupe Mountains?"

"Not a damn thing."

" 'At's what I figgered."

It was silent again, except for the sound of hoof-beats. Duane raised his eyes and saw an eagle high in the sky. What a perspective he must have, Duane thought. Must make that old bird wise. But Duane didn't have time to speculate upon eagle life. He lowered his eyes and checked mesquite trees, juniper bushes, and cholla cactus for a feather tied to an Indian's hair, or war paint on his cheeks.

Duane was curious about Indians, as he was curious about everything else. Their favorite trick was to tie white men head down on wagon wheels, and build fires underneath their heads. I love this land, Duane thought, and if I have to fight for it — that's what I'll do. No Indian's going to cook me over a fire,

and if he tries to steal the boss's cattle, hell —
I'll fight for the brand.

"Y'know," said his companion, "Uncle
Ray was a-fixin' to clean yer clock last night. I
wouldn't push him too hard, I was you."

"He puts something in my bed again, I'll
ram it down his throat."

Ross looked at him coldly. "Yer a little too
big fer yer britches, sonny jim. You ain't
talkin' back to me, are you?"

"You tell me."

Ross spat a gob of brown juice at a pale
green yucca blossom, and said, "Boy, you
don't treat me with respeck, I'll get down
from this horse and whip your ass right
naow."

"The hell you will," Duane replied.

"I guess yer brave now, 'cause the ramrod'll
fire both of us if we git in a fight while we're a-
ridin' the point, but I'll tell you what. Tonight, after supper, you and me — back of the
chuck wagon. What do you say?"

Duane leaned closer and looked into his
eyes. "Sooner or later I'll have to kick the shit
out of somebody in this outfit, and it might as
well be you."

"Children, it gives me great pleasure to introduce Miss Vanessa Fontaine, your new
teacher."

45

Mrs. Gibson stepped out of the way, leaving Vanessa alone before her new students gathered in the parlor of the Gibson home. Each child perched a board across his or her lap, for desks. They looked like a bunch of imps, their beady little eyes focused on her, waiting for her to make a mistake.

"Your parents have hired me," she began, "because they want you to receive a better education. If you don't know arithmetic, can't read, and can't write, you'll be at a disadvantage in the modern world."

"Puhsonally," grumbled a boy, "I'd druther be outside."

"You can't play your life away," Vanessa lectured. "And besides, learning can be fun. I'll bet everybody in this class would like to know something, but you don't know how to find the answer. Why don't we make that our first project? You tell me what you want to know, and that's what we'll do. Any suggestions?"

Nobody said a word, and Vanessa realized that they didn't feel comfortable in her presence. But she was nervous herself, with Mrs. Gibson looking directly at her. "I know that you're shy, but surely there's *something* that you're curious about, such as who invented arithmetic, or where certain words came from. You might even want to know why iron melts, or why water freezes at thirty-two degrees fahrenheit. Can't you think of anything?"

It was silent, and Vanessa knew that she was failing to reach them. If I were little, and I lived in this town, what would I be curious about right now? A whiff of campfire drifted through the window, and a tantalizing possibility came to mind. "Something very significant happened in Shelby recently," she said. "Can anyone tell me what it was?" Again, nobody said a word, so she continued undaunted. "A detachment of soldiers has come, and that doesn't happen every day. Perhaps we should search through every book in town for information about the lives of soldiers. Wouldn't that be fun?"

A little girl with pigtails yawned. "My daddy says that books're full of lies writ by people what couldn't get an honest job."

"I wouldn't want to argue with your father, but if you do enough research, and compare facts, you often can tell who's lying and who isn't. The importance of an education is that it teaches you to evaluate information. I think that all of us should go home tonight, look through the printed material in our homes, and bring in everything about the Army that we find. Then, tomorrow, we'll have a reading session, and find answers to our questions!"

A skinny little boy, wearing thick eye-glasses, wrinkled his nose and crossed his arms over his birdlike chest. "Why don't we just ask one of them soldiers to *tell* us about the Army?"

"I'm sure they're much too busy . . ."

Mrs. Gibson interrupted her. "On the contrary, they seem to have quite a lot of time on their hands. I believe they're waiting to join up with another detachment, and it's two days late."

"Probably massacred by injuns," the boy in the thick eyeglasses said confidently.

Vanessa wondered how the teachers at Miss Dalton's School would handle the situation. She wanted them to actually learn about the army, not listen to old barracks tales from the mouth of a drunkard who'd fought against the South during The Recent Unpleasantness. But on the other hand, it could enable me to establish better rapport with my students.

"Sounds like a good idea," she said. "The next order of business is to elect someone to go to the commanding officer and ask him to deliver an address to the class. Do I have any nominations?"

Every little finger in the room pointed to the new schoomarm, and every little voice shouted in unison, "You!"

The soldiers' tents were lined in a row next to a stream at the edge of town. Wet clothing hung from guylines, while a detail of soldiers repaired a wagon, and others cleaned rifles, mended harnesses, and sewed clothing, everybody keeping busy, but not so busy that they didn't notice the attractive blond woman strolling into their detachment area.

A sergeant with curly red sideburns shot to his feet in front of her. "Can I he'p you, ma'am?"

"I'd like to speak with your commanding officer."

"I'm Sergeant Mahoney, ma'am. Right this way."

He led her toward the largest tent, its front and rear flaps open. Inside, seated behind the desk, she could see the commanding officer.

"Wait right here, ma'am. I'll be out directly."

She glanced at the soldiers, all of whom stared at her as though she were delicious. She'd sung to soldier audiences during her stage career, and knew that they were lonely men, with harsh lives and little money.

Sergeant Mahoney returned, and stood at attention before her. "The lieutenant'll see you now, ma'am. You can go right in."

She entered the tent, where Lieutenant

Dawes stood behind his field desk. "Can I help you, ma'am?"

He had bronzed features, a solid jaw, and wore eyeglasses, which made him appear studious. Evidently he'd been writing something. "I'm the new schoolmarm," she began, "and I'm afraid that I have a rather unusual request, sir."

He raised his right hand. "The name's Dawes. Have a seat. Can I get you some coffee? I don't suppose you'd care for whiskey."

"Wouldn't be schoolmarm here long if I did. I'm Vanessa Fontaine."

"You're just about the most beautiful woman that I've ever seen in my life, Miss Fontaine. What can I do for you?"

Vanessa smiled politely. "My students have invited you to speak to them about what it's like to be in the army."

Lieutenant Dawes opened his mouth to render an unequivocal *no,* but possibly General Sheridan would pass through Shelby someday, and the pretty schoolmarm might tell him about kind, helpful Lieutenant Dawes. "I'd be happy to speak before your students, Miss Fontaine, provided you answer a simple question. What's a rare flower like you doing in such a godforsaken part of Texas?"

"You're very gracious, sir, but perhaps

you've been away from women too long, or the sun is starting to bake your brain, but there's nothing exceptional about me, I assure you. I've come here with the man I'm going to marry. He's looking for work as a cowboy, and I'm the schoolmarm."

She's dirt poor, in other words, Lieutenant Dawes thought. There were many questions that he'd like to ask, but she was betrothed to another man, and Lieutenant Dawes was no bird dog. "What part of the South are you from?"

"Charleston. How about you?"

"I grew up in Washington, and if you're wondering if I fought in the war, I didn't. Besides, it's time to forgive and forget."

"I wouldn't go that far," replied the former Charleston belle.

The cowboys rode into the herd, searching for calves to brand. It was early afternoon, the slightly off-center sun beginning its long drop toward the California canyons. Duane whirled his rope through the air lazily, as he spotted a calf. First he had to check the mother's brand, because range wars started over the misbranding of other people's calves.

The cow carried the Bar T brand, so Duane resumed circling the lasso over his head. He aimed, then let the lasso fly. The calf flinched as the hemp fell over him. Duane pulled him toward the fire, but the calf dug his little hooves into the turf, and bleated pathetically. Thunderbolt paid no attention as he plodded onward.

Duane rocked back and forth in his saddle, noticing other cowboys lining up with their calves. He caught a whiff of burning mesquite mixed with the fragrance of the sage as he came to the end of the line.

He heard somebody clear his throat, and spun around. It was Ross, with a roped calf. The two cowboys looked at each other in silent hatred for a few moments, then Ross grinned. "Hope yer havin' fun today, kid, 'cause tonight I'm a-gonna bust yer haid wide open."

Duane's vivid imagination saw his head splitting like a rotten watermelon. But he knew how to fight a shorter man with less reach, thanks to the lessons of Brother Paolo. Keep him on the ends of your punches, pound him relentlessly, and whatever you do, don't clinch with him.

"Move it up, Braddock!" hollered the ramrod.

Duane pulled the calf closer to the fire, while the little creature fought to break loose. One rastler reached over the calf, grabbed a foreleg, and yanked the animal onto his back.

The rastler held down the calf's foreleg, while another rastler positioned his backlegs. The brander pulled an iron from the fire, blew on the Bar T configuration until it glowed cherry red, and then pressed it against the calf's hide.

Duane closed his eyes, because he couldn't bear to watch the baby's suffering. The odor of burned fur came to his nostrils, the calf wailed as the rastler pulled the iron away. Duane felt relieved that the little animal's misery was over, when suddenly, a man with a knife stepped forward. With a flash of steel, the calf's reproductive organs were removed. The calf screeched horribly as a rastler slathered grease over the wound. Duane's rope was removed from the animal's neck, and the calf was kicked in the rump. The calf ran off bawling, looking for his mother.

Duane broke out into a cold sweat as his Catholic moral training fell upon him like a flaming blanket from hell. Do we have a right to castrate other creatures? In the monastery, his every action had come under intense personal scrutiny for gradations of right and wrong. The secular world was more of a shock than he'd ever imagined. Most people did as they pleased, without regard for the suffering of others. Duane watched the castrated calf disappear into the sea of cattle. But what about him? At least monks don't harm other creatures.

"Somebody's comin!" hollered Ferguson. They turned in the direction of his finger, and saw riders approaching across the mesa. "Looks like a bunch from the Circle K."

McGrath set his mouth in a grim line, and his eyes narrowed into tiny malevolent jewels. "Settle down, boys. We're not a-lookin' fer trouble, but if it comes — I want us to be ready."

Duane took a swig from his canteen, as Bar T cowboys coalesced around McGrath. Duane drifted toward Don Jordan, who was hanging toward the back of the pack. "What's going on?"

"There's bad blood between the Circle K and us," Jordan replied.

"Over what?"

"Cattle, horses, land, water — all the usual stuff."

Duane eased his Colt out of its holster, then let it drop back in, so it would be smoother on the draw. He exercised the joints of his right hand, as the riders advanced closer, led by a big rawboned cowboy in a pearl-colored cowboy hat, red and black checkered shirt, and green bandanna. "Top of the morning to you, Mister McGrath," he said with a wry smile. "Just a-checkin' the stock — that's all."

"It's yer privilege, Mister Krenshaw, but I'll ask you to stay out'n the way of my men, 'cause we've got work to do."

"As long as your men don't lasso the wrong calves, everything'll be fine."

"I don't think you've got much ter worry 'bout there. We know the diff'rence between the Circle K brand and the Bar T."

"Nothin' personal, but I've seen Bar T brands that looked like they was burned on top of Circle K brands. Why is it that the Bar T's herd seems to grow so much faster than everybody else's?"

" 'Cause we work harder, 'stead of goin' around checkin' up on other people. You and your crew'd git a lot more done if you minded yer own bizness."

The Circle K and Bar T riders sat on their mounts only a few feet apart and eyeballed each other across the sunny afternoon. Duane figured that gunplay wasn't out of the question, due to the allegations. He continued to unlimber his fingers.

"When other cowboys put their brands on our calves," Krenshaw said, "it *is* our bizness. Come over to the ranch sometime — I'd be happy to show you some funny brands, though I reckon you've seen 'em before."

Wind rustled the sagebrush, and the moo of a cow could be heard. Duane studied the hands of the men from the Circle K, because it looked like war. Then McGrath said, "We wasted enough time with yer humbug, Mister Krenshaw. Time to git back to work."

The Bar T cowboys wheeled their horses and returned to the herd, while McGrath angled toward the chuck wagon, where the cook stood with a double-barreled shotgun in his hands, gazing back at Krenshaw.

"We'll be a-lookin' fer Circle K stock in this herd," Krenshaw said. "Hope you won't mind."

"Jest stay out of our way," McGrath called over his shoulder.

Duane rode Thunderbolt into the herd, to find another Bar T calf. The atmosphere was tense, with cowboys from different ranches intermingling. One of the Circle K riders moved toward him, and Duane thought he'd try Christian friendliness. "Howdy," he said, touching his finger to the brim of his hat.

The Circle K rider frowned. He was deep-chested, around Duane's height, wearing a brown wide-brimmed hat with a flat crown, and leather leggins. Hatred emanated from his eyes, although he'd never seen Duane in his life. Duane decided to ignore him and search for his next calf.

He moved among the cattle, aware that the Circle K cowboy's eyes were upon him.

Thunderbolt snorted and jerked his head forward. Duane saw the short legs of a calf nudging his mother's teat. He circled around, to make sure that the brand wasn't Bar T.

But the brand was Circle K, and he had to move on. He stood in his stirrups, in an effort to find another calf.

The Circle K cowboy called out, "Bet you would've branded him, if'n I ain't been a-watchin' you, you crooked son of a bitch!"

The insult felt like a slap in the face, although Duane hadn't done anything wrong. I'm going to mind my own business, he thought, and ignore this false accusation. He angled Thunderbolt deeper into the herd, and it wasn't long before his eyes fell on another calf grazing amid a swarm of cattle. It wasn't clear which was the calf's mother, so he'd have to wait and see which cow the calf went to.

He heard a raspy voice behind him. "If'n I wasn't here, bet you would've got that one, too."

Duane looked him in the eye and said levelly, "You'd better be careful that I don't put a brand on you, Mister."

"Like to see you try it, kid."

Duane swung his leg over the saddle and dropped to the ground, surprising the Circle K cowboy, who lowered his hand to his gun.

Before his fingers closed around the grip, he found himself staring into the barrel of Duane's Colt .44. The Circle K cowboy smiled weakly, because he knew that Duane had the right to blow him away.

"A problem over there, Reade?" called Krenshaw, in another part of the herd.

Reade replied, "Caught this feller about to cut one of our calves, but he saw me and backed off."

All eyes turned to Duane, who felt guilty although he hadn't done anything wrong. He raised his Colt, and aimed at the center of Reade's chest. "Get down from that horse."

"Now jest a minute!"

Duane's finger tightened around his trigger. "I'll count to three . . ."

Reade raised his left leg, and stepped down from the stirrup. Duane holstered his gun, and both men stared at each other across ten feet of grass. They were surrounded by swirling masses of cattle, while cowboys from both ranches rode closer.

"You've got a big mouth," Reade said. "I ought to put my boot up yer ass."

Duane felt ice cold, now that violence was about to commence. "You're going to apologize to me, Mister Reade, or I'm going to beat on you."

Reade spat into the dirt. "Apologize, hell."

Before Duane could think, he was running toward Reade, who loaded up his right fist, to catch Duane coming in, but Duane never faltered in his headlong charge. When six feet away, he dove toward Reade, intending to rip him apart.

A nearby steer hooted as Reade launched a right hook to Duane's head. The punch connected, Duane saw stars, then his arms closed around Reade's thighs, and he twisted hard. Reade lost his balance, and both went sprawling into the grass.

Duane tried to find leverage for a solid punch to the head of his adversary. He blocked a flying elbow with his nose, then received a backhand to the left temple. He and Reade rolled and tumbled near the legs of cattle and horses, and kicked up a cloud of dust as they scuffled wildly, throwing punches from all angles.

Duane took a hard fist to the forehead and realized that he was in a serious fistfight, not a mere barroom brawl with a drunken opponent. Duane and Reade jumped to their feet, and Duane dodged a jab down the middle as he threw a hard chopping right to Reade's head, while Reade dug a left into Duane's ribs.

Duane grunted as he wrapped his fingers around Reade's throat, while Reade tried to kick him in his private parts. Duane exploded into a flurry of punches, fists flew like blurs in all directions, both men took heavy shots, and then one of Duane's right leads connected solidly with Reade's jaw. Reade closed his eyes and flopped onto his back, where he lay motionless. The fight had come to an abrupt end.

Duane stood unsteadily, a trickle of blood showing at the corner of his mouth. His hat had fallen off and hung down his back, attached to his neck by the black leather strap. As his head cleared, he saw himself and his opponent ringed with men on horses. Reade opened his eyes, and returned to Texas, 1871.

"Get on your horse," Duane told him evenly.

"Go to hell," replied Reade.

Duane charged again, but this time, when he came within punching range, he darted to the side, in an effort to fake his man out. It worked, the cowboy turned in the new direction, but Duane was already on his way back to the previous one, and when his feet touched the ground, he launched a right to Reade's ear, while Reade whacked him with a paralyzing kidney shot.

The air expelled from Duane's mouth, and he found it difficult to move. Reade smashed

Duane with a left, a right, and then another left to the mouth. Duane backpedaled, trying to elude punches, and looked for an opening. He took one step to the side, ducked a left jab, and countered a right hook. Then he ate another left jab, but managed to land a kidney shot of his own. Reade's eyes squinched with pain, and his fists dropped two inches. Duane slammed him on the forehead with all his weight, and Reade dropped to his knees. Duane watched in morbid fascination as the Circle K cowboy then collapsed slowly onto his face.

Reade didn't move, and a cheer went up from the Bar T cowboys. Duane realized that he'd won the fight, although his kidney still hurt, and his face felt like raw beef. Two beams of light seemed to be drilling into the side of his head, and he turned toward Krenshaw, leader of the Circle K cowboys. Their eyes met, and Duane knew that he'd made an enemy, so why stop there?

"Want to be next?" Duane asked.

"If I get off this horse, boy — I'll kill you."

Duane pointed at the man lying on the ground. "That's what he thought."

"I wouldn't dirty my hands on you."

It was the wrong thing to say to an orphan who fundamentally felt like damaged goods. Duane found himself running toward

Krenshaw, and the leader of the Circle K cowboys heard him coming. Krenshaw went for his gun, but Duane was already launched into the air. He tackled Krenshaw, tore him out of the saddle, and threw him onto the ground with such force that Krenshaw was knocked cold.

A sudden shot was fired, startling everybody. McGrath, smoking pistol in hand, rode toward Duane. "Git on your horse. You got work to do."

Every cowboy in the vicinity had his gun out, and deadly tension crackled like electricity in the air. Duane didn't want to be left out, so he whipped out his Colt, thumbed back the hammer, and wondered who to shoot first.

"Mister Krenshaw," said McGrath, "I think it's time you and your men cleared out of here, otherwise somebody's liable to git kilt."

All eyes turned to Krenshaw, who had regained consciousness. He perched on his knees, then drew himself to his full height, his white shirt streaked with dirt, his hat fallen off. Krenshaw turned to Duane and said thickly, "Maybe some other time."

"You know where to find me," Duane replied.

Krenshaw picked up his hat, punched out

the crown, and climbed onto his horse. The cowboys from the Circle K followed Krenshaw as he rode away, while cattle milled around, unperturbed by the violence that had just occurred. Duane felt jittery as he slapped dirt and dust off his jeans. He took off his black hat, smacked it against his leg, and then restructured the brim. A horse approached, and he looked up to see McGrath, gun in hand.

"If'n I was you," McGrath said, "I'd ride back to the chuck wagon, get my blanket, and light a shuck. Mister Krenshaw, who you just throwed out've his saddle, ain't a-gonna let you live long. Yer so green, you don't even know who he is."

Duane moved his holster so that his gun was in line with his outer thigh. "He's the man who owns the Circle K, right?"

"Wrong. It's even worse than that, 'cause you can reason with Old Man Krenshaw. Jay Krenshaw is his son, and meanness is his middle name. He ain't the type that fergives and fergits."

Duane thought for a few moments, and then said, "Neither do I."

Lieutenant Dawes strode through the detachment area, hands clasped behind his back, cavalry hat low over his eyes. He'd studied the great battles of history, was familiar with the tactics of Caesar and Napoleon, but it meant little in the sagebrush wasteland of West Texas, land of the Comanche and Apache, the most practiced guerrilla fighters in the world.

His father could've obtained a staff position in Washington for his son, but the newly commissioned lieutenant had asked for field duty, and since then served in a succession of forts and posts across the frontier, fighting numerous skirmishes with Indians, and had seen bloody results of Indian depredations. The experience had matured him, but also made him introspective. He was no longer enthusiastic about military life, and even sympathized with the Indians, who made treaties that the white man consistently violated. And if that weren't enough, he thought that many of his fellow officers were idiots.

One of these days, I'll get an arrow through my skull, he thought morbidly. The Indians'll be subdued with me or without me, so what'm I doing here?

Lieutenant Dawes came to stop at the edge of the encampment, and gazed at a flat-topped mountain standing alone like an isolated figure in the dance of time. Solitary, embattled, it reminded him of himself. Lieutenant Dawes was tired of sleeping alone, and couldn't help thinking of Vanessa Fontaine, beautiful, sophisticated, well educated. Now there's potential officer's wife material, he calculated.

Footsteps approached from his rear, and he turned around suddenly. Corporal Hazelwood approached, followed by a small boy. The corporal saluted smartly and said, "Sir, this young gentleman would like to speak with you."

Lieutenant Dawes looked down at the boy, no older that six or seven. "What can I do for you?"

The boy's eyes glittered with worship as he handed the detachment commander a note.

Dear Lieutenant Dawes:
You are cordially invited to supper tonight at our home, six o'clock sharp.
                    Mr. & Mrs. Fred Gibson

Jay Krenshaw tried to behave as though the violent confrontation signified nothing of importance as he led the Circle K cowboys out of the valley. But nothing could be further from the truth. The boss's son was in a murderous mood. The cowboys wouldn't respect a weakling, and there was no doubt that the stranger called Braddock had defeated him.

Crooked outfits steal my daddy's cattle, and we can't be everyplace. Maybe Big Al hired himself a fast hand, but we can do the same, he thought angrily. Jay Krenshaw turned around in his saddle. "Raybart — git yer ass up here!"

A rider detached himself from the pack, and rode forward. Raybart was older than the other cowboys, soft around his middle, and always looked as though he needed a shave. His nose was a small potato suspended above fleshly lips, and he had no discernible chin.

The boss's son leaned toward him. "Know who that feller was back thar?"

"Never see'd him afore."

"McGrath said his name was Braddock. That mean anything to you?"

"There was a Braddock what got shot long time ago."

"This one's got hired gun written all over him. How can I find out about him?"

"He probably stopped off in Shelby. Maybe Gibson knows who he is."

Krenshaw thought for a few moments, as if reaching a decision. Then he said, "Go to town and have a talk with Gibson. See what he knows about Braddock, and then git back to me."

"I just can't walk up to 'im and starting askin' questions, 'cause he'll git suspicious.

I'll have to buy something, and work into it — know what I mean?"

Krenshaw reached into his pocket, pulled out some coins, and passed them to Raybart. "Get going."

CHAPTER 3

Vanessa sat at her window, and watched the copper sun sink through orange streaks of clouds. Somewhere on that measureless range, her husband-to-be was working cattle, otherwise he would've returned home by now with a hangdog expression. At least he won't be a financial liability in the short run, she deduced in the practical lobe of her brain. I barely earn enough to take care of myself as it is.

She looked around her room, a far cry from her boudoir back at the old plantation. She'd had brocade drapes and a big plush feather bed, with a closet filled with fashions from New York, London, and Paris. Now all she possessed were her saloon costumes, which she wouldn't dare wear in Shelby, and some well-tailored but not particularly stylish dresses left from the old days.

Now that money was in short supply, her

clothing was starting to fall apart, and she had a small hole in her right shoe. *I was crazy to run off with Duane. He's so poor.*

Sometimes she wondered what made her tick. *How can a woman of thirty-one fall in love with a man of eighteen, who has no money? Is groping in bed so important that it blots out all other considerations?* She closed her eyes and sighed as she thought of sleeping with Duane, but it didn't pay the bills. *Women who don't plan carefully can end up in deep trouble.*

But a scheming woman can get herself into even more trouble. The dinner invitation had originated in Vanessa's convoluted brain, and she'd dropped the hint to Mrs. Gibson, who'd relayed it to Mr. Gibson. Now the lieutenant was coming, and Vanessa entertained serious doubts about the entire dubious enterprise.

He wore the uniform of the Yankee invader, but obviously was a well-bred man, no raving abolitionist by any means, and even Bobby Lee himself had been opposed to slavery. *But I'm going to be a married woman, and if I flirt, he'll think I'm a slut, which I probably am. Whatever happened to me?* she pondered.

She wasn't sure, but it had something to do with her rootlessness after the war as she traveled from town to town in stagecoaches, meeting a variety of men along the way, most of them liars, villains, and utter swine. Duane's got a good heart, at least. He'd never take advantage of anybody, if he could avoid it, she rationalized.

There was a knock on the door. "Time for dinner, dear."

"Be right there," Vanessa replied in a cheery tone. She looked at herself in the mirror, and hoped she didn't come across as genteel poor, because there was nothing more pathetic. She wore a jade green dress with a high-buttoned collar, and no jewelry or cosmetics. Bringing her face closer to the mirror, she noted a new wrinkle beneath her left eye. I'll be a toothless old schoolmarm in a few years, unless I do something quickly. She pinched color into her cheeks, and ran her tongue over her teeth. Then she narrowed her eyes and attempted to appraise herself objectively. I'm not quite what I was ten years ago, but I'm perfectly presentable, and refinement can be found in my every pore, she told herself.

She realized that her heart raced as she walked down the corridor. What is this madness? Why, I hardly know the man. She entered the ramshackle parlor, where Mr. Gibson sat with his wife and a printed portrait of Sam Houston suspended from the wall.

"Our other guest ain't arrived yet," Mr. Gibson said, rubbing his hands in anticipation of a sumptuous repast.

Vanessa sat on the edge of a chair, because Miss Dalton's school had taught her to keep her back straight at all times. "Perhaps he was detained by army business," she suggested.

Mr. Gibson harumphed, looking like an old walrus. "What army business? They're all just layin' around camp. You can see right into the lieutenant's tent, and all he ever does is read books."

There was a knock on the door, and the conversation came to an end.

"I'll bet that's him now," Mrs. Gibson said, as though they lived in a large town, and any number of gentlemen might be calling. She swept grandly across the room, and opened the door. Standing there, backlit by the moon, stood Lieutenant Clayton Dawes, U.S. Fourth Cavalry.

"Come in, sir," Mrs. Gibson said, with something that appeared a bow.

The West Point officer entered the parlor, and his eyes immediately were drawn to the schoolmarm. "Good evening, Miss Fontaine. So good to see you again."

Vanessa was amused, because they were behaving as if they were at a grand dinner in

Washington, instead of a clapboard shack alongside Comanche territory. But the graduate of Miss Dalton's School had been trained to guard against unwarranted displays of ostentatious manners. Instead, she smiled and said, "How kind of you to take time from your schedule to be with us."

Fading rays of sun glinted on his gold shoulder boards as he stood before her. Mrs. Gibson took the officer's hand. "This way, sir."

She led him to the dining room, and told him where to sit, which happened to be the spot directly opposite Vanessa. The plates were already set, and covered with folded white napkins. We're putting on the dog tonight, Vanessa thought, as she took her seat.

Mrs. Gibson carried in a silver tureen of soup, and placed it on the table. She proceeded to ladle out chicken and vegetables, as Mr. Gibson turned toward the lieutenant. "How much longer do you think your detachment will be in town?"

"Depends on Colonel Mackenzie. Could be permanent."

They slurped soup, and Vanessa glanced at him out the corner of her eye. He was much taller than Duane, with thicker arms. She wanted to say something scintillating, but nothing came to mind.

He turned toward her abruptly. "Understand you've just arrived in town, Miss Fontaine."

"Only a few days before you."

"Where from?"

"Titusville."

"Were you the schoolmarm there?"

"Just passing through."

Lieutenant Dawes had been on the frontier long enough to know the unwritten code: Don't ask too many questions. Close up, in the light of lamps, she appeared almost queenly, with her conservative clothing and erect carriage. She'd shine like a jewel on any army post, and make a great general's wife, he thought. "I hope you won't think me rude, Miss Fontaine, but if I'd had a schoolmarm like you, I might've been a better student."

"I understand that you're a West Pointer," she replied. "What was your favorite nonmilitary subject?"

"History. How about you?"

"I enjoyed reading novels."

"Who's your favorite author?"

"Dickens, of course. Do you have a favorite author?"

"Giovanni Battista Vico. He was an Italian, and said that only philosophers can understand history."

Mr. Gibson decided that it was time to become part of the conversation, although he hadn't the slightest idea of what was being discussed. "History repeats itself," he said. "Rome fell, and so will America one day — mark my words."

"Is the soup all right?" asked Mrs. Gibson, adding her own dissonant note to the conversation.

Lieutenant Dawes wished that he could be alone with Vanessa Fontaine, because he felt that they could have an intelligent conversation. But unfortunately Mr. Gibson wanted to discuss the need for permanent protection against the Indians, and Mrs. Gibson continued to ask about the acceptability of her cuisine.

The next course was roast beef with potatoes and carrots. The harmless but mindless conversation touched a variety of pointless subjects such as the weather, as Lieutenant Dawes waited patiently for a lull. Then he turned toward Vanessa, and said, "I hope you were far away from the fighting during the recent war, Miss Vanessa."

"Unfortunately," she replied, "my home was in the direct path of General Sherman's march to the sea."

"Modern warfare can be very harsh on civilian populations, which is regrettable. But

I was a schoolboy in Washington, D.C., in those days. We expected Bobby Lee to burn the capitol to the ground."

"Too bad he didn't," she replied with a charming smile.

He sliced thoughtfully into his roast beef. Burn the capitol to the ground? He realized that the beautiful lady sitting opposite him was something of a fanatic.

On the other side of the table, Vanessa perceived his change of mood. I went too far that time, she admitted. He probably thinks I'm a diehard Confederate, and I am!

Mr. Gibson realized that his dinner party was in danger of total disarray. "The war was hard on all of us," he declared, "but it's no secret that we in the South suffered most, and some of those scars don't heal so quickly. Sherman's army was not exactly on a mission of Christian charity."

"They were on a mission to break the will of the South," Lieutenant Dawes replied. "Before people make war, perhaps they should ponder the consequences." He turned to Vanessa, and their eyes met. "I value people who speak their minds, instead of making the requisite 'nice' remark. The Civil War has torn this nation apart, and not much good has come from it, except for the freeing of the slaves. But I hope we're not going to get into an argument about slavery. I'd much rather talk about something else, if you don't mind."

A bell rang in the general store, and Lieutenant Dawes instinctively reached for his Colt service revolver. Mr. Gibson wiped his mouth with his napkin, as he rose to his feet. "A customer."

He hurriedly departed the room, and a moment later his wife rose to her feet. "Let me clear the table."

She gathered the dishes, carried them to the kitchen, and disappeared. Vanessa and Lieutenant Dawes were left alone, and a few moments of awkward silence ensued. Vanessa was about to make a banal remark about the weather, when she heard the deep mellifluous voice of Lieutenant Dawes. "I suppose you don't like me very much, because of the uniform I wear. If I were you, I'd probably feel the same way."

The room fell silent again, and she realized that the next move was hers, as though they were playing chess. "You're wrong," she replied, "I don't dislike you at all. And you're right, the war *is* over. It makes no sense to look back, but sometimes I can't help it. As Mr. Gibson said, the scars don't heal so easily."

"I understand," he replied.

She found his voice soothing. This is a sensitive man, yet he's also confident, strong, and steady as a mountain. "Something tells me that you'll go a long way in the army," she said. "It's very easy to be with you."

"Nice of you to say so. I, too, feel a certain affinity between us."

"Why is it that a man like you has never married?"

"There aren't many available women in this part of Texas," he explained.

"But surely some colonel's daughter or general's niece . . ."

"The competition is fierce, and most of them can do better than a mere First Lieutenant."

"But what can a man's rank have to do with true love?"

"Everything."

The customer shuffled a deck of cards at the round table in the general store. Illuminated by a coal oil lamp, he wore his curl-brimmed cowboy hat low over his eyes, shadowing most of his face, as he turned up the ace of spades.

Gibson recognized him as one of the waddies from the Circle K. "What can I do fer you, Mr. Raybart?"

"Three bags of tobacco," said Jay Krenshaw's courier.

Gibson moved to the shelves, to retrieve the

merchandise. "Sounds like the bunkhouse ran out of smokes."

"That's what happened all right."

Gibson dropped tobacco on the table, and accepted payment. "Ain't often that I see you boys in town during the week."

"Whiskey," replied Raybart.

Gibson returned to the counter, picked up a bottle of homemade white lightning, and filled the glass to the halfway mark. Then he served it to Raybart. "If you need me for anythin' else, just ring the bell."

Raybart reached out and grabbed Gibson's wrist. He drew him closer and said in a low voice, "What d'ya know 'bout a feller named Braddock, who rides fer the Bar T?"

Gibson placed his forefinger in front of his lips. "Shhhh. His woman's back there."

"Siddown."

The shopkeeper dropped to a chair. "I don't have much time . . ."

"Is he a hired gun?"

"Not that I know of."

"Where's he from?"

"Titusville, but I'm afraid I really don't know much about him. You don't really think that he's an outlaw, do you?"

"Who's his woman?"

"The new schoolmarm."

Raybart narrowed his eyes skeptically.

"Keep yer ears open. Find out all that you can about them."

"But . . ." Gibson's voice trailed off into the sound of wind rattling the windows of the general store. The unofficial mayor of Shelby felt menaced by the cowboy, whom he barely knew. "Now listen," he said in a shaky voice, "I'm not a spy."

Raybart gazed deeply into his eyes. "You're not dead either, yet."

The cowboys sat around the campfire, gnawing steaks, their eyes half closed with fatigue. Tomorrow they'd be up before dawn for another day of roping and branding. There was little conversation, and the cowboys kept glancing apprehensively at Duane.

All insults had stopped following the encounter with the riders from the Circle K. Even Duane wondered who the wild man was who'd punched strangers in the mouth and yanked them out of saddles. I should've called McGrath over, instead of challenging that cowboy. McGrath is getting paid to be ramrod, not me.

He and Ross were scheduled to battle that evening, but Ross appeared uninterested in pursuing the conflict. They'd all become chary of Duane, treated him with deference; he wasn't the tenderfoot anymore. He'd learned the hard way that in the secular world, naked brutality was considered the pinnacle of human achievement.

Duane didn't know what to think of himself. Violence was clearly a sin, yet Christ physically threw the moneylenders out of the temple precincts. It could be this, or it could be that. Duane wished he could revive the rock-solid certainties of monastery life, but they'd melted like ice in the flames of hell. What could be worse than the hatred, jealousy, and greed of the secular world?

The ramrod's voice came to him from across the campsite. "Braddock — can I talk to you a moment?"

"Yes, sir." Duane was on his feet in an instant, carrying his tin plate, heading toward the great man. The other cowboys watched his progress, as firelight cast writhing shadows on the side of the chuck wagon. Duane sat opposite the ramrod and said, "What's up?"

The ramrod scrutinized Duane carefully. "Who are you, kid?"

"What're you driving at?"

"You nearly got a lot of men killed today. Do you know that?"

"That Circle K cowboy accused me of being a rustler. Was I supposed to lie down and take it?"

"Yes."

The ramrod sliced off a chunk of steak and placed it into his mouth, ruminating like a cow. Duane wondered if he should apologize, but for what? "Nobody calls me a rustler and gets away with it."

"This range don't need another hothead. Old Man Krenshaw's all right, but that son of his is a little loco. Then you ride by and knock him out of the saddle. Jay Krenshaw ain't the type what fergits, and he can hire all the guns he wants. You'd better watch yer back, if you want to see nineteen."

It was midnight when Amos Raybart returned to the Circle K Ranch. All the lights were out except for one in the corner of the main house, while wind whistled the shingles of the barn. Raybart tied his horse to the rail, entered the main house, and the living room was silent, with a few embers glowing dully beneath fireplace ashes. He made his way down the corridor and knocked lightly on a door.

"Come in," said the voice on the other side.

Raybart entered a small, smelly room, where Jay Krenshaw lay fully clothed on a bed. The boss's son rolled over, his eyes half open, and looked at Raybart. "What'd you find out?"

Raybart sat on the wooden chair in the corner. An empty bottle stood on the dresser, and the odor of stale whiskey hung mournfully in the air. "I talked to Mr. Gibson, like you said. He told me that Braddock came from Titusville, and his woman is the new schoolmarm."

Jay Krenshaw sat up in bed. "He's got a *woman?*" The boss's son reached for the whiskey bottle, saw that it was empty, and threw it across the room, where it crashed into the wall, sending shards of glass flying in all directions. Raybart had to raise his arm to protect his eyes.

Jay had slept fitfully since going to bed, because the embarrassment still rankled. And if that wasn't enough, he had to sleep alone while Braddock had his own woman. "What'd she look like?"

"Din't see her."

Jay couldn't forget the horrible incident, which smoldered in his mind like burning rags. I'll never be able to head up this ranch, if I get the reputation that any filthy cowboy can throw me out've my saddle.

"Go to Titusville," Jay said. "Find out all you can about Braddock." He reached into his pocket, and pulled out money. "Don't come back until you know who he is, and what he's done. I think he's an owlhoot, and maybe we can get the law to string him up.

Otherwise we'll have to do it. Are you still here?"

Lieutenant Dawes walked down the deserted street, on his way back to the encampment. His hands were clasped behind his back, head bowed to the ground in deep thought. Miss Fontaine is in difficult straits, he ruminated. The collar of her dress was frayed, and she had a worried expression in her eyes.

Lieutenant Dawes could converse endlessly on topics intellectual or spiritual, but seldom felt warmth for other people. He was basically a lonely soldier boy, but now, after dinner with Vanessa Fontaine, he saw new hope for the happiness that he'd long ago despaired of ever finding. Somehow, I must make sure she doesn't marry, he thought darkly.

Lieutenant Dawes wanted to be an honorable man, and a credit to the officer corps, but needed a wife desperately. He knew that many women married the wrong men out of financial desperation, and wondered if that was driving her into the arms of her cowboy husband-to-be. She probably thinks I'm just another tin soldier, and a damn Yankee to boot.

He pulled aside the tent flap, and Corporal Hazelwood sat at the desk, writing a letter home. Lieutenant Dawes removed his cavalry gloves, as Corporal Hazelwood made his report. Then the corporal departed, leaving Lieutenant Dawes alone in his tent. He looked at the logbook, sat heavily on the canvas cot, and stared into the middle distance. I can't put in twenty years on the frontier without a wife, but if I had Vanessa Fontaine waiting for me at the end of every day, it wouldn't be so bad. How can I broach the subject without making a fool of myself?

Less than three hundred yards away, Vanessa Fontaine lay in bed with her own romantic notions. She was at the crossroads of life, and could go up or down, according to decisions of the next few days. She'd noted the lovesick glaze in Lieutenant Dawes's eyes, and he'd appeared uncomfortable in his uniform. Moreover, she knew that women were scarce in Texas, and men generally considered her attractive. I'm still a desirable commodity, but how much longer can it last?

I'll be an old lady soon, and Duane will start looking for someone his own age. He'll weep and moan, but he'll abandon me nonetheless. On the other hand, a West Point officer closer to my age would be less likely to create a scandal that could jeopardize his career.

Now I'm finally thinking with my mind, instead of my heart. Duane has certain delightful traits, she pondered, but he's really just a plaything, and not a man with whom a woman can build a life. Lieutenant Dawes, on the other hand, is a West Point officer with a better chance for promotion than those who came up through the ranks. I can't throw myself at him, and he can't ask me to marry him, since I'm already engaged. Maybe I should get unengaged, but if I do it so soon, people will think that I'm silly, callous, or a schemer, which in fact I am. And then, if it all works out, how could I tell Duane? With his temper, he's liable to shoot somebody.

Duane lay on the dirt near the cold embers of the campfire. Men snored all around him, but he wasn't accustomed to sleeping on the ground, and didn't know where to put his hip. He tried to find a comfortable position, but there was none on the cold, hard ground.

His muscles ached, a demon drilled a hole through his brain, and his stomach struggled to digest the massive poundage of beef that he'd devoured that evening. Unable to fall asleep, he recalled the run-in with the Circle K. He was in trouble again, because other people wouldn't leave him alone.

What is it about me that bothers them? he

wondered. Why didn't that Circle K cowboy pick on somebody else? And he knew that the incident wasn't over. Once again, he'd have to watch his back.

You can always return to the monastery, he said to himself. Just get down on your knees, apologize to the abbot, and he'll forgive you. But how can you live without women?

He'd noticed pretty Mexican girls at Mass in the monastery church, and had experienced impure thoughts. The craving became so intense, he decided to leave, but didn't have courage to tell the abbot. So he got into a fight, and the abbot had thrown him out, resolving his dilemma. Then, a few weeks later, he'd run into Vanessa Fontaine. He recalled the advice of Saint Paul the Apostle. *It is better to marry than burn.*

Duane was anxious for Saturday night to arrive. He also considered Vanessa his best friend and advisor. She'd always demonstrated good sense, except when she'd run off with him. I'll bet she's as lonely and unhappy as I am right now, and misses me as much as I miss her.

Lieutenant Dawes appeared at the general store at the appointed hour next morning. A buffalo hunter sat at the round table, drinking whiskey, while Gibson filled an order for beans, molasses, and flour. "They're awaitin' fer you," he said.

Lieutenant Dawes headed for the corridor behind the counter, spine straight, stomach in, chest out. His stomach rumbled with anxiety, because the detachment commander didn't feel comfortable with little children who weren't subject to his orders. And he had to make the best possible impression on Miss Fontaine.

He found the parlor, where children sat on chairs, the sofa, and the floor. The schoolmarm faced them behind the rickety writing table that served as her desk. "Our guest has arrived," she declared warmly. "Class, I'd like you to meet Lieutenant Clayton Dawes."

The children applauded politely, as she'd taught them. Lieutenant Dawes tried to smile, but looked as if he'd just been out-flanked by six thousand Comanches. "I've been asked to tell you about army life," he began, "but I don't exactly know where to begin, because the army is quite a complex subject. So I thought that I'd just answer any questions that you might have. Who wants to be first?"

Nobody moved for several seconds, as children eyed him suspiciously. Then a hand warily raised into the air. "How come you wear a uniform? Why can't you dress like an ordinary person?"

"Uniforms originated because soldiers couldn't recognize friend from foe in the confusion of battle. My particular uniform was designed by people in Washington, D.C., who've never seen Texas in their lives. Any other questions?"

"How much do soldiers get paid?" a different boy asked.

"Not much, but most men don't join for the money. They become soldiers because they want to serve their country."

A little girl with a pink bow in her blond hair offered, "My father told me that men become soldiers 'cause they're no good fer nawthin' else."

"Tell your father," the lieutenant replied, "that Ulysses S. Grant used to be a soldier, and now he's President of the United States. Robert E. Lee was a soldier, and now he's built one of the finest universities in the South. Soldiering requires many skills, such as tactics, engineering, and supply, but most of all, I'd say that a soldier has to have common sense."

"Ever kill an injun?" asked a skinny little boy with a big nose, a fiendish grin on his face.

"A few."

"What'd it feel like?"

Lieutenant Dawes was seldom at a loss for words, but how could he explain terror, triumph, blood, and guts? "I guess I was glad to kill him before he killed me. Next question?"

It was silent, and Lieutenant Dawes realized that he'd been too abrupt. His troopers had to tolerate his imperious manner, but not the children of Shelby. He cast his eyes over them and remembered when he was a child, with a bright mischievous mind, and the innocence of a lamb.

The silence was rescued by the voice of the schoolmarm, who interrupted with the unerring instinct of a sophisticated social animal. "Could you tell us about West Point, Lieutenant?"

"I spent the best years of my life there, and

I'll always carry it with me wherever I go. Most people don't know that the Point is one of the best engineering schools in the world, and any American can go there, free of charge. All it takes is the desire to serve your country, and hard work."

Vanessa listened to him describe a day in the life of a cadet, and she had to admit that he cut the splendid figure of a man. The more she thought of it, the more she questioned running off with a poor ex-monk so much younger than she. Duane had many wonderful qualities, but no money, no prospects, and no specialized skills, except for his talent with guns, which probably would get him killed before long.

After the lecture, Vanessa escorted Lieutenant Dawes to the door. "Thank you for agreeing to speak to us, Lieutenant. It was a most enlightening lecture."

Their bodies were close, in the long corridor that led to the general store. She felt his rugged physicality, while the lone soldier was enchanted by her narrow waist. Each knew that they'd never speak again, but he didn't dare make an untoward suggestion to a woman about to be married, and she couldn't simply flirt like a dance hall girl.

They stepped onto the main street of Shelby. Straight ahead was a wagon, the big draft horses looking at them curiously. Schoolmarm and officer fumbled for words, their eyes met, and a silent communication passed between them. He knew that he had to speak, or forever hold his peace. What would my father say under the circumstances? he wondered. He'd say whatever was on his mind, and let the devil take the hindmost. Lieutenant Dawes cleared his throat, and his voice sounded strange and reedy to his ears. "I understand that you'll be getting married in a few days, Miss Fontaine."

"It's the truth," she replied, a frown coming over her face.

There was silence. Somehow the hurdle must be surmounted, but neither knew how. Then Lieutenant Dawes muttered, "You don't sound very happy about it."

"To be honest, sometimes I wonder if I'm doing the right thing."

He took a deep breath to steady himself. "If you're not sure, perhaps you shouldn't go through with it."

"It's not good for a woman to be alone, if you know what I mean."

He tried to grin. "As long as there are men like me, women like you will never be alone."

"It's been my observation that men grow tired of women rather quickly."

"Depends on the woman, I'd say. You'll

probably remain beautiful forever, because you have perfect bone structure. But true beauty comes from within, and is ageless. As I said before, I'm surprised to find a woman like you in Shelby. Do you like it here?"

"Not very much, I'm afraid, and I certainly don't look forward to spending the rest of my life here."

"Why can't you leave?"

"Sometimes people get locked into difficult situations from which they can't readily extricate themselves."

"Are you speaking of yourself, Miss Fontaine?"

"Perhaps."

They gazed deeply into each other's eyes, then glanced away nervously. This is it, he thought. "Sometimes, people think they're trapped, but they're really not. If you don't want to marry Mister Braddock, you can . . . well . . . this may sound rather strange . . . but you can marry me."

She didn't know whether to blush, laugh, or cry. "You shouldn't joke with a poor girl's heart, Lieutenant."

"I need a wife, and it appears that you need someone to take care of you. Perhaps we can arrange something, but it wouldn't work if you found me unattractive."

"Oh no — you're quite attractive," she admitted. "The army uniform was made for a man like you. It's just that you've taken me by surprise."

"Surely you've noticed that I've been looking at you with lust in my heart."

She touched her hair. "I thought you saw me as a dried-up old schoolmarm."

"You're much more than that."

Both felt relieved, because the barrier had been passed. "This is very unexpected," she said. "I don't receive a proposal every day. You *have* made a proposal, haven't you?"

"Absolutely."

"I'm scheduled to marry another man this Sunday, but your offer is most compelling. I'd like to think it over, if you don't mind. In war and love, one mustn't make hasty decisions."

"We could help each other," he explained. "I'm going on a scout in the morning, and perhaps you'll have an answer when I return?" He bowed slightly, a sunbeam rolling across his left shoulder board. "I place myself at your disposal, Miss Fontaine."

Duane twirled his lasso over his head, as Thunderbolt leapt over a cholla cactus. They were chasing a spirited calf who wasn't in the mood for a red-hot brand. The calf dodged from side to side, squealing for his mother, but Thunderbolt stayed after him, tongue hanging out, enjoying the chase.

Duane threw the rope, and it flew through the air. The calf saw it coming, bleated in misery, but couldn't get out of the way. The ring of doom dropped over his neck, and Duane tied his end around the pommel. "Gotcha!"

He dragged the struggling calf toward the fire, and couldn't remember when he'd ever felt so vigorous. *I always knew that this was the job for me!* The sky was bright blue, with no clouds in sight. He felt warm, the top three buttons of his shirt unfastened, his red bandanna loose around his throat. A substantial quantity of thick black cowboy coffee made him wide awake and keyed for action.

It's not a bad life, he acknowledged. *And on Saturday night, I'll sleep with my beautiful future bride. What am I always complaining about? It looks like everything's finally going my way.*

Lieutenant Dawes sat at his desk, studying his map. His orders were to sweep south, to insure that no Comanches were marauding in the area. He traced his finger along the proposed route and hoped to reach a certain water hole by nightfall.

The image of Vanessa floated through his mind, interrupting his concentration. After years of living in the Bachelor Officers' Quarters, the mere thought of sleeping with Vanessa Fontaine excited him beyond his wildest hallucinations. *My misery will be over, if she says yes.*

Sergeant Mahoney approached, throwing a salute. "Ready to move out, sir."

Lieutenant Dawes drew himself to his full height, and surveyed the scene before him. The detachment was formed in two ranks, with the wagon to the right, and the guidon fluttering in the breeze. He marched to his horse, whose reins were held by a private with a chin cut during his morning's shave. Lieutenant Dawes raised himself into the saddle, and hollered, "Detachment — left face!"

The men reined their horses in that direction as Lieutenant Dawes rode to their head. He was surprised to note a gathering of children at the edge of town, clumped around their tall, blond schoolmarm. He felt like a knight of the round table going off to war, cheered by his lady love.

He took his position at the head of the column as his horse pranced nervously, raring to go. Lieutenant Dawes raised his right hand in the air, and shouted, "Detachment — forward — hoooooo!"

He lowered his hand and put his spurs to the horse. The animal stepped out proudly, moving his head up and down, as Lieutenant

Dawes sat firmly in his saddle, cavalry hat slanted low over his eyes.

Ahead, the children and their schoolmarm congregated alongside the path of the oncoming soldiers. The little girls clapped their hands gleefully, while boys stared in awe at soldiers riding off to fight the dreaded Comanche. Lieutenant Dawes drew closer, and admired the woman he hoped to marry. He raised his right hand, fingers extended stiffly, and tossed her a salute.

A light rain fell that night. The cowboys from the Bar T dined on the usual steak dinner, but the biscuits were soggy, and rivulets of rainwater flowed among the beans. McSweeny swore at the fire sputtering beneath the makeshift tarpaulin shelter, as if that would make the coffee boil faster.

Duane sat in silence among the other cowboys. They all wore their ponchos, their feet wet, and a chill was on the range. Duane swallowed his last chunk of nearly raw steak, and washed it down with water from his canteen. He dipped his plate into the bucket of tepid water, cleaned it, and stacked it on the rainsoaked chuck wagon counter. Then he headed for his bedroll. He wanted to go to bed early, because McGrath had assigned him the second watch.

Rain poured on him as he unrolled his blankets and tarpaulin. Then he pulled off his boots, removed his hat, and squirmed out from beneath his drenched poncho. In an instant he was inside his bedroll, his head withdrawing like a turtle's.

Rain pelted him steadily, but the tarpaulin kept him dry. The storm howled around him, lashing the canvas atop the chuck wagon. A bolt of thunder rippled over the ground, and the earth heaved.

The dramatic weather caused him to think of his wife-to-be in Shelby. I can't wait to see her on Saturday, he thought, hugging the blankets closer. What a great time we'll have.

Fifteen miles away, a lone rider made his way across the rainswept plain. He slouched in his saddle, and the hood of his poncho make him look like a strange mad monk on an incomprehensible quest.

But he was no monk, and his mission wasn't religious. Amos Raybart's eyes were closed, and he slept fitfully, transported through the night on the back of his soaking horse. The animal plodded onward, because Comanches offered more misery than cowboys, and if a horse became tired, the Comanche ate his liver.

Raybart traveled at night, and slept during

the day. The cowboy had been wanted once, and knew all the tricks. He drowsed in the saddle, and rain didn't bother him. He didn't have to punch cows, and was making extra money. What more could a man want?

Somewhere in the pouring rain — Titusville. Raybart hoped to arrive on Saturday, unless he was delayed by Comanches. He saw himself lying on the plain, stripped naked, his bones whitening in the sun, while a Comanche wore his hat.

He opened his eyes and perused the blackness that surrounded him. The rain hissed as if it disapproved of him. He'd been a thief, had killed a man in Arkansas, and sold whiskey to Osage warriors. The son of a mud hut farmer, he'd been poor all his life, and didn't expect anything significant to change.

Just a few more days, he thought, fingering the coins. I'll get me a nice hotel room, and then I'll go to the cribs. Might as well have some fun while I'm at it, he thought as he rode toward the darkness at the edge of the storm.

CHAPTER 5

The cowboys returned to the Bar T Saturday afternoon. They herded the horses into the corral, and proceeded to feed and water them, while the Ramrod made his way to the main house.

The front door was opened by Myrtle Thornton. "No trouble, I hope."

"Only once." McGrath removed his cowboy hat. "The boss in?"

Myrtle led McGrath to Big Al Thornton, who was seated with his daughter on wooden chairs behind the house, facing the open range. Phyllis wore a pink dress with a high buttoned collar, while the top three buttons of the rancher's shirt were undone.

"Have a seat, McGrath," Myrtle said. "Let's hear about it."

McGrath smelled of sweat, tobacco, and horses as he dropped onto a chair. "We had a blowout with the Circle K. They showed up

1785989

while we was on the north range, and Jay said we was abrandin' their calves. One thing led to another, and before I knew it, that new man you hired beat the hell out of Billie Reade, then he knocked Jay out of the saddle, and I thought for sure there'd be gunplay. You never told me that Braddock was a professional."

Thornton appeared surprised. "I din't know it myself!"

"His hand moved awful fast."

Myrtle Thornton interjected: "I told you that he was an owlhoot."

"Just because he's got a fast hand," Big Al replied, "that don't mean he's a hired gun. But we don't need no more hotheads around here than we've got already. Tell Braddock that I want to talk to him."

The cavalry detachment saw no Comanches, witnessed no atrocities, and now were back at their encampment, anxious to prepare for their big Saturday night on the town.

The troopers lined up in front of Lieutenant Dawes, and he inspected them with merciless objectivity. They were covered with dust, wilted in their saddles. If Comanches had attacked on the way in, no telling what might've happened.

Sergeant Mahoney rode toward him, and

threw a salute. "Any special orders, sir?"

"I'm going into town for about a half hour. Carry on."

The detachment commander felt as though his legs were permanently bowed, as he climbed down from his horse. He knew that he should take a bath, shave, and change clothes, but couldn't wait that long. He tossed his reins to the orderly, then headed toward the general store.

Vanessa had been on his mind throughout the patrol, and his future hung in the balance of her decision. Perhaps she changed her mind, he thought, but how could a rational woman prefer an ordinary cowboy to me? He considered himself a first-rate candidate for marriage, but if Vanessa rejected him — it would devastate his vanity, and he'd resume his depressing bachelor career. One day he'd get careless, and somebody's husband would shoot him, or a Comanche would get his hair.

Please say yes, he implored silently, as he strolled down Shelby's only street, headed for Gibson's General Store.

Fred Gibson fretted behind his store window, as he observed the Army encampment on the edge of town. He'd laid in a special stock of white lightning, prepared in a washtub with the aid of his wife, because he'd foreseen demand increasing during the months ahead, as both the Bar T and Circle K added more cowboys, and the Army camp became a permanent adjunct to the town.

Gibson needed capital, his fondest ambition a full-fledged saloon with gambling tables and girls. Maybe Mr. Phipps and I can build it, and between the two of us, we can become rich men!

The door opened, interrupting his luxurious reverie. Lieutenant Dawes appeared filthy, as if he'd crawled down main street on his belly. "Glad to see you back, sir," said Gibson, flashing his shopkeeper's smile. "Have a whiskey on me."

He poured the glass, and Lieutenant Dawes accepted it with shaky hand. He sipped off an inch, then asked: "Is Miss Fontaine in?"

"Don't know where else she'd be. You look like you've had a rough patrol. Hope there weren't no trouble with injuns."

"Would you tell Miss Fontaine that I'd like to see her?"

Mr. Gibson departed for the back of the building, and Lieutenant Dawes pushed the glass away, because he didn't dare get drunk at this crucial juncture. Vanessa Fontaine could hurt him far worse than any Comanche, and he tried to calm himself, but believed deeply that his last chance for happiness was on the line. Sure, he might meet another desirable single woman someday, but it was unlikely in remote West Texas. And if he did find another, she'd probably want a rich man, not a mere Lieutenant in the Fourth Calvary.

Mr. Gibson reappeared through the curtain, and lowered his eyes demurely. "Miss Fontaine is waiting for you in the parlor."

Lieutenant Dawes passed into the corridor, and found Vanessa seated next to the fireplace. She arose as he approached, and they beheld each other tentatively.

"I apologize for my appearance," he said stiffly, "but I was anxious to see you. Have you reached a decision concerning . . ."

His voice trailed off, because he was afraid to say it. He felt awkward, despicable, and bedraggled as he awaited her verdict. She opened her mouth to speak, and he thought he'd faint from suspense.

"I've given considerable thought to your proposal," she began, "and I've realized how fortunate I am to have found you. We're not children anymore, blinded by foolish passions, but a man and a woman with a good share of experience behind us. I believe that we can have a happy life together."

He felt as if a sunflower burst inside him, as he took her in his arms. "I've dreamed of you every night," he whispered into her ear. "I'll try to be a good husband — I promise."

He closed his eyes, and felt her tall lithe body against him. This is the pinnacle of my life, he thought. With this woman at my side — I cannot fail.

"But there's just one problem," she whispered softly. "Somehow, I'll have to tell Duane."

"You wanted to see me, sir?"

Big Al was seated alone in his backyard and casually examined Duane Braddock standing above him. Braddock had a wispy beard, and his rumpled clothes were covered with dried mud. "Have a seat."

Duane dropped to the chair, wondering if he was going to get fired. "I heard you had a little problem with the Circle K," Big Al began. "What's yer side of it?"

"One of the Circle K cowboys called me out, then Jay Krenshaw braced me."

Big Al leaned forward and looked into Duane's eyes. "Are you a professional?"

"Not me, but what would *you* do if Jay Krenshaw drew on you?"

Big Al stared at him. "Let me explain the lay of the land. Jay's father and I are old friends, but Jay's been a hellion practically from the day he could walk, and he's got a mean streak a mile wide. Anyhow, we generally tolerate his ornery nature, because we don't need gunplay on this range. So next time you see Jay Krenshaw — back off."

"If nobody stands up to him," Duane countered, "he'll get worse. Sooner or later somebody'll get shot, and do you want it to be one of your cowboys, or one of his?"

Thornton was surprised by the answer, because most cowboys generally clammed up when called before the boss. "Don't you like to work here, boy?"

"Nobody calls me a rustler and gets away with it."

"A man fights to defend what's right, and not just work the poison out of his system. Whether you realize it or not, you've made an enemy for life. Keep your holster oiled, and take care of your right hand. I'm a-telling you, as sure as I'm sitting here — Jay Krenshaw will try to kill you afore long."

Phyllis Thornton watched from behind her curtain as Duane headed back to the bunkhouse. Her eyes roved over his hips, the tilt of his hat, his cowboy swagger. There was something about him that made her nervous, and she chewed her lower lip absent-mindedly, wondering whether she should actually get down from her high horse and *do* something to attract his attention.

Most girls flirted like harlots, and if all else failed, they showed a little leg, but she detested hypocrisy and pretense. On the other hand, Duane Braddock was the best-looking boy she'd ever seen.

She looked in the mirror, and saw imaginary wrinkles around her eyes. It appeared that she was getting a double chin. Her hips were too wide. I don't want to be an old maid — that's all I know. She left the bedroom, and found her father in the backyard, watching the sun sink toward the horizon. He spun around and reached for his gun. Phyllis sometimes wondered whether her father adorned an old wanted poster in a faraway post office.

She plunked onto the chair beside him and thrust out her lower lip. "I'm unhappy," she declared. "It's the same routine day after day. I wish we could have some fun once in a while."

Big Al Thornton narrowed his eyes as he scrutinized his one and only daughter. She was a fussy child, and possessed a vitriolic temper, reminding him of himself when he was young, always restless, looking for excitement. "Perhaps you might want to visit your Aunt Lulu in Denver, although I'd hate to lose you to a Shoshoni warrior along the way. Is there anything that we can do here?"

"Yes, but as soon as I say something, you'd tell me that it's impractical, or costs too much."

"You're not even giving your father a chance!"

"Well, since you put it that way . . . I think it might be nice for you to throw a big shindig. You could invite people from across the county, and maybe there'd be less trouble on this range if we all had some fun together."

Big Al sucked a tooth and wondered what game she was playing this time. "Wa'al, if you think we all need a shindig *that* bad, work it out with your mother. As far as the cost goes — don't worry — I'll pay. What else are fathers for?"

Duane shaved in a mirror with a diagonal crack in a rusting frame. It was nailed to a cottonwood tree behind the bunkhouse, near the table maintaining the wash basin and pitcher. He cut himself twice, dried himself with the towel, and returned to the bunkhouse.

The others were preparing for Saturday night. Ross said, "Ramrod wants to talk to you, Braddock."

Duane buttoned his shirt as he made his way toward the ramrod's shack. He knocked on the door, and it was opened a few moments later by the great man himself.

"I got a job fer you, kid. We need a cat, 'cuzz we got too many damned rats. It's up to you to get one."

"But I don't know anything about cats, ramrod. Where should I go?"

"That's yer problem." The door slammed in Duane's face.

Titusville twinkled straight ahead as the sun merged with the horizon. Amos Raybart was pleased that the first leg of his journey was finally coming to an end. Now he could get a drink of whiskey, a hotel room, and a bath.

He was surprised that Titusville was so huge, because the surrounding range didn't appear very populated. He could perceive buildings in various stages of abandoned construction. On the main street, many buildings were deserted, with windows boarded up. The town seemed to be dying, but Raybart had seen many go bust as gold mines petered out, investment dried up, or the men on Wall Street routed the railroad someplace else.

It felt eerie to be riding down the main street of a mostly unpopulated large town. Raybart kept his right hand near his gun, in case somebody tried to bushwhack him. Farther down the street, he saw more boarded-up saloons and stores, but one drinking establishment wasn't closed, and lights glowed in both windows. The sign above the door said: LONGHORN SALOON.

Raybart licked his lips in anticipation as he reined his horse toward the hitching rail, stepped down from the saddle, and loosened the cinch. The horse drank thirstily from the trough in front of the saloon, as Raybart hitched up his pants. Then he headed for the batwing doors.

A few cowboys sat at the bar, while others were gathered at tables, playing cards, reading old newspapers, or staring mindlessly into space. Above the bar hung a painting of naked women cavorting in a bath, but it was marred by bullet holes. Raybart slouched to the bar, placed his foot on the rail, and said: "Whiskey."

The bartender filled a glass and pushed it toward him. "First one's on the house."

Raybart flipped a few coins on the bar. "What the hell happened to this town?"

"The railroad was supposed to come, but it din't. Let me tell you — this was a real wildass place fer awhile there. We had a killin' damn near every Saturday night, and one night there was *six* killin's. But thank God it's settled down. Hard to think straight, when lead is flyin' around."

The bartender waited on another cus-

tomer, while Raybart tossed down his whiskey. "Hit me again."

The bartender returned with his bottle, and
topped off Raybart's glass. Raybart leaned
closer and said, "I'm a-lookin' fer somebody.
You ever hear of Duane Braddock?"

The bartender's eyes bugged out. "That's
the Pecos Kid — the feller what's done most
of the killin'!"

Now it was Raybart's turn to register surprise. "Is he a hired gun?"

The bartender pointed over his shoulder.
"You want to know about the Pecos Kid, that
man a-sit-tin' at the table over thar, the one in
the stovepipe hat — he knows him about as
well as anybody. His name's Farnsworth, and
he used to run the newspaper, but now he's a-
drinkin' hisself to death."

Raybart stared at a rotund man sitting in a
corner, staring into a glass and mumbling.

"Is he loco?"

"If he ain't, he's damn close."

Raybart approached the newspaperman
cautiously, because Farnsworth gave the appearance of a maniac about to blow his cork.
Bedraggled blond hair poked beneath his hat,
the crown of which was dented on the side.
He hadn't shaved for several days, and the
odor of whiskey radiated from his being.
Raybart stopped in front of the table and said:

"I'm a-lookin' fer Duane Braddock."

"Ungrateful little bastard," Farnsworth replied. He blinked as his watery eyes recognized a new face. "Who're you?"

"It's don't matter," replied Raybart, as he sat opposite Farnsworth. "What d'ya know about 'im?"

"Last thing I heard, he was headed south."

"The bartender said he shot some people here."

"Five to be exact."

"Is he a hired gun?"

"There's some that says he is, and some that says he ain't, so you tell me? But I saw him shoot Saul Klevins outside on Main Street, and Klevins was the fastest gun in these parts."

"If Braddock wasn't a hired gun, how could he shoot the fastest gun in these parts?"

"He had a good teacher, for one thing. You ever heard of Clyde Butterfield?"

Raybart nodded sagely. "They say he was one of the best what ever was."

"Butterfield taught him everything he knew, and then some. But that doesn't explain anything. Duane had to have something for Butterfield to mold in the first place. Sometimes I ask myself: Did I create the Pecos Kid, or did he create me?"

"I'm a-tryin' ter figger out who Braddock

really is. Do you know anything about whar he come from?"

"He grew up in a monastery in the Guadalupe Mountains. They say he was studying to become a priest."

Raybart was astonished by this news. "Maybe they lied. Do you know if Braddock is wanted by anybody?"

"If he is, I pity the lawman who's on his tail."

"What else can you tell me about him?"

"He ran off with the most beautiful woman in town, and I wonder where he is now. What did you say your name was?"

Raybart leaned closer, and gazed into the journalist's eyes. "You never met me, and we never had this conversation."

Vanessa felt as though God had smiled upon her, as she sat by the window of her room. At last she was getting married to a gentleman of substance, and the past would return in slightly altered form. She'd be treated like a lady again, instead of a loose woman on the deck of life.

As for the bed part, she wasn't wildly in love with Lieutenant Dawes, but felt superior to silly romantic nonsense. Duane would arrive in town soon, and she wondered how to break the news. If she told the truth, there was the possibility that he'd become violent. I'll have to lead into it slowly, and reassure him every step of the way. He must understand that I'll always reserve a special place in my heart for him.

She thought of being naked with Duane, and a flush came to her cheek. Her mind filled with images that the average Christian would consider lewd. Except for her deceased first love, she'd never enjoyed it as much as with Duane.

It's time to make rational decisions for a change, she lectured herself. I'll have to speak with him alone. She found Mrs. Gibson in the kitchen, preparing roast beef sandwiches for the multitude of cowboys and soldiers who were supposed to show up that evening.

"I've come to ask you a favor, Mrs. Gibson," Vanessa said. "This may come as a shock, but I've decided not to marry Duane Braddock. I know it sounds terrible, but please try to understand."

"A woman mustn't rush into these things," Mrs. Gibson replied, "and cowboys don't exactly make the best husbands. But a West Pointer is quite another matter."

Vanessa's jaw dropped open. "You know!"

"I seen how both of you look at each other. It's none of my business, but I think you'd be far better off with Lieutenant Dawes. My dear, women like you are not supposed to marry cowboys. You're a lady, and you require a gentleman like Lieutenant Dawes. I consider him an extremely handsome officer, by the way." Mrs. Gibson giggled like a schoolgirl at her indiscretion.

"That brings me to the favor I need to ask," Vanessa said quickly. "I need to tell Duane of my decision, and I'd like to speak with him alone, where he can feel comfortable. Would you mind awfully if I invited him to my room?"

"We wouldn't want a public display, would we? When he arrives, Mr. Gibson will send him directly to wherever you prefer."

In Titusville, a prostitute with a gimp leg led Amos Raybart down a corridor lined with canvas walls. Her left arm was semiparalyzed, and she held it like the front paw of a squirrel. Meanwhile, on the other side of the shack, a customer groaned like a buffalo during mating season. Raybart's prostitute was pretty if you like big-boned farm girls.

They entered her tiny room, and it too had canvas walls. Her cot was narrow, jammed against the wall, and she had a dresser dotted with tiny bottles of cosmetics. "Fifty cents," she said.

He dropped the coins into her hand, while

the oil lamp cast shadows over his unshaven features. "I want to ask you a few questions."

She became suspicious immediately, and made sure that he had nothing in his hands. "Questions 'bout what?"

He looked into her eyes. "I want you to tell me everythin' you know about Duane Braddock. I understand that he screwed you onc't."

Her eyes widened at the sound of the name from her past. "He was only here fer a few minutes. It's not like we was friends."

"Did he say anything 'bout hisself?"

Her caution grew, and she took a step backwards. "What you wanna know fer?"

He grabbed her arm, yanked his Remington, and pointed it at her nose. "I'll ask yer agin'. Did he say anythin'?"

"The onliest thang I remember 'bout Duane Braddock was that while he was here, he got in a fight with three other cowboys, and before it was over, they damn near beat him to death."

"He took on *three* other cowboys, you say?"

"I know it sounds loco, but ask any of the other girls — you don't believe me."

Raybart maintained his aim on her nose. "You ever see 'im again, you better not tell him about me. Understand?"

"I never saw you a-fore in my life, mister."

He grinned fiendishly, as he holstered his gun. "You can take yer clothes off now."

It was dark when the Bar T cowboys rode into Shelby. They came to a halt in front of the general store, and tied their horses to the hitching rail.

"Braddock!" shouted the ramrod.

Duane shambled forward. "What d'ya want?"

McGrath pointed his finger at Duane's nose. "I don't care if you get drunk, pass out in an alley, or shoot somebody, but don't fergit the cat."

"If there's a cat in this town, you can bet your bottom dollar that I'll get him, ramrod."

McGrath looked at him dubiously, then moved toward the front door, followed by his crew. Duane untied a gunnysack from the back of his saddle and threw it over his shoulders. His plan was to stuff a cat into the gunnysack, and ride him back to the bunkhouse.

He looked around at the few shacks that comprised Shelby and didn't see any cats. Where should I go? he wondered. He decided to worry about it after he saw Vanessa, and a smile creased his face at the mere prospect of kissing her again. It had been so long since he'd seen her, he'd dreamed about her every night, and now at last they could be together again. He suspected that she'd made arrangements for their imminent wedding, and hoped somebody would give them a cat for a wedding present.

He opened the door of the general store. Before him were soldiers and cowboys sitting at the round table, or on the floor. Another contingent was crowded around the counter, which had become a bar. Mr. and Mrs. Gibson worked frenziedly behind it, pouring whiskey and collecting money, their eyes aglitter with naked greed. Duane tried to attract their attention, but had to compete with shouting soldiers and cowboys.

Then Mr. Gibson noticed the silver conchos reflecting light off his two oil lamps. "In back!"

Duane circled the gang at the bar and came to the curtained door that led to the rear of the house. He pushed it aside and disappeared from view.

Meanwhile, seated in the corner, Lieutenant Dawes watched him go. He'd been curious about Vanessa's former husband-to-be, and now at last had seen him. Just the kind of pretty face that ladies love, he thought cynically, as he raised the bottle of white lightning to his lips.

The voice of Corporal Hazelwood came to him from the far side of the room. "You fel-

lers see that galoot what just walked in here —
the one with the fancy hat?"

"What about 'im?" asked Private Cruik-
shank.

"That's the Pecos Kid!"

"Who's the Pecos Kid?"

"When I was in Titusville a few weeks ago,
on my way back from furlough, I saw 'im
shoot Saul Klevins!"

"Who's Saul Klevins?"

"The fastest gunfighter in Texas, some
said, but he weren't faster than the Pecos Kid.
Shot him right through the fuckin' heart, and
I was there — I saw 'im do it!"

Lieutenant Dawes was astonished by the
news. He hadn't realized that his wife-to-be
had been living with a killer! It put a new complexion on the enterprise. If he makes any
trouble here, I'll personally arrest him, and I
don't care who the little son-of-a-bitch shot.

Duane paused for a look at the parlor, ever
fascinated by real homes, where people sat together in the glow of familial love. The priests
and brothers at the monastery had been pa-
tient, but not parents. Duane desired his own
family, and his key to happiness resided right
down the hall. He knocked on her door, and
waited impatiently as footsteps crossed the
floor on the other side.

The door opened, and Vanessa smiled nervously. "Hello Duane — won't you come in?"

Duane was surprised by her formality. Usually, when they met, they ripped off each other's clothes and caught up on events afterwards. Something seemed out of place, but he chose to ignore it.

She took a deep breath. "I have to talk with you, so you'd better sit down. Would you like a drink?"

He had the premonition that something terrible was going to happen. His lungs deflated, he sat on the chair, tipped up the front brim of his hat, and stretched out his left leg. "What's going on, Vanessa?"

She sat opposite him, looked into his eyes, and said, "We're not getting married."

The cavern in his stomach opened wide, and he felt like gagging. "What're you talking about?"

"Please stay calm?"

"I'm calm."

"Promise me that you won't tear the place up?"

"Maybe I'd better have that whiskey now."

She opened a drawer and took out a pint of Mr. Gibson's homemade white lightning. He accepted it from her hand, pulled the cork, and took a copious swig. It went down like fire, his brain sizzled, and he was jolted into a keener awareness of his emerging situation.

She kneeled in front of him, placed her hands on his knees, and tears filled her eyes. "I'm sorry, Duane, but I've been thinking that we're not such a good couple after all. I'm much older than you, and my needs are far different. Surely you can understand that."

He couldn't understand anything, and the ache was becoming unbearable. "I always thought we got along fine," he mumbled.

"What future could we have together with no money? It's just hardscrabble existence, and in ten years we'll both be worn out."

He scowled. "You don't believe in me, because I'm younger than you. You think I'm an idiot, but you're wrong. We have something special between us. You can't just throw it away."

"Every blade of grass and grain of sand is special, but money is the only protection we have against the harshness of the world. It can actually *buy happiness.*"

He hung his head and looked at the floor. "You don't love me."

"It's out of love that I'm doing this. You shouldn't be tied down to an old hag like me for the rest of your life. When you're thirty — I'll be forty-two. Think about it."

He stood abruptly. "Now you're trying to

humbug me. If I know you — you wouldn't dump one man unless you had another. Who is he?"

"Please don't raise your voice. They can hear you all over the house. I'm the new schoolmarm, and can't tolerate scandal."

"What's the weasel's name?"

"I don't think your knowing his name would help anything."

"I'll find out anyway, so what is it?"

Her eyelashes fluttered, and she appeared as though she were undergoing a tremendous ordeal. "He's in the army," she said softly.

Duane felt as if someone had hit him over the head with a two-by-four. He staggered from side to side, as he recalled the general store full of soldiers guzzling white lightning. "You're marrying one of those drunkards!"

She drew herself to her full height, raised her nose, and said, "He's an officer."

Duane smiled cruelly. "An officer in fancy pants, and you grabbed him like the desperate woman that you are. It didn't even matter that he's wearing a *blue* uniform."

"The war is over, and it's time to put it behind us. Besides, I don't know how someone your age can talk about the war. You didn't go through it and couldn't possibly know what it was like."

He took another swig of whiskey, but his

heart was ripping down the middle. "You've never taken me seriously."

"Duane, look at me." She took his face in her hands and gently turned him toward her. "If I didn't take you seriously, I would never've let you touch me, and I certainly wouldn't've run off with you. But Lieutenant Dawes is a West Point graduate, and could become a general someday."

"And an Apache might cut off his head. If you loved me, it wouldn't matter where I went to school, and whether I'll be a general."

"If you were ten years older, and ten years richer, I could never leave you. But I don't think that God intended me to be a schoolmarm for the rest of my life."

"The only person you've ever loved is yourself!"

"Now you're being mean."

"It was nice knowing you."

He headed for the door, but she blocked his path. "Please don't be angry, Duane. Try to understand."

"You dumped me for a blue uniform."

She kissed his cheek. "You'll find another girl. Who could resist you? You're so beautiful — even I, who should know better — I've done things with you that I'd never done before, not even with the man I was supposed to marry."

He wanted to say something vicious, but a tear rolled down his cheek. He wished he could punch her through the wall, but at the same time wanted to hold her like the old days. "I was just a toy that you played with," he said bitterly.

She wrapped her arms around his waist and tenderly kissed his tears away. "Dear Duane," she mused. "What will become of you?"

"I can take care of myself," he said gruffly.

"Promise me that you won't get into any trouble?"

He was silent.

"Please?" She hugged him closer. "Don't ever say that I didn't love you, because I do."

"I'll never believe you again. I'm sure you and that Yankee officer deserve each other."

He wriggled out of her grasp, lurched toward the door, and was gone. She heard his footsteps recede down the corridor, and the bedroom seemed dark and lonely. She sat on the edge of the bed, a blank expression on her face. I've done it.

Duane entered the main room of the general store and pushed his way to the bar. "Gimme a bottle," he snarled.

Mr. Gibson placed white lightning before him, Duane snatched it out of his hand, pulled the cork, took three quick swallows, and waited for the kick. It caught him in the chest, he coughed, and took a step backward, bumping into a soldier.

"What whar yer goin', sonny."

Duane hoped the soldier would shoot him, to end the pain. She never loved me in the first place, he thought. I was just her lapdog. He found an empty length of wall, sat, and looked at cowboys and soldiers filling the air with garbled conversation, arguments, declarations, and drunken ravings. He was surprised to notice several of them looking at him and wondered if a scorpion was crawling across his shirt.

He spotted an officer's shoulder boards on a stool across the room, and realized that he was looking at his rival. Before Duane knew what he was doing, he was on his feet, headed toward the bluecoat. Lieutenant Dawes saw him coming and stood up. Duane drew closer, sparks flying out of his eyes, and came to a stop in front of the lieutenant. "You son-of-a-bitch!" he said evenly, looking into his eyes.

The general store was small, and white lightning amplified Duane's voice. Everything became silent, and all eyes turned in his direction. Lieutenant Dawes towered over the young cowboy; it looked like war, and then the officer said, "You give me any trouble, Mr. Pecos, and I'll arrest you."

Duane leaned forward. "You're a lowdown skunk!"

"They'll throw me out of the army if I whip you before so many witnesses. Care to go outside?"

Duane was poised to attack, when McGrath's hand dropped onto his shoulder. "You better settle down, boy. Yer in way over yer head. That's the Fourth Calvary yer a-talkin' to, an' if you fight one, you gotta fight 'em all."

Duane was ready to fight them all, if that would win back Vanessa's love. He looked at Lieutenant Dawes's weatherbeaten features. "You'd better take good care of her," he warned, "otherwise I'll kill you, and I don't make idle threats."

The general store was a spinning carousel as Duane lurched toward the door. He stepped outside, and stumbled among the shacks that comprised Shelby. He felt lost, defeated, and dismayed, catching strange flashes of a baby in a wagon, being driven to the monastery in the clouds.

He sat heavily against the side of a building, out of sight of the saloon, and gazed at the open range. Two flat-topped mountains stood like sentinels overlooking rolling hills backlit by blazing stars. The truth of the universe blasted Duane loose from his moorings, and all he could do was bow his head to the Glory of God. *Father in Heaven, forgive me.*

Now he understood why priests and brothers were celibate. *Women make men crazy enough to kill each other, just like bucks during mating season. I threatened that officer, and he had a roomful of armed men with him. If I'd punched him, I'd be in shackles and chains right now, on my way to the stockade.*

Duane heard footsteps, and his hand dove toward his gun. McGrath turned the corner of the building. "How're you doin'?"

Duane shrugged. McGrath sat next to him, and rolled a cigarette slowly and deliberately with his callused hands. "Are you really the Pecos Kid?"

"So what if I am?"

"I don't know what's eatin' you, but it must be pretty bad."

"My woman just told me that she's marrying that lieutenant, and I'm not feeling so hot."

"What'd you 'spect from a woman? One day they want this — next day they want that — can't ever make up their minds! I been married to two, and lived with a few more, and I still don't understand 'em."

"She told me that she loved me, but I guess she lied."

"She probably did, but they change their minds all the time, and don't know what the hell they want. You'd best settle down, otherwise you'll spend Christmas at Fort Leavenworth. Just take three deep breaths, and one step backward. And if'n you don't have a cat in that gunnysack when you get back to the ranch, you'd better start alookin' fer another job."

Lieutenant Dawes knocked on Vanessa's door, then waited patiently. The faint sound of sobbing could be heard through the wooden planks. He turned the knob and saw her facedown on the bed, perfectly still. For a moment he thought she was dead, and Duane Braddock had murdered her, but she turned her tearstained face toward him. "Please leave me alone."

"Did he do something to you?"

She shook her head and sniffled. "I've broken his heart, poor little boy."

"And he just threatened to kill me — poor little boy my ass! I can't imagine how you could be serious about someone like that!"

"You should've seen the look on his face when I told him. He actually cried real tears."

"You should've seen the look on his face when he was threatening to kill me. When it comes to sheer viciousness, he'd be hard to beat. I'm tempted to lock him up, but out of love for you, my dear, I'll let it ride."

She raised herself to a sitting position, and he lowered himself beside her. She kissed his cheek. "Thank you for being so understanding. You won't regret it, I promise."

The door was opened by a man with a long horsey face. "May I help you."

Duane removed his hat and smiled. "Sorry to disturb you, but I wonder if you could tell me where I might find a cat."

The man raised his eyebrows. "Got a rat problem?"

"Real big ones — like this." Duane held out his hands to show the average measurement of the beasts he'd seen in the bunkhouse.

"Mrs. Phipps's cat just had a litter of kittens, but they couldn't handle a rat of that size. Don't believe I've ever seen you before. Who are you?"

"Duane Braddock. I work for the Bar T."

The man snapped his fingers. "Duane Braddock? Why, I'm supposed to marry you tomorrow morning!" He shook Duane's hand vigorously. "I'm Parson Jones."

"I guess you haven't heard that the wedding has been called off," Duane replied. "My bride-to-be has decided to marry somebody else."

Parson Jones blinked in disbelief. "You poor boy — how you must be suffering. Is there any comfort that I can provide? Perhaps we can pray together."

"If you really want to help me, you'll tell me where I can find a cat."

"I don't know of any cats, but there's a stray dog that's been roaming around here, with his ribs showing. He came in from the range one day last week, looking more dead than alive. I'd say that he could kill a rat if he put his mind to it. Just offer him something to eat, and maybe you can convince him to go back to the ranch with you."

The crew from the Circle K rode into Shelby, led by Jay Krenshaw. They climbed down from their saddles before the general store, and Jay noticed Bar T brands on some of the horses lined at the rails. He was certain that Duane Braddock was there, and then the fun would begin.

Jay had been thinking about Braddock all week, cursing himself for not whipping him when he'd had the chance. Meanwhile, his men crowded around, because they knew that a brawl was coming. They looked at Jay, who said, "Let's do it."

The men from the Circle K swept into the saloon, looking for Duane Braddock. They advanced across the crowded little room and gathered together at the bar.

"Guess he ain't here yet," said Reade, a note of disappointment in his voice.

"Then we'll wait fer 'im," Jay replied.

Duane couldn't understand how Vanessa could be his woman on Monday, and somebody else's Saturday. He was on his way back to the general store, the gunny sack slung over his shoulder. He felt as if his blood had turned to sludge, and his shoulders drooped as he came to the main street. Soldiers and cowboys could be seen, passing bottles of white lightning. They held loud conversations, with much wild gesticulations, but a few were sprawled on the ground, drooling onto the dirt.

Don Jordan detached himself from the crowd and headed toward Duane. "Jay Krenshaw and his boys are in the general store, and I think they're looking for you."

Duane knew that he should jump onto Thunderbolt and ride out of town immediately, but couldn't move his feet backward. Heartsick, demoralized, catless, he didn't want to fight the Fourth Calvary, but the Circle K might do.

Jordan gazed with trepidation toward the front door of the general store. "I wouldn't wait around too long if I was you."

Just then the door opened, and Jay Krenshaw appeared, accompanied by Reade, followed by his other cowboys.

"There's still time," said Jordan. "Let's get a move on, pardner."

Duane shook out the fingers of his right hand and felt the wild sensation of mortal combat. Jay Krenshaw gazed hatefully at him for a few seconds, then Jay stepped forward. Duane knew that a fight was coming, and got set. It could be guns, knives, fists, but he was ready to roll. Jay promenaded closer, and glanced coldly at Duane. "Remember me?"

"I never forget an ugly face," Duane replied.

"You punched me the other day, when I wasn't looking. Go ahead — try it again."

Duane's right fist zoomed through the air, before Jay could raise his guard, and Duane's knuckles cracked into Jay's forehead. Jay suddenly found himself on his butt, in a flash knockdown. He jumped quickly to his feet, handed his hat to one of his cowboys, and dove toward Duane, but Duane threw a stiff left jab. It pulped Jay's lips, but Jay countered with a left hook to Duane's right kidney. Duane felt as if somebody had stuck a knife into him, as he backed away. Jay caught him with a right cross, and Duane went sprawling backward, tripped over his spurs, and fell onto his back.

Jay jumped on top of him, throwing punches from all directions, most of them landing. Duane took a deep breath, clenched his teeth, and bucked like a wild horse. Jay was thrown off him, and both combatants leapt to their feet. Before Jay could get set, Duane launched a right hook with all his weight behind it. It landed on Jay's right temple, and Jay's eyes closed. He fell like a tree hit by lightning and landed with a splat in the middle of the street. The fight had come to a sudden end.

"Hold it right there!" called a voice in front of the general store.

Everyone turned to Lieutenant Dawes, service revolver in hand, his shirt half unbuttoned, hatless, and Duane wondered if he'd just got out of bed with Vanessa Fontaine. Lieutenant Dawes moved toward Duane, holding his gun pointed at Duane's chest. Duane wondered if he could roll out and get off a fast shot, but then noticed McGrath and other Bar T cowboys at the edge of the crowd, and didn't want to shoot the wrong person by mistake.

"Anybody see what happened here?" Lieutenant Dawes asked.

Sergeant Mahoney replied, "They got into

an argument, and the Kid threw the first punch."

Dawes looked meaningfully at Duane. "I thought I warned you."

"I hit him before he hit me. So what?"

"I should arrest you, that's what."

McGrath maneuvered between them, his belly hanging over his belt. "Jay Krenshaw was a-lookin' fer a fight from the moment he come to town. He egged the Kid on."

Lieutenant Dawes searched for someone to give an alternate view, and this time Reade made his views known. "It was the Kid who started it. He's a killer from Titusville, and everybody knows it."

Lieutenant Dawes turned his official gaze back to Duane. "I warned you once, and now I'm warning you again. Stay out of trouble, or else."

Duane took three deep breaths and another step backward. "Yes, sir." He spat into the dirt, then headed toward the front door of the general store, where Fred Gibson stood, face pale. "I hope you're not going to shoot anybody."

"I want two roast beef sandwiches and another bottle of white lightning."

Mr. Gibson's heart was heavy with anxiety as he returned to his store. He and his wife were enjoying the most lucrative night of their marriage, but he worried that Shelby was losing the pristine quality that had attracted him in the first place.

His sweat-stained wife made more sandwiches at the counter. "What happened?"

"A little fight. If you hear gunshots, just duck behind the counter."

Fred Gibson gathered two sandwiches and another bottle of white lightning, then carried them outside to Duane. In the middle of the street, a few Circle K cowboys helped Jay Krenshaw to his feet. "I'm all right," growled the boss's son.

Duane dodged into the nearest alley, tucking the sandwiches underneath his arm. He made his way to the back of the general store, and glanced up at Vanessa's window. The light was out, and he was certain that Lieutenant Dawes had just been there. Duane felt like putting his fist through the wall.

He came to the open range, placed a sandwich on the ground, sat crosslegged a few feet away, and rolled a cigarette. Now I've got the Circle K *and* the Fourth Calvary mad at me, and my bride-to-be is screwing somebody else. What next?

Lieutenant Dawes returned to Vanessa's bedroom, and tossed his hat onto the bedpost. "It was a fight, and guess who was in the middle of it — your boy Duane Braddock again."

She lay beneath the covers, her long golden hair flowing over the pillow. "Did he get hurt?"

"Not yet, but I wouldn't give you a plugged nickel for his life. He just beat up Jay Krenshaw, the most dangerous man in this town."

Vanessa sighed in exasperation. "Sometimes I think Duane's crazy. All those years with the priests and monks have taken their toll."

"I hope you won't be angry, but I think that's all a big bald lie. A man doesn't spend his life in a monastery and then get into fights like that."

"You don't know Duane very well. He's one of a kind."

"He's a cold-blooded killer, and you were going to marry him?"

"He needs somebody to take care of him."

"He makes any more trouble, *I'll* take care of him. He'll end up at the end of a rope, and I don't care how unique he is."

Duane sat on the ground like an Indian, hoping that the dog would appear, but so far he'd seen nothing except a heaven full of stars and the mountains of the moon. He wished he could be on that glowing crescent, or any-where else except inside his skin. From the first moment he'd met Vanessa Fontaine, he'd been lost. She was, quite simply, the most beautiful woman he'd ever imagined, nearly perfect in every way, except that she didn't love him.

He couldn't understand how she could dump him so quickly. It dispirited him to think that he'd never touch that long, lissome body again. He wanted to keel over and die, the pain was unbearable, and he gasped for air. I'm ugly, disgusting, and repulsive, which is why she doesn't love me. What made me think that I deserved a woman like that? He drew his gun, thumbed back the hammer, and pointed it at his right temple. Squeeze the trigger, and you won't have to think about Vanessa anymore.

Something moved straight ahead, and Duane froze. A medium-size dog material-ized out of the darkness, creeping ever closer to the sandwich on the ground. All thoughts of suicide vanished from Duane's mind in an instant. "It's all right, boy," he whispered. "Go ahead — take a bite."

The dog growled suspiciously, as if warning Duane to keep his distance. It advanced, snatched the sandwich in his jaws, and put on a burst of speed. One moment Duane saw him, and the next he was gone. Duane knew that the mutt was out there someplace, gulping down the sandwich, looking over his shoulder for wildcats and coyotes, not to mention nighthawks that swept out of the sky, grabbed you in their talons, and carried you off.

Duane held the second sandwich in his hand. "When you're finished with that one, I've got another."

Two ferocious little eyes appeared in the darkness, examining him carefully. The creature stepped forward apprehensively, his little black nose twitching. He had a coyote's face, a beagle's body, and a terrier's hair, matted and filthy. One-quarter of his left floppy ear had been torn off by animal or animals unknown. If cleaned, he'd probably be white with black spots, one of them surrounding his right eye, giving him a comical aspect.

"Go ahead — take it," Duane said. "I brought it for you."

The dog cocked his head to the side, and appeared to say, *why?*

"I've got a job for you. All the rats you can eat, and if you run out of rats, we've got more beef than we know what to do with. You play your cards right, you can be the mascot of the Bar T."

The dog shivered with excitement as he

took the sandwich out of Duane's hand. The sole survivor of a wagon train massacred by Comanches, he'd made his way to Shelby, and now at last had found legitimate employment. He gulped the sandwich swiftly, burped, and looked expectantly at his new boss.

"Just one problem," Duane said as he led the dog back to the general store. "You'll have to convince the ramrod that you're as good as a cat."

It was quiet in Titusville, compared to the days when saloons and whorehouses burst at the seams with Saturday night revelers. Now, only a few horses were tethered in front of two saloons still open, the rest of Main Street nearly deserted.

In front of the Carrington Arms Hotel, a lone figure tied a bedroll to the back of his saddle. Amos Raybart glanced around, to make sure nobody was about to bushwhack him from a blind alley. Then he rode up the street, heading for the open range, a bent cigarette dangling out of the corner of his mouth.

A tin badge lay in his jacket pocket. He'd bought it under false pretenses from the blacksmith, who'd hammered SHERIFF across its face for a few extra coins. A long journey

138

lay ahead, and it might come in handy up the road.

He'd elicited sufficient information for Jay Krenshaw, but Raybart himself had become curious about the Pecos Kid. Was he an innocent man fresh from a monastery, or a murderous galoot who lied as fast as he drew his Colt?

Could it be possible that an orphan raised in a far-off monastery could become, within the space of a few weeks, the Pecos Kid? According to testimony, he'd shot five people, made a trip to the cribs, and then ran off with the most beautiful woman in town. Raybart had never heard of anyone like Duane Braddock.

What's the truth? Raybart wondered. Is he a saint, the son of the devil, or a little of both?

Duane ambled back to the general store, and was certain that the fissure in his heart would never heal. Vanessa was probably in bed with Lieutenant Dawes at that very moment, and the mere thought nearly drove Duane to his knees.

He tried to catch his breath. The pain was worse than being punched. The dog looked up at him, an expression of concern on his canine features. Duane scratched the animal's ear, and tried to focus on the business at hand. "We're going to see the ramrod, and if he doesn't like you, you don't get the job. So try to look good, all right?"

The dog barked, and Duane looked him over once more. He didn't appear impressive, and in fact was one of the mangiest dogs that Duane had ever seen. With his black eye, he looked like he'd just been in a saloon brawl. "I think I'll call you . . . Sparky," Duane said. "Let's talk to the ramrod, and for Chrissakes, don't bite him."

They came to the square in front of the general store, where groups of cowboys and soldiers drank whiskey, threw dice, conversed in loud tones, or lay flat on the ground, passed out from excessive white lightning. Duane spotted Uncle Ray in the crowd. "You see the ramrod around?"

"Inside."

Duane snapped his finger, and Sparky followed, nose raised, tail high in the air, pumping himself up for his job interview. They entered the general store, and it reeked with sweat, tobacco smoke, and whiskey. Duane picked up the dog and carried him like a babe in his arms as he searched for McGrath, finally noticing the stalwart cattle expert seated alone in a corner, legs splayed before him, a bottle in his hands.

Duane dropped to one knee in front of him

and placed the dog on the floor. "Ramrod, are you awake?"

"I stay awake," McGrath uttered, one eye open and the other closed.

"I've been all over town, and the only cats they've got available are kittens who'd probably make little snacks for the rats in the bunkhouse. But then I ran into Parson Jones, and he told me that the best thing for big rats is a dog about this size."

Duane pointed to Sparky, and McGrath opened his other eye. "What the hell is it?"

"It's a rat-catcher. Haven't you ever seen one before?"

McGrath gazed suspiciously at Duane. "Are you tryin' to bullshit me, boy?"

"This dog can catch any rat that ever lived. He'll clean out that bunkhouse in no time at all."

McGrath wrinkled his venous red nose. "He don't look like much."

A growl emitted from Sparky's mouth as he barred his fangs and tensed his legs, about to leap. The ramrod raised his hand. "Okay — okay. I believe you — calm down."

"This dog could whip a wildcat if he put his mind to it," Duane said.

"He don't git rid of them rats, I'll kick his ass off the Bar T."

Duane patted Sparky's head. "Sounds like

you've got the job on a trial basis."

Duane looked at McGrath in gratitude and realized that the old ramrod had a soft heart beneath his leathery exterior. The mission was accomplished, so Duane dropped down beside the ramrod, put his back to the wall, and rolled a cigarette. Sparky lay at Duane's feet, placed his chin on his paws, and closed his eyes.

"You'll have to clean him up," McGrath said. "He looks like hell."

"I'll toss him into the first stream I find. He'll be all right."

The ramrod handed Duane the bottle, and Duane took a swig. Ramrod and newest hand sat side by side, facing a roomful of men in advanced stages of inebriation, mouthing garbled sentences to each other, or attempting to play cards in the darkness, while at the counter, Mr. and Mrs. Gibson counted the take thus far.

Duane felt emptiness in the pit of his stomach as he recalled Vanessa Fontaine in a room at the back of the building, in bed with Lieutenant Dawes. He moaned, and closed his eyes.

"You poor son-of-a-bitch," McGrath declared. "Nothin' can fuck up a man like a woman. When they're not a-naggin', they're a-lyin'."

The ramrod spat tobacco juice toward the nearest spittoon, but missed by four inches, hitting the boot of a cowboy trying to read a wrinkled old newspaper. "When a man gits mixed up with a woman, it gener'ly starts real nice, don't it? But then, not too long after, it starts a-gittin' pretty bad."

Duane looked at the wise old ramrod of the plains, and somehow he didn't seem so foreboding now. "Ramrod," he said, "there's something I've been wanting to talk with you about. When I first met you, you said something about an old-time gunfighter named Joe Braddock. I pretended that I didn't know him, but . . . to tell you the truth, he was my old man. I be mighty grateful if you'd tell me what you know about him."

The ramrod became more alert, as he examined Duane's face. "Afraid I don't know a helluva lot. As I recall, Joe Braddock was in a gang that operated south of here, so they could slip over the border when things got hot. They got mixed up in a range war and was strung up by some vigilantes in one of them little border towns."

Duane had suspected that his father had been hung, and now it was confirmed by the venerable ramrod. He didn't know whether to cry, laugh, or yank out his Colt and shoot a hole through the ceiling. Why didn't you just be a cowboy, Daddy? How come that wasn't good enough? "You ever hear anything about

Joe Braddock's woman, ramrod?"

"Don't get me wrong, Kid. Joe Braddock's just a name to me, and maybe I've got him mixed up with some other outlaw. You know how it is with fast hands. They all come to a bad end."

All lights were out at the Circle K ranch, except for one coal oil lamp burning in the bedroom of Jay Krenshaw. The son of the boss stood in front of his mirror and examined his left eye, which had turned a hideous purple. He couldn't see out of it, his nose felt broken, and his jaw was loose on its hinges. Worst of all, one front tooth had been knocked out. He forced himself to smile, and appeared an imbecile with the big black gap.

Jay bellowed like a wounded buffalo and banged his fist on the dresser. Then he screamed like a woman, because he thought that he'd broken his hand. If Duane Braddock were standing in front of him, Jay would shoot him between the eyes.

He thought of Raybart traveling across the wilderness, tracking down Duane Braddock's past. *I hope he gets back soon, so I'll know what I'm dealing with. If he's who I think he is, I'll hire the fastest gun in West Texas to kill him. It'll cost plenty, but that little son-of-a-bitch has got to die.*

CHAPTER 6

Duane opened his eyes. It was Sunday morning, and he was alone in the bunkhouse. He'd returned from town early, accompanied by the new Bar T mascot, but none of the other cowboys had come back yet. The bunkhouse was as silent as the monastery in the clouds, as a shaft of light broke through the filthy window.

Duane was seized by the urge to go outside. He pulled on his pants, jumped into his boots, wrapped his blanket around his shoulders, and was out the door. The yard spread before him, basking in the sun, and beyond, a mesa covered with grass and mesquite stretched toward the horizon, where a mountain range glowed purple and gold.

Duane felt the power of the universe in his bones. He dropped to his knees, clasped his hands together, and prayed. "My Lord, thank you for the bounty of this day. Thank you for my job, and good health. Please forgive my many transgressions, and please help me to forget Miss Vanessa Fontaine."

Then, in the middle of the prayer, something prompted him to open his eyes. To his astonishment, Phyllis Thornton stood twenty yards away, looking at him curiously. "Didn't mean to disturb you," she said. "I was just taking a walk, and there you were."

She looked like the Virgin of Guadalupe with her black hair and tanned features. Taken by surprise, he rose to his feet. "Good morning," he spluttered.

"You didn't go to town with the other cowboys?"

"Yes, but I came back early."

"I've never seen a cowboy pray before. You're very different from the others."

She reminded him of a newly ripened peach, and he wanted to bite her fanny, but then realized that it was Sunday morning, and lust was the work of the devil. He turned toward the mountains and tried to catch his breath. They stood in awkward silence for a few moments.

"What do you do around here?" Duane asked.

"I milk the cow, and then help Mother in the kitchen. In the afternoons, my father usually has work for me in the office, and sometimes I run errands for him. Why did you come back from town so soon?"

"I'd rather be here, because it's so quiet. It reminds me of church, but you probably think I'm being foolish."

"You're not being foolish at all," she said indignantly. "I can't understand how anybody can look at those mountains, and not believe that there's a God."

He noticed the gentle curve of her nose, and her lower lip protruding slightly, tantalizingly. They gazed into each other's eyes, and he coughed to clear his throat. "I've got to make breakfast. Nice talking with you."

That's the kind of woman who'd make the perfect wife for a rancher, he thought, as he headed back to the bunkhouse. But unfortunately, I don't have a ranch. I'd better stay away from her, otherwise I'm liable to get fired.

"Dearly beloved, we are gathered here today . . ." Parson Jones began the wedding ceremony in the parlor of the Gibson home, as Vanessa and Lieutenant Dawes stood before him, with Fred Gibson as best man, and Mrs. Gibson as matron of honor. Lingering odors of whiskey and tobacco smoke from the general store permeated the atmosphere.

"Do you, Lieutenant Clayton Dawes,

Fourth Cavalry, take this woman, Vanessa Fontaine . . ."

The parson droned through the ancient Christian ritual, adding his own special flourishes, while Lieutenant Dawes and Vanessa entered the holy estate of matrimony. A beatific smile creased Mrs. Gibson's face, for she loved weddings, while Mr. Gibson wondered how soon he and the blacksmith could build the whorehouse that would make them rich.

"Do you, Miss Vanessa Fontaine, take this man, Lieutenant Clayton Dawes, Fourth Cavalry, to be your . . ."

Vanessa realized that her long travail was finally over, and she was safe at last. "I do!" she replied emphatically.

Parson Jones continued with the ceremony, and Lieutenant Dawes couldn't believe his exceedingly good fortune. Now he wouldn't have to spend his life drinking whiskey, playing cards, and chasing whores. He'd have a genuine woman to sleep with every night, an impossible dream just a few months ago.

"I pronounce you man and wife." Parson Jones closed his Bible dramatically. "You may kiss the bride."

The intrepid officer pecked his wife's cheek, while the Gibsons threw handfuls of rice. The deed is done, thought Vanessa, as her lips touched her new husband. But somehow, inexplicably, she found herself thinking about Duane Braddock. *I wonder what happened to him,* she speculated, as her husband's arms wrapped around her. *I hope he's all right.*

After breakfast, behind the bunkhouse, Duane set up a row of cans on a plank between two barrels. Then he stood about twenty yards away and assumed his gunfighter stance, with his legs slightly bent, shoulders hunched, right hand just above his Colt .44. He pretended that Lieutenant Clayton Dawes stood before him, reaching for his iron.

Duane's shoulder jerked, his gun flew into his hand, he raised the barrel, took aim, and pulled the trigger. The gun bucked in his hand, as the can flew into the air. Duane held his arm straight as he continued to fire, the air filled with gunsmoke, and finally his hammer went *click*.

He counted five cans for five bullets, a perfect score. After loading five more cartridges, he holstered the Colt. He pretended to be strolling away from the cans, when suddenly he spun out, yanked the Colt, fired three cartridges in rapid succession, and three more cans were demolished. He holstered the gun, turned in another direction, took a few steps, then dove to the ground, rolled over, and fired the final two cartridges. The first landed on target, but the second went astray.

He loaded the Colt again, then pretended to give it to someone. Suddenly, he flipped it around and drilled a can through the middle. He tossed the gun into the air, caught it behind his back, and ventilated the next can. But he knew from bitter experience that it was considerably more difficult to hit a target that was firing back. And he realized that no matter how fast a gunfighter, there was always somebody faster.

He loaded the chambers again and noticed a blue dress appear around the corner of the bunkhouse. "I thought the Comanches were attacking," said Phyllis Thornton. "What're you doing?"

"Just practicing."

She moved closer. "Mind if I watch."

"It's your ranch, Miss Thornton."

"Where'd you learn to shoot?"

"A friend taught me."

"I've never seen tricks like that. Do you think you could teach some to me? I've fired guns before, and I know the basics."

"Your Daddy might not want me to."

"I think he'd be pleased. It's important to know how to shoot."

"In that case, the first lesson is never point a loaded gun at anybody, unless you intend to kill him." He passed the gun to her. "I'll set up some cans."

Duane pulled an armful out of the gunnysack, while Phyllis felt the warmth from his hand on the walnut grip. He wore black pants, a black shirt, and a red bandanna, with his silver conchos hatband flashing rays in all directions.

"Go ahead," he told her, stepping out of the line of fire.

She raised the gun, thumbed back the hammer, and sighted along the barrel.

"Lock your elbow," Duane said. "And maybe you'd better put a leg behind you, because that gun kicks like a mule. Here, I'll show you."

He came up behind her, took her wrist in one hand, and her shoulder in the other. "Like this."

Their bodies touched, and her hand trembled slightly. She felt strange, but grit her teeth as she locked her elbow. "Okay to fire?"

He stepped back. "Whenever you're ready."

The gun exploded, simultaneously kicking into the air. It knocked her against Duane, who thrilled at the touch of her body. But she didn't put a hole through anything. "I had it in my sights," she complained.

"You're supposed to hold your breath, and *squeeze* the trigger. Go ahead — try again."

She lined up the sights on a can, while he checked her posture. She was healthy, full-bodied, and made Vanessa Fontaine look like a beanpole, although he still considered Vanessa extremely beautiful, and he missed her with all his heart. He noticed the tip of her tongue sticking out of the corner of her mouth like a berry. The gun exploded, and a can was launched into space, a hole drilled through the top.

"Not bad," Duane said.

Big Al Thornton came into view around the bunkhouse. "What the hell's a-goin' on here!"

Duane's eyes darted nervously as he searched for an avenue of escape, but Phyllis turned to her father and said, "Duane was teaching me how to fire his gun."

Duane held up his hands. "I figured that everybody should know how to shoot."

Big Al looked at him coldly, then said, out the corner of his mouth: "Phyllis, I believe yer mother wants you fer somethin'."

She passed the gun to Duane, and their eyes met. "Thanks for the lessons." Then she headed toward the main house, and Duane gazed at her retreating posterior view, in many ways more beautiful than her front, but then realized that he was leering at the boss's daughter! He tried to smile. "She's a good learner," he said to Big Al.

The rancher looked down at Duane, and Duane felt like crawling beneath the nearest rock. "I was a cowboy myself once," Big Al said, "and I know what yer up to, so let me make somethin' perfeckly clear. You ever lay hands on her — I'll kill you. Understand?"

Duane tried to smile. "Yessir."

Without another word, Big Al walked back to the house.

Big Al was grumbling beneath his breath as he opened the front door. Phyllis stood in the middle of the parlor, her arms crossed. "What did you say to him?" she inquired.

"I know cowboys better than you. They'll do anything to get what they want from a woman, and Duane Braddock has prob'ly kilt a few people in his day. You don't handle a gun like that unless yer a professional."

"Then he's the ideal teacher, but you've scared him away. He'll probably run next time he sees me."

"He'd better," Big Al said as he inclined toward his office. He hung his hat on the peg, sat in his chair, and lit a cigar. His head became enveloped in blue smoke as he contemplated imminent discord in his family. He knew that he was too protective of Phyllis, but only because he didn't want her hurt by some fast-talking cowboy. I don't care how good with guns he is. I'll come up behind him with a shotgun and blow his goddamned head off.

The door to his office flew open, and his wife stood there, with his daughter. Big Al considered jumping through the window and running for his life.

"What have you done!" his wife demanded, fists on her hips, as she charged like the Fourth Cavalry into his office. "Phyllis was talking with a nice young man, and you embarrassed her? Have you gone loco? How is she ever going to get married if you scare away potential husbands?"

"That weren't no potential husband," Big Al replied. "He's a cowboy, and I told him that I'd *shoot* him if he ever stepped out of line with her!"

"You old buffalo!" she hollered. "That's not how you get your daughter married off, or don't you want her to have a husband?"

"She's not marryin' no cowboy as long as I'm alive!"

"No matter who he is — you'd find something wrong with him."

"Duane Braddock is headed for jail or a grave. Fast hands don't make the best husbands."

"I'd rather have a husband who's a fast hand," Phyllis chimed in, "than a slow hand."

Big Al looked skeptically at his daughter. "I can see that he's pulled the wool over yer eyes, but he don't fool me one bit. I know what's in that varmint's mind, and if I ever catch him with one little finger on you, I'll tear him apart with my bare hands."

It was silent as the family reflected upon the patriarch's last remark. Then his wife's voice came like the edge of a Bowie knife. "I know what's wrong with you, you old buzzard. You don't want anybody else to have her, so she can be your own little girl forever, but she's not a little girl anymore, and it's time she got married. You'd better not interfere, or else you'll have to deal with me!"

Big Al feared no man, but couldn't cope with his wife and daughter allied against him. "She's too young to get married," he protested weakly.

"She's older'n most women when they get married. I don't want you interfering with her friends anymore. Is that clear?"

He knew that if he offered resistance, it would be cold meals and a cold bed, not to mention malevolent glares and no conversation until he surrendered unconditionally. He ran the ranch, but his wife ran his life, and he was too old to find another woman. "All right," he muttered, "but if she marries a desperado who gets shot someday, don't come a-cryin' to me."

Duane examined the steak sizzling in the pan, then flipped the fried potatoes, and smelled bread toasting atop the stove.

It was still peaceful in the bunkhouse, and no one had returned from town yet. It was becoming the most spiritual Sunday since he'd left the monastery in the clouds, except for the few moments when the boss had threatened his life.

Phyllis reminded him of a newly opened rose, while Vanessa was a shrine to Old Dixie. Vanessa was better educated, and worlds above him in manners, but Phyllis Thornton was a frontier kid like he, and they understood each other. Unfortunately, her father hadn't been very friendly.

Duane shoveled dinner onto a tin plate and carried it to the table. Someone knocked on the door, and he thought it might be John the Baptist. "Come on in."

Phyllis Thornton stood in the entry, backlit by the sky. "I apologize for my father," she said, as if reciting a lecture in school. "He didn't mean anything personal. My mother and I had a talk with him, and he's agreed to let me continue shooting lessons."

"I'm free for the rest of the day," Duane replied. "I'm willing to take the chance, if you are."

He wolfed down his food, while she stood in the doorway, becoming aware of the incredible filth of the bunkhouse. It exuded a powerful reek, clothing was strewn everywhere, not one bed was made, and cigarette butts littered the floor, along with a variety of stains, not to mention bones of unnameable creatures.

She turned to the cowboy eating ravenously at the table and observed his aquiline nose, high cheekbones, and long black sideburns. He's a prince living in a junkpile, she ruminated. "I'll be back in about an hour."

The door closed as he slathered a slice of bread with butter. Phyllis possessed a wonderfully rounded caboose, and the mere thought of touching her anatomy caused a delightful sensation. Vanessa Fontaine was a frail, fairy princess, whereas Phyllis was sturdy, steady, and ready. He wanted to take her back to his bunk, but instead had to give her shooting lessons.

He washed the tin plates in the basin behind the bunkhouse, and realized that rats could no longer be heard gnawing. He filled buckets with water and poured them into the tub atop the stove. Then he tossed in his dirty clothes and soap shavings.

He stirred the clothes with a wooden paddle, and thought of Phyllis changing clothes at the main house. Whatever I do, I mustn't step over the line. If her father ever caught us, he'd kill me — no doubt about it.

Phyllis paced the floor of her bedroom, her brow creased with concern. Then she sat on the edge of her bed and chewed her thumbnail. She felt an unfamiliar and indescribable disturbance, and couldn't quite fathom what it meant.

She couldn't sit still, so she arose and resumed strolling across the floor. There was something about Duane with his long body and big shoulders that she couldn't put out of her mind. He'd eaten heartily, and she found that stimulating, the movements of his sinuous lips.

I think I'm falling in *love* with him, she realized with dismay. The sensations were peculiar, for it had never happened before. I wonder what he thinks of me? A frown came over her bright youthful features. He's nice to me because I'm the boss's daughter, that's all. If he met me under other circumstances, he wouldn't even look twice. But I don't want a man to marry me because he's in love with my father's ranch. I would never use my father's wealth to get what I want, or would I?

She undressed in front of the mirror, trying to appraise herself objectively, noticing blemishes and deficiencies that existed only in her imagination. A boy like Duane could get any girl he wants, and wouldn't waste his time with the likes of me, if I weren't the boss's daughter. She changed into her cowboy clothes, arguing with herself. At least I'll get some shooting lessons out of the deal.

Duane strapped on his Colt and positioned it low for a fast easy draw. Then he tied the leather thong to his leg, gunfighter style. He put on his hat and slanted it low over his eyes, the silver conchos flashing sunlight through the windows. Outside, Sparky stood ten feet in front of the door, and it appeared that he'd gained considerable weight since Duane had seen him last.

Duane patted him on the belly. "You don't have to eat them all," he counseled. "Just *kill* them all."

Sparky barked, and Duane had the uncanny impression that the dog understood every word he said. The faithful animal followed Duane to the shooting gallery behind the bunkhouse, lay in the shade of a cottonwood tree, and observed him carefully.

Duane lined up tin cans and bottles on the

board, then sat on the ground beside Sparky and placed his hand on the animal's back. Duane didn't want to waste ammunition, because he couldn't buy more for a week. He twirled the chamber, holstered the gun, and waited for Phyllis to arrive. The sun shone upon him, and his future appeared full of glittering possibilities. Vanessa still danced in his heart, but now he had somebody new to occupy his thoughts.

After an interval, she came into view, wearing her cowboy outfit, a big ten-gallon hat shading her features, and she carried four boxes of cartridges. "Daddy gave us these," she said cheerily, "so that you won't have to use your own."

He made no clever remark about getting shot, and maintained his respectful distance. "Practice is the most important part of shooting, so just stand where you are and shoot at the targets. If I see you doing anything wrong, I'll tell you. When your aim improves sufficiently, I'll show you some tricks."

He drew his gun, tossed it into the air, caught it behind his back, dropped to one knee, and fired. A bottle exploded atop the board, and the plains echoed with the sound.

She couldn't help smiling. "How'd you do that?"

"Practice, that's all." He handed her the

gun, grip first. "Don't forget to keep your elbow straight. The more rigid you are, the better."

She turned toward the row of bottles and cans, spread her legs, held the gun with both hands, narrowed one eye, and stuck the tip of her tongue out the corner of her mouth. He took a step backward and evaluated her scientifically. This is a woman who was made for bearing children, he comprehended. She wore black jeans and a red and white polka dot cowboy shirt. There was something jaunty and fearless about her, a full-bodied outdoors girl who rode horses and shot guns just like he.

The Colt fired, her hands kicked into the air, but no can was drilled, and no bottle shattered. She frowned. "Missed."

"Hold the gun steady, line up the sights, and squeeze the trigger. Don't wait so long."

She raised the gun in both hands, while Duane moved a few steps for the side view. The artery in his throat began to throb as he noticed the rise of her breasts. The cartridge detonated, and a can rocketed backward, a bullet hole through the label.

"Do it again," he said.

She shifted aim for another shot, and he took a few steps backward, for the long view. She fired, and blew a bottle to smithereens.

161

"Good shot," called a voice behind Duane.

Myrtle Thornton wore a long gray dress with a white apron, as she arrived on the scene, eager to see the man who'd captured the heart of her daughter. She found him sensitive looking, with dramatic cheekbones and piercing eyes. "You must be a good teacher," she said.

He didn't know how to reply, while Phyllis appeared embarrassed. The mother scrutinized the shifty-eyed young man, and still was certain that a sheriff was looking for him somewhere. "Phyllis said that you do gun tricks. Mind showing me one?"

Duane loaded his gun and holstered it easily. Then he scratched his nose thoughtfully, as if he were distracted by a wayward fly, when suddenly his hand darted to his gun, he whirled, and a crescendo of gunfire rocked the solitude of the morning. Four cans and one bottle were demolished nearly simultaneously.

"Who taught you how to shoot like that?" Mrs. Thornton asked.

"Friend of mine."

Mrs. Thornton could understand why her daughter was so taken with him. She hoped that Phyllis wouldn't commit any foolish indiscretions, but didn't want to be a meddling mother either.

"I've got work to do," she said. "Duane — thank you for giving Phyllis shooting lessons."

The boss lady walked away, and Duane breathed a sigh of relief. The woman terrified him, for some bizarre reason.

"I think that my mother likes you," Phyllis said.

"She thinks I'm an outlaw."

"Aren't you?"

They looked into each other's eyes, and Duane saw the spotless innocence of her soul. He took three deep breaths, and one step backward. Then he reloaded the gun, and passed it to her.

She took it from his hands and aimed down the barrel at an empty bottle of Old Crow, as he sized her once more. We'd be perfect together, he realized. She squeezed the trigger, and shards of glass exploded into the sunny morning, glittering like a rainbow.

CHAPTER 7

Amos Raybart leaned forward on his saddle as he rode up the winding mountain path. The air filled with the fragrance of ponderosa pines, and birds flitted among the branches. It was midafternoon, and he'd been on horseback for most of the past week.

The monastery lay straight ahead, according to what he'd been told in the town below. Soon he'd know the truth about Duane Braddock, better known as the Pecos Kid. Was he a priest, a trigger-happy killer, or just a dumb kid?

The bone that stuck most in Raybart's craw was that Duane had run off with the most beautiful woman in Titusville. The rodentlike cowboy was jealous, for he'd never got anything from women unless he paid cash on the barrelhead. *Why did God make me ugly, and Duane Braddock a lady's man?*

He turned a bend in the trail, and a scattering of log buildings could be seen. One was substantially larger than the others, with a tall spire and big cross nailed to the front wall. Raybart realized that he'd finally arrived at the monastery in the clouds.

The ground leveled, and in the distance, through brilliantly clear air, he saw an array of mountain peaks bristling with trees. He felt as though he were in heaven, far above the filth and blood of the cowboy world. Men in brown robes worked a large field, while cows and sheep grazed nearby.

Raybart climbed down from his horse, threw the reins over the rail in front of the church, and pushed the front of his hat back. He looked for a source of information, and his eyes fell on a young man in a brown robe, pushing a wheelbarrow full of boulders. Raybart slunk toward him, trying to smile warmly, but it looked like a cross between a leer and a grimace. "Howdy. I'm a-tryin' to track down a feller who used to live here, name of Duane Braddock. Ever hear of 'im?"

The young monk let down his wheelbarrow, and his face froze into an expression of suppressed horror. "What's he done?"

"He used to live here?"

The monk looked at the phony badge shining on the front of Raybart's black leather vest. "He kill somebody?"

Raybart cocked an eye. "What makes you say that?"

"If you want to find out about Duane Braddock, sir, talk to the abbot. He probably knew Duane better than anybody. You'll find him in that building over there."

"Could you get some water for my horse?"

The young monk dutifully lead the horse toward the stable, and Raybart soon found himself in a moderate-size room with a middle-aged monk writing in a ledger. "May I help you, sir?"

"I'd like to speak with the abbot."

"He's in there."

Raybart opened the door and was struck with the stark image of an aged man in a black skullcap reading a book at his desk. Raybart approached on his tiptoes, so as not to disturb him. The abbot was extremely thin, with a salt and pepper beard. The bogus lawman waited patiently for the holy man to acknowledge his presence.

But the abbot seemed completely absorbed in his reading, and Raybart wondered what it was. Raybart wasn't a churchgoing man, and tried not to think about God, because he'd committed numerous sins throughout his life. He wanted to believe that when you die, that's it. No God or Judgment Day. But other times he believed every word in the Bible, and figured he'd spend eternity in the devil's frying pan.

Slowly the abbot raised his head and looked into his eyes. "God forgives all sins," he said. "Have a seat."

Raybart was taken aback, and he had an impulse to run out of the abbot's office, jump onto his horse, and ride away, but then caught himself, and sat. "I'm a lawman," he began. "I'm a-lookin' fer Duane Braddock."

"What's he done?" asked the abbot.

"What makes you think he's done anything?"

"Has he killed someone?"

Their eyes were fastened upon each other, and it was flint on steel. "More than one, I'm afraid," Raybart confessed.

The abbot appeared to deflate as he leaned backward in his chair. "My God," he muttered, clasping his hands together. Then he shook his head sadly from side to side. "How'd it happen?"

"It's hard to know the truth. Some folks say he used to be a priest. Is that so?"

"Duane was never ordained, but he spent most of his life here, studying and praying with the rest of us. He was a pious boy, but he had a terrible temper. He nearly killed one of the other boys, and that's when we had to send him away. He's very sensitive, perhaps because of his parents."

"Who were they?"

The abbot sighed, and it didn't occur to him that the man before him might be wearing a tin badge that he'd bought for a few pennies. "Well, his father evidently was an outlaw, and his mother . . . she was one of those ladies who works in saloons."

"A whore?" Raybart offered.

The abbot nodded knowingly. "Some of the boys found out, and one of them began to ridicule Duane, calling him a . . . bastard . . . in front of the others. That's the one Duane nearly killed. What's he done now?"

"He's shot five people, but some people say it was self-defense, while others think he's a hired gun called the Pecos Kid."

The abbot fingered the wooden cross that hung from his neck. "Duane had the makings of a good priest, with deep feelings for God. But he hurts inside, and it makes him angry. Are you going to arrest him?"

"He ain't wanted fer nothin'," Raybart blurted.

"Then why are you looking for him?"

Raybart realized that he'd given himself away, but smiled with the confidence of an ex-outlaw. "Official investigation."

"You're welcome to stay overnight as our guest. You might want to stop off at the church. Duane spent a lot of time there."

Raybart swaggered out of the monastery office with his precious information, but it was growing dark, and he didn't dare go down the mountain when he couldn't see the trail. His eyes fell on the church where Duane had spent so much time. It seemed incredible, but Duane Braddock actually had been raised in the monastery, and then shot five men. The Pecos Kid may've been the partial invention of a drunken reporter, but that didn't make Braddock less deadly.

Raybart passed from bright sunlight to the darkness of the church interior, and his vision was drawn to a carved wooden statue of the Virgin bathed in candlelight. Raybart moved toward it in strange fascination. He wasn't a Roman Catholic, and preferred whiskey-toting Bible-bashing preachers who ranted against the workings of the devil.

The closer he came to the statue, the more crude it appeared, painted in bright garish colors. It seemed odd that someone would worship such a thing, but he liked the serenity of the church, and it sounded as if choirs sang softly in the rafters. He sat in a pew and looked at the rough-hewn altar facing a crucifix of Jesus twisting on the cross, drops of red blood on his breast.

Raybart had attended many prayer meetings in his life and knew what Christianity demanded. You repented, washed yourself in the blood, and were saved. But Raybart had never stepped forward, because he didn't believe *that* much, and besides, preachers were in it mainly for the money, weren't they? He figured religion was just another crooked business.

He looked around the church curiously and tried to imagine Duane Braddock praying. The gun-happy cowboy and Bible-toting acolyte didn't fit together somehow. Where'd he get his fast hand? Raybart wondered. He felt an urge to get down on his knees, and lowered himself to the floor. "My God," he whispered, clasping his hands together. "I guess I'm a no-good son of a bitch." He thought of the things he'd stolen, the people he'd punched, the lies he'd told, and the times he'd dealt from the bottom of the deck. A terrible remorse came over him, because he knew that his soul had been besmirched by a lifetime of dirty deeds.

But there was a way to wash them off, according to the preachers. You say that you're sorry from the depths of your heart, and start anew, cleansed by forgiveness of Jesus. Raybart felt alien to himself as he clasped his hands together in the pew. Maybe it's time to be a decent Christian fer a change.

A delicious feeling came over him, as if he were being bathed in warm blood. He shuddered in the pew, and tears ran down his cheeks. I've been a no-good weasel fer most of my life, but I don't have to be one no longer. I don't want to burn forever in the fires of Hell. What if there's really a God?

The Bar T cowboys returned to the ranch late Saturday afternoon two weeks later. They headed for the corral, while the ramrod tied his cayuse in front of the main house. He spat out the plug of tobacco and headed for the front door.

It was opened by Phyllis, a concerned expression on her face. "How'd it go?"

"Same as last week. Where's yer dad?"

"His office."

He made his way down the hall as she rushed to the window, peering sideways from behind the curtain at cowboys disappearing around the corner of the barn. She caught a glimpse of *him* atop his favorite horse, and then he was gone.

"Looking for something?" asked her mother, who'd silently entered the parlor.

Phyllis turned around. "The cowboys are back," she explained.

"Could there be a special cowboy that you've been worrying about, ruining your appetite, keeping you up at night?"

Phyllis blushed to the roots of her hair.

"I know everything about you, young lady," her mother said. "I think it's time you and I had a little talk."

The ramrod found Big Al seated at his desk, reading a report on the Texas cattle industry. Big Al looked up, and McGrath could see his boss's eyes bleary from paperwork.

"We've got most of the calves branded," he said. "Another week on the north range should do it."

"See any injuns?"

"A few in the distance. Reckon they steal a beeve whenever they get hungry."

"I don't mind a beeve once in a while, as long as nobody gets killed. See the Circle K?"

"No, thank God."

Big Al leaned back in his chair. "The air has got so poisoned 'twixt the Circle K and us, the missus and I've decided that we should throw a big shindig, and invite everybody in the territory, so's we can have some fun fer a change. It'll be next Saturday night, and we'll have plenny to eat and drink, with musicians and all. Natcherly we want you and the cowboys to be there, but I don't want no fights, and no trouble, so pass the word along."

McGrath wrinkled his forehead in disapproval. "You invite the Circle K here, somebody'll git shot. They hate us, and we hate them."

"I'm going to palaver with old Lew Krenshaw, to make sure there's no gunplay. We're all on this range together, and we've got to git along, like in the old days."

"Tell that to Jay Krenshaw."

"I will, and you tell them cowboys of your'n that they'd better be a-wearin' clean clothes, and take baths, 'cause I don't tolerate no pigs around my daughter. And if any of them gets the notion to start trouble, he'll have to deal with me. By the way, how's that new feller doin' — Braddock?"

"Hard worker. Keeps to 'imself. No trouble a'tall."

Big Al didn't want to ask more questions about Duane, because he didn't want the ramrod to know his interest. "Git cleaned up, and tell the boys what I said."

McGrath departed, and Big Al scratched his chin thoughtfully as he gazed out the window. The mark of a man could be found in his work, and Duane was acceptable to the ramrod, a harsh taskmaster. At least he's not completely useless, Big Al thought.

He had the unsettling feeling that he was losing his daughter. She'd worshiped him throughout her life, but now he had a rival, and knew that the man who'd changed her diapers would become second-best to a saddle tramp who rode in out of nowhere, with owlhoot written all over him. Big Al scowled as he lit a fresh cigar, filling the air with blue tobacco smoke. People will ask who my daughter married, and I'll tell them *The Pecos Kid.*

McGrath stomped into the bunkhouse, reared back his head, and hollered, "The boss is a-givin' a big shindig next Saturday night, and yer all invited!"

The bunkhouse erupted with howls of delight. McGrath waited patiently for them to quiet down, but they jumped about like a circus full of monkeys, and Ross swung from the rafters, kicking his legs in the air.

"Settle down!" McGrath shouted. "I ain't finished. There'll be gals here, and Miss Phyllis, too, so you'd better watch yer manners. And every man will take a bath aforehand, and wear his best duds, because we don't want to look like a bunch of bummers, do we?"

The bunkhouse rocked on its foundations as cowboys shouted and jumped gleefully. "Gals!" one of them shouted. "Goddamn!"

McGrath headed for his shack to prepare for Saturday night at Gibson's General Store, while in the bunkhouse, the men set to work heating water for baths. In the far corner, Duane pulled off his cowboy boots and lay on his bunk.

"Coming to town?" asked Don Jordan, a few bunks away.

"It's not that much of a town," Duane replied.

His intention was to spend another peaceful Saturday night alone in the bunkhouse, and save money for the ranch he hoped to own someday. In addition, he didn't want to run into Vanessa Fontaine and her new husband, the fancy-pants lieutenant.

He dozed on his bunk, as others took baths, changed clothes, and prepared for town. Eventually they rode off, and the bunkhouse quieted except for an occasional gust of wind whistling past shingles. Duane lit the lamp, heated water, and took his bath. Then he put on blue jeans, a red shirt, and a green bandanna. He ate steak and biscuits at the table, reveling in his solitude.

He had to admit that he'd never felt better in his life. The outdoors seemed to agree with him, his face had become deeply bronzed, and he looked like an Indian.

After supper, he decided to look at Thunderbolt, and then search for something, anything to read. It was dark as he approached

the barn, but an oil lamp sent golden efful-
gence through the windows. Duane stepped
inside and saw that the lantern was halfway
down the stalls, on the left. A cowboy was
brushing a horse, but Duane had thought all
the cowboys went to town. Then he noticed a
certain curvature of the hip as Phyllis Thornton turned around. "Oh — it's you, Duane.
You're not going to town again?"

"I'd rather take it easy here."

She bent over to brush Suzie's forelocks,
and Duane caught a glimpse of perfect form.
Ashamed of himself, he turned in another direction. She glanced at him over her shoulder.

"Heard about the shindig?"

"Yes — McGrath told us."

"People will come from miles around, and
if the governor wasn't a scalawag, we'd invite
him, too. We'll have a band and dancing all
night long. Do you know how to dance,
Duane?"

"Not a step," he admitted.

"Then you'll have to learn. Maybe I should
teach you, as payment for your shooting lessons. I've been practicing with one of my father's Colts while you were away, and I'm
getting real good. Maybe you can show me
some fancy tricks, like when you catch the
gun behind your back."

"You're liable to shoot your leg off. It's best

to stick with the basics."

He noticed that she was sweaty from her exertions, and her complexion glowed with vitality. Her movements were firm and strong, and she was no fragile wraith like Vanessa Fontaine. Duane wondered what it would be like to walk behind her and grab her breasts.

He swallowed hard, and the artery in his throat pulsated insistently. His foul thoughts embarrassed him, and he took three deep breaths. Meanwhile, she stood erectly and wiped her forehead with the back of her arm, the gesture pulling her blue plaid cowboy shirt against her breasts, revealing more of their shapes than Duane usually saw.

He appeared in a trance, and she didn't know if it was good or bad. "Could you at least show me how to fast-draw?"

They were alone in the barn, and the cowboys had gone to town. "Anytime you want."

Her innocent eyes twinkled with mischief, and she became awkwardly flirtatious. "Will you dance with me at the party?"

"I told you that I don't know how to dance."

"And I told you that I'll teach you. It's much less complicated than firing a gun."

"I believe your father said he'd shoot me if I ever laid a hand on you."

"I believe *I* told you that he'd apologized for that barbarian remark."

Duane smiled. "I'd be happy to dance with you, Miss Phyllis."

He pondered whether to invite her to the hayloft, for a little stargazing. Meanwhile, she gathered her brushes and combs. "I've got to get back to the house. Can I have a shooting lesson after breakfast?"

"Sure, and by the way, do you have anything interesting to read in the house?"

"I'll see what I can find. Where will you be?"

"The corral."

She headed for the door, and once more he admired a certain outstanding segment of her anatomy, which was set off to perfection by her tight jeans. Duane blew out the lamp, then made his way out of the barn. As he approached the corral, he saw the dark forms of horses in the moonlight, milling around, free of saddles and bridles, having their own special sabbath evening.

He came to a stop at the rail fence, rested his arms on the top rung, and peered inside at sleek muscular animals. He considered them the most beautiful creatures in the world, and wondered what they thought of the two-legged creatures who had enslaved them.

One horse detached himself from the mass

178

and moved toward Duane cautiously. Duane reached into his shirt pocket and removed a handful of raisins, which he held out. Thunderbolt lowered his head and scooped up the tasty kernels with his lips.

Duane patted Thunderbolt's neck, feeling his incredible power. God creates horses, and we ride them into the ground. I'll bet there's much that you could teach me, Thunderbolt. Sometimes I wish that I could be a horse, and run free, but the Comanches would capture me, or the cowboys, and I'd be locked in a corral every night like you.

Duane often wanted to turn Thunderbolt loose, but a man needed a horse if he wanted to survive on the massive distances of Texas. Besides, Thunderbolt was worth at least forty dollars, more than a month's pay.

Thunderbolt made a sound in his throat, as if he understood what Duane was thinking. Duane often thought that Thunderbolt was more intelligent than he. Patting the shock of hair between Thunderbolt's ears, Duane said, "I'll take care of you, and you'll take care of me, all right?"

Thunderbolt snorted suddenly and gazed apprehensively over Duane's shoulder. Duane spun around, reaching for his Colt. His shoulders relaxed when he saw Phyllis approaching with a thick, old, leather-bound tome. "We have an extra Bible, and my mother said I could give it to you. It's a little dog-eared, but no pages are missing."

"Today I was wishing that I had my own Bible," Duane confessed. "Thank your mother for me."

Their fingers touched as the Bible passed hands. Thunderbolt examined them curiously, as a coyote howled mournfully in a far-off cave. Phyllis knew that she should return to the main house, but her feet wouldn't move. Duane struggled to find something socially acceptable to say, but wanted to wrap his arms around her.

"Is that your horse?" she asked.

"Yes — I broke him myself, and it's something that I'm not very proud of."

The rancher's daughter appeared surprised. "Why not?"

"He doesn't sit on me, so why should I sit on him? Sometimes I think that I should turn him loose."

"But you need a horse, don't you?"

"That's the problem."

"Didn't God say that animals were put here for us?"

"I don't think that Thunderbolt would agree, but he's a very good horse, fast as the wind. If you appreciate a spirited animal, you might take a ride with him sometime."

Phyllis wondered if Duane were talking about Thunderbolt or himself when he referred to the *spirited animal,* and taking a ride with him. Meanwhile, Thunderbolt was aware that three was a crowd. With a whinny, he turned around and headed back toward the other horses, watching the human beings cautiously.

Phyllis looked up into Duane's swirling eyes. "Why don't you go to town like the other cowboys?"

"It's just a few shacks nailed together. There's nothing to do except get drunk and fall on your face."

"My father said that Mister Gibson is building an addition to the general store, with chairs and tables."

"You meet the strangest people in saloons."

"Don't people get killed from time to time?"

Duane pulled out his Colt. "That's what this is for."

She looked at the gun, then raised her eyes and examined his facial characteristics close up. He'd cut his chin while shaving, but otherwise was extremely handsome in a roguish way. "I've never met anybody like you," she admitted.

"That's probably because you haven't met many people period. Limited choice, it's called."

"I think you're special."

He wanted to be charming and devil-may-care, but decided to stick with the truth. "I think you're special, too. If things were a little different, I'd . . ." His voice trailed off into the night.

She wouldn't let him off the hook so easily. "You'd what?"

He became ill at ease, but again resolved to be honest. "You're the kind of woman who I'd want to settle down with. We're very similar, you know."

"If that's the way you truly feel," she replied, "well — why don't we just get married?"

Everything became silent, and even the coyote stopped howling in his far-off cave. "If I give you a ring," Duane said, "your father will give me a bullet. I have no money, a bad reputation, and my prospects are poor. I think you could do much better."

"My mother owned more than my father when they got married, but they've been together for nearly eighteen years. I don't think I'd ever find anybody better than you, Duane."

It pleased Duane's vanity that she found him appealing, and he imagined himself writhing naked in the hayloft with her, but then a glimmer of rationality beamed through his surging animal lust.

"Marriage is a big step," he lectured, as if he were much older than she. "We can't run into it blindly, and I don't want to elope, because I'm convinced that your father would shoot me."

"We should be sensible," she agreed. "Otherwise no one'll take us seriously. What do you think we should do?"

He thought of the hayloft, the bunkhouse, and numerous other comfortable spots where two human beings could recline, but then Christian morality overcame him, accompanied by Victorian prudery. He cleared his throat, and said, "Tomorrow morning I'm giving you a shooting lesson, and that's all I can handle right now."

"I'd better go back to the house, or my mother will worry. Do you think, under the circumstances, since we're thinking about getting married, that we could kiss good night?"

His willpower failed totally as he glanced around to make sure that her father wasn't sneaking up on them. Then he held his arms stiffly down his sides and lowered his lips to her. Meanwhile, she stood on her tiptoes and clasped her hands behind her back.

Their lips drew closer, and his heart leapt with anticipation of her spotless beauty. He opened his eyes at the last moment, their noses almost crashed, then their lips touched softly, gently, tenderly, and his head spun with ecstasy. He thought it the most scrumptious sensation he'd ever known as the fragrance of prairie flowers arose from her bosom. His hands touched her waist, and he felt her go limp against him.

Her lips were strawberries, and his brain became inflamed. Her dovelike palms came to rest upon his shoulders, their bodies touched, her sixteen-year-old nipples jutted into his shirt. Duane thought he was going mad and struggled to control himself. He tried to take three deep breaths, but her mouth was all over him like petals of the softest flower. He was about to rip off her dress, when he realized that she was a decent Christian girl, and you didn't violate her unless you placed a ring on her finger first. And then he recalled a famous line: *If you ever lay hands on her — I'll kill you.*

Duane summoned his strength and pushed her away. Her eyes were ablaze with strange catlike madness, her complexion mottled by emotional confusion.

"I never kissed anybody before," she said plaintively, her voice trailing off.

"I have," he admitted, "but never as sweet as that."

Her eyes glittered in the darkness. "I love you, Duane. Do you think that we could do that again?"

"If we do, I'll probably end up taking your clothes off."

Each took a step backward, and looked at each other longingly.

"Well, we can't have that," she said.

"If we're going to get married," he replied, "that means we wait a decent interval, and get engaged. About a year later, we'll get married."

She held out her hand, just like Big Al Thornton. "It's a deal."

They shook as if they'd just sold and bought three thousand head of cattle.

"I think you'd better go back to the house now," he said, gazing at her heaving bosom.

She leapt forward suddenly, touched her lips to his, then turned and fled, her boot heels kicking high in the air. Duane was surprised by her impulse, and could taste her upon his tongue. With trembling hand, he pulled out his little white bag of tobacco. Another moment I would've had her on a haystack, yanking at her buttons.

He strolled out of the barn, looked at ranch buildings, the corral, and the vast range full of Bar T cattle. If I marry Phyllis, this'll be mine someday! The more he thought about it, the more profound it became. It appeared as if all his dreams were finally coming true. It just goes to show you that if you try to lead a Christian life, the Lord will reward you. As it says in Jeremiah:

Blessed is the man that trusteth in the Lord.

In back of Gibson's General Store, Vanessa was sitting to dinner with her new husband. In the middle of the table, a platter of roast beef emitted trails of steam. Vanessa had prepared it under the tutelage of Mrs. Gibson, along with fried potatoes and onions.

Lieutenant Dawes carved thick slabs of meat, as he said, "We'll have army engineers here in a week, and their first project, after my headquarters, will be our home. You can design it yourself, and supervise construction. Make sure you work in an extra bedroom for our first child." He awaited her response and noticed that she was gazing past his shoulder at a blank space of wall behind him. "Are you all right, Vanessa?"

She appeared startled, as if she'd just awakened from a dream. "I'm fine," she said in a faraway voice.

"You seem distracted lately, my dear. What's wrong?"

"Nothing."

"You don't want to tell me, but I know what it is. You're thinking about your former boyfriend, the one who likes to shoot people for the fun of it."

She glanced at him crossly. "You don't know Duane at all."

"Perhaps I know him better than you, because all you see is his pretty face, and can't perceive his violent and bloodthirsty nature, not to mention his outright lies."

"I wish you weren't so jealous of him," she replied. "He's just a boy — can't you tell? If I knew he was all right, I could forget him. But he tends to get into trouble. For some reason, people like you hate him."

"I don't hate him, but I have a certain skepticism that you evidently lack. Perhaps it comes from my military training, or maybe I'm just a skeptic at heart. We've been married two weeks, and all you ever do is think about him."

She touched her hand to his arm. "You're exaggerating, because you know very well that's not *all* I do."

He placed his hand on hers. "Perhaps I'm being ridiculous."

"I just want to know how he's doing, that's all. Can't you ask one of the cowboys from the Bar T?"

"Do you expect me to walk up to the ramrod and say, *Can you tell me how my wife's former beau is doing?*"

"Then I'll have to ask him myself."

"You're my wife, and you're going to inquire about the health of your former boyfriend? That will make both of us look like fools! Why can't you forget him?"

"It's an impossible situation," she agreed.

"I'll drink to that."

He reached for his glass of white lightning in his rough soldierly manner, and she couldn't blame him for being jealous. *What would I do if he had an old girlfriend who he talked about all the time?*

But she knew that Duane hadn't come to town for two Saturday nights in a row, and she hoped that he wasn't brooding with his gun, working himself into a murderous mood. *He's not my responsibility*, she tried to convince herself. *He'll have to get along without me now.*

But somehow, despite everything, she couldn't stop imagining him in her bedroom, unbuttoning his shirt.

It was after midnight as Amos Raybart rode toward the main house of the Circle K Ranch. He was slouched in his saddle, for he'd ridden many long miles, and he'd even been chased by Comanches for several terrifying hours.

188

Raybart felt as if he'd been plunged into hell after his rarified hours at the monastery in the clouds. The world of ordinary men seemed foul and wicked to his born-again eyes. He hadn't even taken a drink of white lightning at the general store in Shelby, where he'd gone to look for Jay Krenshaw, but the Circle K cowboys had told him that the rancher's son didn't come to town.

I'll git my pay at the end of the month and give it to the abbot, Raybart thought. Then I'll stay at the monastery fer the rest of my life. He stopped his horse in front of the rail, climbed down from the saddle, and hitched up his belt. Then he entered the house and made his way down the long dark corridor to the room at the end.

He knocked, but there was no answer. Opening the door, he stepped into the small smelly bedroom. A slanted ray of moonshine revealed Jay Krenshaw sprawled facedown on his bed, clothes on, boots off. Raybart lit the lamp on the dresser, revealing bottles everywhere. It appeared as though Jay Krenshaw was in a drunken stupor.

Raybart didn't care to wake up Jay, because some drunks throw punches upon arising. Perhaps I should pray for him. Raybart clasped his hands together and bowed his head. "Dear Lord," he whispered, "please put yer healin' power on this poor soul, and give him . . ."

"Who's 'ere?" grumbled Jay Krenshaw, rolling over slowly in his mucked-up bed.

"Amos Raybart, sir."

Jay raised one eye, but the other refused to open. He stared at Raybart in confusion and disbelief, then brought his legs around and sat upright. "Took you long enough," he muttered. "I was about to send somebody after you."

"After Titusville, I rode into the Guadalupe Mountains," Raybart explained, "where Braddock was raised at a monastery."

"He was really a priest!" Jay asked.

"He didn't git that fur, but he was close to it. The abbot said he was a good boy, 'cept he had a bad temper. He nearly killed one of the other orphans in a fight, and they threw him out. That's when he went to Titusville, where he met Clyde Butterfield, the old gunfighter — you ever heard of him?"

"They say he was one of the fastest."

"He taught Duane his tricks, and that's how Duane could beat Saul Klevins. Then Braddock ran off with the purtiest woman in Titusville, and come here."

Jay Krenshaw leaned forward and looked into Raybart's eyes. "It sounds like a crock of shit to me."

"I tracked down the information myself, and it weren't easy. Accordin' to the abbot, the Kid's loco 'cause of his parents. His father was an outlaw who got shot or hung someplace, and his momma was a whore who died of some disease. They never bothered to git hitched."

Krenshaw smiled. "He's a little bastard, eh?"

"He's also real good with a gun, accordin' to the folks what seen him shoot Saul Klevins. I was you, I'd give 'im plenty of room."

"You ain't me." Jay Krenshaw took a sip of whiskey, rammed the cork back in with the heel of his hand, and leaned toward Raybart again. "Who's the fastest gun you ever heard of — who's still in business?"

Raybart shrugged. "There's lots of 'em."

"I want somebody who don't live far from here, and I don't care what it costs. Yer a low-down skunk, Raybart, and if anybody knows — you do."

Raybart wiped his mouth with the back of his hand as he searched through his memory. "Wa'al, you put it like that — how's about Otis Puckett from Laredo?"

CHAPTER 8

Gibson and his carpentry crew heard a large number of riders headed toward town on Monday morning. At first they thought it was an Indian raid, but then Mr. Phipps shouted from atop the roof, "It's Big Al Thornton!"

A smile wreathed Mr. Gibson's face, because the Bar T was the source of considerable business. Money was rolling in everywhere, and he could barely believe it. He'd struggled for years, opening stores across the frontier, losing his shirt every time, but now at last he'd landed in the right place at the right time. He wiped his hands on his apron and headed toward the middle of the street, to see the great man. The storekeeper fairly drooled in anticipation of the big order he expected to receive.

Big Al rode his white gelding down the main street, followed by his men and the clatter of hoofbeats. He wore a big silverbelly hat with a wide flaring brim, and a cigar stuck out the corner of his mouth. "Howdy, Mr. Gibson," he said. "I've come to invite you and the missus, and everybody else in this town, to a shindig at the ranch next Saturday afternoon. There'll be a barbecue, free drinks, and we're even a-gittin' together a band!"

The cogs of Gibson's mercantile mind spun furiously. "Need any white lightning?"

"I figger about three kegs ought to do it."

"Could brew some beer," Mr. Gibson offered. "And how's about a few sucklin' pigs?"

"Got my own pigs," said Big Al as he put the spurs to his horse.

The wealthy rancher rode down the street, followed by his cowboy escort, headed toward the army encampment. He held his reins in his left hand, his right fist resting on his hip as he surveyed new construction underway. The town was growing, the region becoming more prosperous, and now they even had an army camp, although it was just some tents squatting on the edge of town.

A freckle-faced sentry stepped forward, holding his rifle high. "Halt!" he said. "Who goes there?"

Big Al tipped his cowboy hat. "I wanna palaver with yer commandin' officer," he replied, not bothering to stop or identify himself further.

"But . . . but . . ."

The sentry sputtered as he dodged oncoming horses. The cowboys passed by, headed for the big white tent at the center of the encampment. Soldiers crowded around, and the rancher touched his forefinger to the brim of his hat as he smiled cordially. A tall, husky officer emerged from the tent, his campaign hat tilted jauntily over his eyes. Big Al climbed down from his horse and threw the reins at a private standing nearby, his jaw hanging open in surprise.

Lieutenant Dawes held out his hand. "You must be Big Al Thornton."

"And yer Lieutenant Dawes. I want to say that my family has felt a lot safer since you and yer men've been in the vicinity. The only thing them goddamned injuns understand is lead, but that ain't why I'm here today. I'm a-havin' a big shindig at my ranch next Saturday, and I'd like you and yer men to come as my guests, stay as long as you like, eat and drink all you want."

Lieutenant Dawes grinned. "I accept your invitation on their behalf. You can be sure that we'll be there, and if any of them gets a little drunk, I'll handle him myself."

"I heard you got yerself hitched not long

ago. Don't forget to bring the little woman along. We've heard a lot about her, and my wife would love to meet her."

"Mrs. Dawes'll be happy to hear that," the officer replied, "and she loves parties. It'd take an act of war to keep her away."

Not all Bar T cowboys were traveling with Big Al Thornton on that glorious day. Approximately half the crew had remained at the ranch, performing their usual jobs. Duane was one of them, and the ramrod had told him to sweep across the western range with Don Jordan and Uncle Ray, keeping their eyes peeled for screwworms and unknown cowboys with long ropes and peculiar branding irons.

The three cowboys rode down the side of an incline, and a vast grass-covered plateau lay before them, adorned with groups of cattle grazing in the sun. On the distant horizon, a row of hills sprawled like rounded teeth.

Duane knew that everything before him would be his someday, and he was astonished yet again by his great good fortune. *I couldn't ask for a better woman than Phyllis Thornton, and she comes with all this!* He imagined himself removing her garments slowly, and kissing whatever was revealed. It was almost too much to hope for, a ripe young woman, pure as newly fallen snow, together with the Bar T ranch. All I have to do is not get into fights, and keep my hands off her until our wedding night. I hope I can hold off that long.

There was a knock on the door, and Jay Krenshaw opened his eyes. "Who is it?"

"Riders comin', boss."

Jay pulled on his boots quickly, then grabbed a gunbelt hanging from the bedpost. He strapped it on, tucked in part of his shirt, put on his hat, and took down the Henry rifle from the wall. Then he jacked the lever, a cartridge rammed into the chamber, and he opened the door, hoping it wasn't Comanches.

He heard shouting in the yard as his cowboys prepared for the visitors. Jay stepped onto the porch and saw the cloud of dust approaching. "You men take cover," he said. "This could be trouble."

He ducked behind a water barrel and snaked his neck around so he could observe the advancing riders. It didn't look like a Comanche attack, but the Circle K was in a remote corner of Texas, and unannounced strangers weren't necessarily on missions of mercy.

"Looks like the Bar T," said Morris Standfield, his ramrod.

"If they're a-lookin' fer lead," Jay replied, "we'll give 'em aplenty."

He stepped from behind the barrel and strolled toward the middle of the yard. His men joined him, and all carried loaded rifles, ready for anything. The riders from the Bar T galloped closer, and Big Al held up his hand as whorls of dust arose among their ranks. It appeared as though they were being borne forward on a white cloud.

Big Al's white horse came to a stop in front of Jay Krenshaw, and Big Al leaned forward, resting his forearm on his pommel. "This is a helluva welcoming party," he said in his booming voice. "Did you think we was injuns?"

Jay spread his legs and pointed his forefinger at Big Al. "If yer a-lookin' fer trouble — you come to the right place!"

"Trouble?" asked Big Al. Then he laughed. "I'm hyar to invite you and yer cowboys to the big shindig I'm a-throwin' next Saturday. I'll invite yer daddy meself." Big Al made a move to climb down from the saddle.

"Hold on!" shouted Jay. "My daddy don't talk to nobody! He asked me to keep folks away!"

Big Al climbed down from the saddle and looked Jay in the eye. "I ain't folks, so get out've my goddamned road."

Jay could offer no resistance, because Big Al and Jay's father had known each other since San Jacinto, where a bunch of ranchers, cowboys, sheepherders, and dirt farmers had fought off the Mexican Army, and established the Republic of Texas. Old Lew Krenshaw and Big Al Thornton were considered founding fathers, almost godlike in the eyes of the younger generation.

Big Al strolled around the main house and headed toward a small cottage in back, with a big cottonwood growing near the front door. He knocked on the door, and a voice inside hollered, "Who the hell is it!"

"It's *me,* you old horned toad!"

"Wa'al I'll be damned! Come on in!"

Big Al opened the door on a skinny old man with a long white beard and sorrowful eyes sitting at the edge of a cot, his bony knees sticking into the air. Big Al held out his hand. "Yer lookin' more like Rip Van Winkle every day, Lew!"

"Have a seat, you old varmint."

Lewton Krenshaw reached underneath his pillow, extracted a bottle of whiskey, and tossed it to Big Al, who pulled the cork and took a deep long swig as his eyes scanned the interior of the cottage. Books and pamphlets were piled everywhere, clothes hung from nails, everything covered with dust. Big Al sat on the only chair and looked at his longtime friend. "You look like hell, if'n you don't mind me a-sayin' so, Lew."

"Feel weak," Lew Krenshaw said. "Sleep all the time. Lost me appetite. Nawthin' to live fer."

"What happened?"

"Don't feel like a-talkin' 'bout it."

Big Al slapped his hand on his old friend's shoulder. "Snap out of it, Lew. Whatever it is, it cain't be *that* bad. Why don't you git it off'n yer chest — you'll feel better."

Lew looked down at the floor glumly. "You know what it is."

"Jay?"

"The missus and me, we give him everythin' he wanted, but he was an ornery li'l cuss from the day he was borned, just like yer daughter was a sweetheart from the day *she* was borned. I had my hopes on him, but he's . . . maybe I'd better not say it."

"Why don't you kick his ass out've here? Let 'im git along on his own fer a while, and find out what life's about?"

"He won't work, and somebody'd prob'ly shoot him."

"What's that got to do with you a-holin' up here like a lizard?"

Lew Krenshaw pointed to stacks of books. "I been a-tryin' to understand, but I jest git more confused. One feller says this, the other feller says that, and some of 'em have writ that God is dead, and we're all on our own down hyar."

"Them fellers wouldn't know a bull's ass from a banjo. God ain't no person, so he can't die!"

"If'n he's up there a-lookin' at us all the time, how come there's so much sufferin' and badness in the world?"

"I'll ask the big feller next time I see 'im, but I come here today to invite you to a shindig at my ranch next Saturday."

"I don't travel no more, Al. Feel better in me little shack."

"We'll have a band, and you used to stomp with the best of 'em. You'll have a good time — I guarantee it!"

"Folks'll laugh at me."

"That's 'cause you ain't cut yer beard fer five years. You got to pull out of this hole yer in, Lew. It ain't yer fault that yer son's a no-good little fuck."

"But I'm too old fer parties."

"To hell with old. You know what I'm a-gonna do if'n I see Death a-comin' fer me?" Big Al reached behind his belt and pulled his big Bowie knife out of its sheath. "I'll cut his balls off."

"Why is it," Lew asked, "that yer like you

always was, and I'm so damned old?"

"Cause yer always a-lookin' back, 'stead of alookin' ahead. If you don't come to my shindig, I'll hog-tie you and carry you on the back of my horse, and if that crazy son of your'n gives me any shit, I'll punch him through a window."

CHAPTER 9

Sam Wheatly sat behind the counter of his post office, general store, and real estate office in Laredo. It was a slow day, the region sparsely populated, and few people stopped by. He wore a green eyeshade, long drooping mustache, and baggy eyes.

Once in a while banditos passed through, but Wheatly made it a practice never to argue with loaded guns. Then the cavalry would arrive and spend enough to make up for what the banditos had stolen.

He tabulated bags of coffee and cans of tomatoes, making careful notations on his ledger. Laredo was a small town of saloons, a barber shop, a few whorehouses, and Wheatly's General Store. Peaceful during the day, Laredo could get fairly wild at night, but he closed the establishment at six, and retired to the back rooms with his wife and three children.

The store was unusually quiet, for his children were in school, and his wife visiting a sick friend. He lit a cigar and blew smoke into the air, content with his humble lot. The store earned a decent living, and he had every expectation that it would continue to prosper as trade increased between Texas and Mexico. I'll be just fine, as long as no bandito shoots me.

The door opened and a fat man was silhouetted in bright sunlight, his black hat low over his eyes. "Howdy, Mister Puckett," Wheatly said. "Got a letter fer you."

Puckett was shaped like an egg, narrow in the shoulders, wide in the waist, with heavy jowls and a dour expression. He advanced toward the counter, spurs jangling, and held out his hand.

Wheatly dropped the envelope into it. He'd often wondered about Otis Puckett, who'd ride out of nowhere about once every two weeks, to get his mail. He lived in Mexico, but Wheatly didn't know where.

"Nice day," Wheatly said, trying to make conversation, and draw out Puckett.

"What's so nice about it?" Puckett growled as he headed for the door.

On the dirt sidewalk, Puckett read the return address on the envelope. Then he tore it open, read the letter, and a cynical smile came over his face. He spat into the street, tucked the letter into his back pocket, and headed for the nearest saloon.

It was a large adobe hut, and a few Mexicans sat bleary-eyed among the tables, with more at the bar. Puckett waddled toward it and said to the bartender, "Tequila."

The bartender filled a glass and Puckett carried it to a solitary table, where he sat with his back to the wall. Then he reread the letter. His services were requested in Shelby, fifty dollars upon arrival, and another fifty upon completion of the job.

It was the only proposition he'd received all month, because he lived far from main population centers, and folks tended to forget fast hands, as younger men came to the fore. Puckett was forty-two years old and had been a hired killer for most of his life. Across the West, whenever fast hands were discussed, his name would invariably come up. But he lived in Mexico, because he wanted normal family life.

Puckett had an eighteen-year-old Mexican wife, plus a little son. Between jobs, he worked his few head of cattle, and his garden. It was a decent life, and the extra money really helped out.

Sometimes he wanted to move to San

Antone or El Paso, so he'd be available for more assignments, but he preferred remote Mexico with his little family. Rosita actually seemed to love him, although he was old enough to be her father, and much too fat.

He placed his hand upon the great solid mass of his stomach. No matter what he did, it kept getting bigger. He knew that he appeared ridiculous to other people, but if they said anything insulting, their lives would come to abrupt ends.

He relaxed, sipped tequila, made plans. I'll go back to the *ranchero,* say goodbye to Rosita, then hit the trail. Should take about a week, provided the Apaches don't get me.

He wondered vaguely who he'd have to kill this time, and why. In dreams, he'd seen a gunfighter in a black cowboy outfit, with a halo around his head: the Angel of Death. Sometimes, in the morning, the smell of the grave had been in his bedclothes. He knew that one dark night, like every other mortal being, he'd die, but expected that far in the future, and didn't think anyone could defeat him in a standard gunfight.

I wonder what my man is doing right now, and if he knows that he's going to die.

CHAPTER 10

Two steers sizzled and spattered over hot coals, sending a cloud of smoke roiling across the Bar T. It was the morning of Big Al's shindig, and a crew of cowboys ran bright-colored ribbons from the main house to the barn, and then to the bunkhouse. Other cowboys tuned their guitars and fiddles, attempting to practice, while more cleared wagons, barrels, and refuse from the front yard, where the dancing would take place. A different crew hammered together long rough-hewn tables for the food and drink.

An atmosphere of excitement permeated the Bar T, and even Big Al could feel it in his office. It was a day to stuff your belly, meet new people, and have a grand time that you could talk about for the rest of your life.

He remembered when he was young, traveling for days to a party, and raising merry hell. But now he was a parent, and Duane

Braddock was giving his daughter shooting lessons. He'd heard that she was becoming a dead shot, and falling in love with him. Big Al had seen the sickly glaze in her eyes when she'd returned from target practice.

He didn't like it, but Myrtle had taken Phyllis's side. Big Al could barely handle one of them, but not both. So he kept his mouth shut, bided his time, and waited for Duane Braddock to step out of line.

Big Al knew that a cowboy would do anything necessary to get his hands on a woman, including lying, cheating, and stealing, and he suspected that Duane Braddock was attempting to seduce his daughter.

I'll watch 'im like a hawk, Big Al thought grumpily. Let 'im put one hand in the wrong place — I'll shoot it off.

Meanwhile, Phyllis was buttoning on her favorite white dress. She'd washed it yesterday, and had to lower the hem, because she was growing so rapidly. She looked at herself in the mirror turning from side to side, trying to see herself from every possible angle. She wanted to look perfect for her father, so that he'd be proud of her.

Her complexion flushed with excitement, and her eyes danced brightly. This was the day she'd planned for, and she looked forward to seeing girls and boys whom she'd met over the years at weddings, funerals, and other shindigs. Most of all, she wanted to dance with Duane.

She examined herself critically and thought her ears too big, nose too small, and she was getting fat. In a few years, I'll be an old lady, but at least I'll have today. She felt as if her body belonged to somebody named Duane Braddock.

She looked into the courtyard, where steer and hog carcasses turned on spits, basted with a secret concoction by Seamus McSweeny, the cowboy cook. Gaily colored ribbons fluttered in the breeze, and then she spotted *him* sitting atop the barn roof, nailing a ribbon to the beam. He looked down at the point of contact, his hatbrim covering his face, and light flashed on his silver concho hatband as he raised the hammer high.

She experienced a strange sensation as she observed the hammer fall. Maybe it was the rhythm, or he looked like a Greek god seated atop the barn. Something delicate gave way inside her, and she felt afraid of him, for she *needed* him.

He glanced up, and their eyes met across the courtyard. She raised her fingers to her lips and blew him a kiss. He didn't move for a few moments, and she wondered if he'd actually seen her, when suddenly he threw back his head, and roared: "Yiiippppeeeeeeeee!" his voice ricocheting across the hills, melting into the morning breeze.

"Detachment — right face!" shouted Sergeant Mahoney. "First squad — column of two's from the right, forward hoooo!"

Horses' hooves slammed into the ground, and equipment jangled as the detachment moved out, trailed by the townspeople's wagons. It was nearly ten o'clock in the morning, a few wisps of cloud floated across the sky, and everyone anticipated the big shindig at the Bar T.

Lieutenant Dawes rode at the head of the long column, his yellow bandanna flying in the breeze, brass and leather shining. He chewed his lips nervously, because he knew that Duane Braddock would be at the shindig, and believed Vanessa still was in love with him. Maybe I married her too quickly, he speculated darkly.

Behind Lieutenant Dawes rode his detachment of cavalry soldiers, and they, too, were spruced for the shindig, their heads aswim with expectations. They led brutal, dangerous lives, were poorly paid, and were considered lazy, worthless imbeciles by large numbers of taxpayers. The best they could hope for were dank, filthy saloons serving the most horrific whiskey imaginable, and whatever warmth could be provided by fifty cents' worth of prostitution.

But now they were going to a real shindig, with decent people, and real women would be there. Each trooper dreamed that he'd find the prairie princess of his dreams, and she'd fall madly and hopelessly in love with him.

In the end of the column, accompanied by their own special cavalry escort, came five wagons full of men, women, and children wearing their best Sunday clothing. They chattered incessantly about the day that lay ahead, who would be there, and what they'd eat. Like the soldiers, the townspeople led difficult, repetitive lives, their only entertainment an old newspaper or magazine, or one of the books that was passed from hand to hand, coming apart at the seams.

Seated among them, next to Parson Jones, was Vanessa Fontaine, and the day was going from bad to worse for her. That morning she'd had her first intensive argument with her husband as he'd accused her of being in love with Duane Braddock, and she'd called him a jealous idiot. If that wasn't enough, her husband spent most of his time with the detachment, while she had an empty room for a companion.

But her main worry was Duane Braddock. She didn't know what he'd do when he saw her at the party. He probably hates me, she thought worriedly, and might even shoot Clayton. Maybe I can talk sense to him, but I doubt it. Something tells me that this is going to be the worst day of my life.

Fifteen riders made their way across the range, led by Jay Krenshaw. Their horse's hooves kicked up dust that trailed all the way back to the Circle K as a flock of birds flew over their heads. The cowboys wore their newest outfits, with boots shined and hats brushed clean. They, too, hoped that women would fall in love with them, although they knew it extremely unlikely.

Jay owned a dark business suit, but refused to wear it to the party. Instead, he had on one of his regular rumpled black and white check-ered shirts, with a blue bandanna, and a white hat. He'd bathed, shaved, and wanted to look his best, because he knew that Phyllis Thornton would be there, and he'd loved her in his twisted, malignant way for most of his life.

They'd met as children, but never got on well. Jay had the impression that Phyllis thought him beneath her, which made him angry because he actually did feel inferior to her. She could read and write better than he, and his tongue always stuck to the roof of his mouth whenever he tried to speak with her.

But he had a special advantage: the Circle K Ranch. Jay's father had made no secret about his desire for Jay to marry Phyllis someday, but Phyllis was too young to see practical benefits. Time is on my side, Jay reckoned. The older she gets, the more sense it'll make to her. I'll get my hands on her someday, if I just bide my time.

Next to him, his father sat atop a sorrel stallion, surveying the vast sprawling ranch land. He'd come here as a boy from Louisiana, full of hope and dreams, and now, many years later, he'd achieved his highest aspirations. But somehow it gave him no pleasure, because he knew that he was going to die within the next five to ten years. Sometimes he thought it was better not to've been born.

He glanced at his son and wondered where he and his deceased wife had gone wrong. Instead of a man to take over the Circle K, Jay was erratic, moody, and drank too much. Every cow and building will be gone not long after they plant me in the ground, he predicted.

But Lew Krenshaw had an ace in the hole. He believed that a good woman could redeem a man, and he'd always hoped that Phyllis Thornton would marry Jay. Then Jay would have a family, and settle down, but on the other hand, Jay might continue in his present direction, and become a rotten husband and father. Lew wondered what was bothering his son, and what made him so . . . stupid.

I tried to lead a decent life, Lew said to himself. I believed in God and fought for Texas. What'd I do to deserve such a lazy, useless son of a bitch?

Cowboys positioned chairs around a low rough-hewn table in front of the house, with a view overlooking the yard. Then Big Al made his grand entrance, wearing striped pants and a white shirt with ruffles in front, and a black string tie. He strolled across the lawn, sat on a chair, stretched his legs, and said, "I'm not doin' one goddamned lick of work for the rest of the day."

A cowboy brought him a glass of whiskey, he took a sip, and then leaned back, proud of all he'd achieved. The ranch was sound financially, if beef prices held. His family would never starve, as long the grass grew. Sometimes he thought about running for Congress, but didn't want to spend the rest of his life fighting liars in Washington. No, he'd rather stay in West Texas, and it gave him satisfaction to be able to entertain his friends and neighbors, for he knew that they worked hard and deserved some fun. "It was a great idea to

213

have this party," he muttered to himself. "I'm glad I thought of it."

"Are you talking to yourself again, Daddy?" Phyllis descended the stairs of the veranda, wearing her white dress with red velvet trim.

"Cain't help it," he replied. "I'm the most interesting man I know."

She raised her hand to shade her eyes. "I believe somebody's coming."

He squinted in the direction of her gaze. "Cain't see nawthin'."

"Looks like the army."

They watched silently, the daughter standing and her father sprawled on the chair, a glass of whiskey in his hand, as the detachment rode into the yard, accompanied by a cloud of dust. Their brawny commanding officer shouted orders, and then dismounted. He walked toward the wagons, picked up a blond woman by the waist, and gently lowered her to the ground. Then he took her hand and led her toward Big Al.

"Looks like she's the one everybody's a-talkin' about," Big Al said. "Lordy, is she a tall drink of water, or what?"

"I think she could use a decent meal," his daughter replied sarcastically.

He glanced at her, because the reactions of women fascinated him. "I would've thought that you and her would be friends, since yer both around the same age."

"She's practically an old lady!"

The lieutenant escorted his elegant wife up the lawn, and Big Al noted her narrow waist, small breasts, and gleaming golden hair. He'd heard of Duane Braddock's romance with her, and wondered how a woman of such poise and dignity could get mixed up with a dumb cowboy.

Lieutenant Dawes cleared his throat. "May I present my wife, Vanessa?"

The golden goddess held out her hand, and Big Al didn't know whether to kiss it, shake it, or get down on his knees and kiss her shoes, but she sensed his confusion and boldly grabbed his paw, giving it a warm squeeze. Her smile dazzled him, as she said, "I've heard so much about you, sir."

Her voice carried magnolia blossoms and mint juleps, and he realized that she was a former belle. "I'm happy to know you, ma'am. If there's anythin' you need, jest ask."

Phyllis glided behind her father and kicked him in the calf. He let go Vanessa's hand, then grabbed the lieutenant's. "It's always a pleasure to see the army. Is it true that you'll be a-stayin' in the neighborhood fer a while?"

"We're building a small camp here. Thirty-forty men, probably."

Big Al leaned forward and narrowed his

eye. "I guess you'll be a-needin' ter buy beef fer the troops."

"Reckon so," replied Lieutenant Dawes, drifting into the area of dollars and cents that tended to cause trouble for officers. "If you want to make your bid for the contract, you'll have to speak to Colonel Mackenzie."

"In the meantime, who's a-buyin' yer beef?"

"Me, I suppose."

Big Al grinned, and sunlight sparkled off his front gold tooth. "We'll talk about this some other time, but now, let me introduce my daughter, Phyllis."

Phyllis curtsied and fluttered her eyebrows in the appropriate virginal manner. Lieutenant Dawes judged her a ripe young plum ready to be plucked, and she'd inherit the biggest ranch in the territory. *Too bad I didn't come for a visit before I met Vanessa,* he conjectured. "How do you do."

Phyllis thought him stiff and affected. "Welcome to the Bar T, Lieutenant."

The front door of the house opened, and everyone turned to the queen of the Bar T. Attired in a purple dress with yellow trim, she swept down the lawn, and her husband introduced her to the gathering. A conversation of social platitudes ensued on the surface, while Lieutenant Dawes continued to examine Phyllis slyly out the corners of his eyes. Her beauty captivated him, and also caught the attention of Vanessa, who was surprised to find such a delightful creature in the wilderness of West Texas.

Meanwhile, Vanessa noticed that Phyllis was distracted, and then saw a faint smile come over the younger woman's face. Phyllis was looking toward the barn, and Vanessa turned in that direction. Her blood ran cold when her eyes fell on a slim young man wearing a black cowboy hat with flashing silver conchos. Is this what he's been up to behind my back? Vanessa wondered.

Midway between the Bar T Ranch and the Rio Grande was an open stretch of country populated mainly by armadillos, gila monsters, and rattlesnakes. Occasionally a stagecoach might pass through, followed by a detachment of cavalry, or possibly a raiding party of Commanches, but otherwise the land had been still and untrammeled for thousands of years.

Somewhere in that tangled tractless wilderness, a pear-shaped man sat beside a fire, roasting the tenderloin of an antelope shot earlier in the day. Otis Puckett prepared his dinner, for he wouldn't let anything interfere with meals. He'd shot an animal nearly every day, leaving most of it for buzzards and wild dogs.

As the meal cooked, he prepared mentally for the gun duel that lay ahead. He preferred not to shoot a man in the back, like some of his more unsporting brethren. He'd rather kill before a crowd if possible, so he could impress potential customers.

One moment he was sitting by the fire, turning the antelope loin, and the next second he was on his feet, hauling iron. He shot a red blossom off a barrel cactus, the yellow blossom off a sea urchin cactus, and the white blossom off a whiskey cactus. Dropping to one knee, he drilled a devil's head cactus through the middle, and then blew away the arm of a cholla cactus.

His gun was smoking, as, with a half smile, he thumbed new loads into the chambers. He was pleased with his performance, and seldom missed a target. He'd been given a wonderful gift, and no one could ever steal it away. He considered himself fortunate, and particularly loved the magic moment when an adversary dropped before him, as if in acknowledgment of his great skill.

A rivulet of sweat rolled down his temple as he thought of Rosita and his son back in Mexico, waiting for him to return, or at least that's what he hoped. He found it difficult to trust Rosita completely, for he had flabby flesh around his middle, and the face of a bulldog. He knew she didn't love him deeply, but hoped she feared him. She'd seen him kill in the dirty cantina where she'd been a prostitute, and knew his capabilities.

No stagecoaches or trains went to Shelby, so he had to travel on horseback through hostile country. The shooting performance had been for the Comanches, to show that many would die if they tried to steal his horse.

But he knew deep in his heart that one day, on a shaded street or open prairie, his aim might be slightly off, or his hand too tardy in the classic fast draw, and he'd meet his own dark destiny. He tried not to think about it, and knew it was unlikely, but he wasn't the only talented fast hand in the world.

He'd lived with Sister Death so long, she was an old friend sitting silently on a nearby boulder, wearing a black cloak encrusted with diamonds, watching the fat man perform his fast draw, while the antelope loin crackled and spat at the fire.

Farther north, clouds of smoke arose from another fire, wafting over the crowd at the Bar T Ranch. The cowboy musicians tuned up for the first dance, when a new horde of riders appeared over the top of a hill.

"It's the Circle K!" hollered Uncle Ray.

Every Bar T cowboy checked his armament once last time. Meanwhile, on the front lawn, Big Al gazed at the approaching riders. The success of the shindig would depend upon how well Big Al handled Jay Krenshaw and his unruly cowboys.

The Circle K cowboys rode into the front yard, and Jay Krenshaw sat firmly in his saddle, hat low over his eyes, as he scanned the gathering. His eyes fell on a silver concho hatband beside the barn, and he ground his teeth together angrily, intensifying an ache in his jaw that had been bothering him ever since Duane had punched him out.

The disgraceful day came back with full force, and Krenshaw felt volcanic rage. He wanted to draw his gun and ride straight for Duane, shooting him down like a dog, but knew full well that the opposite outcome probably would occur, for Duane Braddock was the Pecos Kid, and he'd shot Saul Klevins in Titusville. I'm just a-gonna bide my time, Jay counseled himself. Otis Plunkett'll show up one of these days, and that'll be the end of one little son of a bitch in a funny hat.

Meanwhile, riding among the Circle K cowboys, Amos Raybart and his beady eyes sought out Duane Braddock; it didn't take long to spot the silver conchos. Maybe I'll have a talk with 'im later, and find out what he's about, he thought.

Big Al strolled down the lawn, a smile on his face, followed by his wife and daughter. They headed for the wizened old man on the sorrel gelding.

"So you made it — you wooly, old bear!" Big Al hollered at Lew Krenshaw. "Come on down, and let me shake your hand!"

Lew Krenshaw laboriously raised his leg over the saddle, then lowered himself to the ground. Big Al grabbed his hand, they shook solidly, then embraced each other like brothers. It was a dramatic and clear signal that a day of peace would exist henceforth between the Circle K and Bar T.

Lew Krenshaw gazed through rheumy eyes at the ranch house, barn, and other buildings. "You sure got the place all spruced up!"

"It ain't that we've got it spruced," Big Al replied. "It's that yer spread is so damned run down. Say hello to the missus."

Mrs. Thornton wrapped her arms around her old friend and neighbor, while spindly Lew Krenshaw nearly disappeared in her ample bosom. Then Phyllis said, "Remember me?"

Lew's jaw dropped open as he stared at her. "I'll be hornswaggled — you must be little

Phyllis, only you ain't so little anymores." His eyes roved over her, and he thought, now that there's the kind of woman who can give a man sons. "You know my Jay, don't you?" He grabbed a sleeve and pulled his son forward.

Jay felt like jumping out of his skin, but said in a muffled self-conscious voice, "Howdy."

They looked awkwardly at each other, and then she stepped back to the side of her father. Meanwhile, approximately ten yards away, Lieutenant Dawes sat near his wife, observing the newcomers.

"Do you see that man talking to Miss Thornton?" Lieutenant Dawes asked Vanessa. "That's Jay Krenshaw. You may recall me telling you that he hates your former lover's guts." Lieutenant Dawes placed his hand reassuringly on his wife's arm. "If they start shooting, just hit the dirt."

"In my best dress?"

The band broke into a quadrille, and the crowd applauded. Big Al gallantly took his wife's hand and led her to the yard. Everybody watched as he placed one hand on her waist, held her palm, and danced her away, her skirts whirling through the air.

Then the cowboys moved inexorably toward the daughters of farmers and ranchers who lived throughout the county. The cow-

boys tried to comport themselves like gentlemen, and no one chewed tobacco as they
asked women to dance. Soon the yard filled
with country folk whirling in time to the music.

Phyllis knew that Duane wouldn't dare ask
her to dance, out of fear that her father would
shoot him. That meant that some other cowboy would ask her, and she couldn't say no. A
dark shadow passed between her and the sun,
and she realized that Jay Krenshaw was standing in front of her.

"Wanna dance?" he asked awkwardly.

She looked at his sallow cheeks, dull eyes,
and droopy lips. There appeared something
demented about him, and she'd perceived it
even when they'd been children. All she could
do was smile and say, "Love to, Jay."

He took her hand and led her to the yard.
She looked him over critically, trying to figure
out what it was that she despised, and noticed
that his shirt was too small, pants too big, he
had no discernable hindquarters, his shoulders slouched, and he reminded her of a
camel.

They came to the section of the yard that
had been designated the dance floor. He held
her hand and waist and gazed deeply into her
eyes, hoping to ignite a fire with his desire, but
she merely glanced at Duane sitting against

the barn. Jay tried to lead her into the dance, but he had no sense of rhythm, and immediately stepped on her left toe.

"Sorry," he mumbled.

"I've got nine more," she replied, hoping to settle him down.

"Don't dance much," he admitted.

"Why don't you let me lead you?"

He shook his head. "Wouldn't be right."

"Who cares? Let's go."

"We'll go when I'm good and ready," he replied testily.

She tried to smile, but he'd bathed with a perfumed soap that furled her throat. Again, he took her hand and waist, clumsily moving her across the yard, while she kept her feet out of the way as much possible, but it was arduous with a man galumping haltingly.

This is the party that I've been planning six months, she thought, and I'm having a terrible time. She tried to adjust to Jay's elusive timing, not to mention his quirky motions, as other dancers hopped and bucked gaily all around her.

Guests with hearty appetites lined up anxiously at the main table, where Seamus McSweeny cut fat strips of juicy barbecued beef off steaming carcasses, and stacked them on platters, surrounded by bowls of potato salad, beans, pickles, and loaves of bread. A pot of coffee bubbled atop another fire, adding to the fragrance, and at the end of the table were arrayed a mouth-watering variety of pies and cakes, for every woman had brought her specialty to the party.

The fiddler drew his bow back and forth, while the guitarist strummed chords. The first keg of whiskey was half empty, and some of the cowboys swaggered about as though in their favorite saloons.

Big Al returned to his chair and sat heavily. *When I was a kid*, he thought, *I could dance all night, then go to work at dawn. Now, I dance a few steps, and that's it.*

His gigantic chest rose and fell with his respirations, and the first thing he reached for was his glass of whiskey. He slurped amber liquid, then leaned back in his chair, smiling happily as his eyes fell on his beloved daughter trying to dance with Jay Krenshaw. *She'll never marry that bow-legged polecat, even though it's the best thing for this ranch.*

Big Al turned his gaze to Duane Braddock, who smoked a cigarette and leaned against the barn, watching the show. Big Al lit a cigar as he tried to view Duane Braddock from a woman's viewpoint. *Wa'al, he ain't an* ugly *feller, and he ain't afraid of nawthin'. Still young enough to learn, and prob'ly wishes* somebody'd teach him, just as I did when I was his age. Mebbe I'll have a little talk with 'im later, and see what he's made of.

The dance came to an end, and the participants applauded the band. The corners of Big Al's mouth turned down as he watched his beloved daughter turn away from Jay Krenshaw, and it appeared that she was heading toward Duane Braddock! She wouldn't be so brazen as to ask that boy for a dance in front of the rest of us, would she?

Duane stiffened as he wondered what Phyllis was doing. She appeared to be walking straight toward him, and everybody was looking at her. An odd smile played on her face, and she betrayed a certain bounce in every step. "Care to dance, Mister Braddock?"

"Have you gone loco?" he asked between his teeth. "Your father is looking right over here."

"I planned this party so's I could dance with you, and since you haven't asked me to dance, I'll have to ask you. Besides, it's time that he found out about us, don't you think? I hope you're not going to be a fraidy-cat."

She took his hand, and before he knew it, she was leading him toward the dance ground. All he could do was follow, like a dog on a leash.

★ ★ ★

"Did you see that?" Lieutenant Dawes nudged his wife. "It appears that she's set her cap for your ex-lover."

At that moment, Vanessa hated Lieutenant Dawes. Before she could purge the poisonous emotion, she said, "Well, he's a very handsome boy."

"If you like boys."

His remark made her feel like a lecherous old lady who'd seduced a mere youth, although the truth was that she and Duane had blundered into each other's arms under unusual circumstances, similar to how she'd wandered into her current husband's bed. My life, since the war, has been a series of desperate moves, she concluded.

Lieutenant Dawes guffawed. "It appears that he doesn't even know how to dance."

On the dance ground, Phyllis took Duane's hand, and then touched his shoulder. "You're supposed to place your free hand on my waist," she said.

He did as he was told, expecting a bullet from Big Al at any moment. "Do you think we could sit down?" he asked in a chocked voice.

"It's disgraceful that you don't know how to dance at your age," she retorted, "but I guess it's due to your life in the monastery.

Dancing is easy, but you must *feel* the music inside you, and then you move in time to it, like this."

She maneuvered him to the left, but his big toe tripped over his ankle, he lost his balance, and held out his arm before his head crashed into the ground. Laughter burbled around him, and his ears turned red as he arose. The loudest voice belonged to Jay Krenshaw standing on the far side of the clearing, surrounded by his cowboys, a glass of whiskey in his hand.

Phyllis noticed the expression on Duane's face and realized that she'd embarrassed him. Supremely sure of herself a few moments before, she became confused.

He noticed her bewilderment and saw that he was making her uncomfortable. "Wa'al," he declared, trying to effect a certain cowboy nonchalance, "I guess I'm not a-goin' to win any dance contests here today, but do you think we can try it again, Miss Phyllis?"

If she'd had any remaining doubts about him, they melted away at that moment. Her confidence returned, and she took his hand once more. "It's one step to the left, and two to the right. That's not so difficult to memorize, is it?"

"We'll see," he replied.

"Loosen up. You might even like it."

She eased him to the side, but this time he didn't lose his balance. Her feet advanced in one direction, while his retreated in another. Somehow he couldn't catch up with her, and then he tripped over his feet again.

"You're not listening to the rhythm, Duane."

He tried to adjust to her movements, moved his feet as best he could, and suddenly, to his amazement, discovered that he was actually dancing! Two to the left and one to the right, he said to himself, as he let her maneuver him across the floor. Her form was fluid, she seemed floating on air, while he struggled to be in the correct spot at the exact time.

"Now you've got it," she said.

The dance wasn't as complicated as he'd thought, and even an idiot such as himself could remember one to the left and two to the right. He became aware that his hand was on Phyllis's slim waist, and her small callused palm rested easily in his. He couldn't help contrasting her country body with the cosmopolitan former Miss Vanessa Fontaine. "You're the woman for me," he murmured. "I wish we could get married today, so that we could be together all the time."

"Maybe we can get engaged on Christmas."

"Your father would never tolerate it."

"Leave him to my mother and me. Everything'll be fine, you'll see. Don't you understand that I want the same thing as you?"

They undressed each other with their eyes as they moved smoothly among the other dancers. He saw a nubile maiden with bright cheeks and laughing eyes, while she observed a long lanky cowboy with wide shoulders and black hair on his chest. Their eyes met, and an unmistakable communication passed between them. Both knew that one day they'd be together, regardless of earthquakes, tornadoes, Indian raids, or civil insurrections.

"They seem to be getting along rather well," Lieutenant Dawes drawled to his wife as they sat side by side on the lawn. "Phyllis is an only child, and the Pecos Kid has his eyes on the family ranch, evidently."

Vanessa knew that she should keep her big mouth shut, but it was impossible. "Duane could never be coldly calculating like that!"

"Just like he'd never kill somebody, I suppose. I can't help wondering why you keep defending him."

"Why do you persist in attacking him? He's only a boy, for God's sakes."

"If he's only a boy, then why did you sleep

with him? I can't understand what you ever saw in him. He's not *that* good looking."

"Perhaps not to you."

"To you?" he asked, sitting straighter in his chair.

She became cross. "Do you think we could talk about something else?"

He knew that envy was getting the better of him, but couldn't stop. "Are you saying that you still find him attractive?"

"In an aesthetic sense — yes — but he was extremely immature and silly at times. Yet, despite his youth, he never insulted me."

Lieutenant Dawes raised his eyebrows. "When have I ever insulted you?"

"Every time you mention his name. I'm going to tell you something right now, my dear husband. You keep it up, and you'll regret it."

He could see that she was becoming angry, and didn't want a public scene. "I'm sorry. I thought we were joking."

"Perhaps you were, but I wasn't. I think it best if we never mentioned Duane Braddock again. Otherwise I'll leave you, because anything's better than this."

He'd be the laughingstock of the officers' club when word got around that he'd met a strange woman, married her a week later, and then was divorced. Senior commanders might surmise that something was wrong with his mind, and pass him over for promotion.

"I apologize from the bottom of my heart," he said. "You can be sure that I'll never mention that person again."

The dance ended, and Phyllis clapped her hands while the musicians bowed, doffed their hats, and headed for the main table groaning beneath pounds of food.

"Let's get something to eat," she said to Duane.

"I don't think we should spend the rest of the afternoon together," he replied. "I don't want to make your father angry."

"It's only a party, Duane." She grabbed a handful of his sleeve and pulled him toward the food. All he could do was follow, worried about possible retaliation from his future father-in-law. If he weren't so exhilarated by her presence, he would've noticed a far more serious threat on the other side of the clearing, where Jay Krenshaw sipped a glass of white lightning.

Jay could see that the Pecos Kid was a far better dancer than he, and Phyllis preferred his company. It rankled like acid poured onto Jay's guts. He wanted desperately to be viewed as a great man like his father, but whatever he did, he always fell short.

If these people knew who Duane Braddock's mother and father were, they'd be in for a big surprise. I should tell Big Al, but I'd look like a sneaky son of a bitch. Maybe I should just wait for Otis Puckett to get here. He'll take care of the Pecos Kid, and then maybe I'll have a chance with little Phyllis.

Lew Krenshaw sat next to Big Al and ate from a massive plate of sliced beef. "You put on a good feed," he said, his mouth full. "I ain't had a meal like this since I can't remember when."

"You look it!" Big Al boomed. "Mebbe it's time you hired a cook, or you might even think of a-gittin' married agin'. I'll bet there's plenny of women who'd love to marry Lew Krenshaw."

"I don't want nobody to marry me fer my ranch, and besides, love is fer the young, like that galoot what was a-dancin' with yer Phyllis. Who the hell is he?"

Big Al growled. "One of my cowboys."

Myrtle leaned forward and looked at Lew Krenshaw. "His name's Duane Braddock."

"I think she's sweet on him."

"Like hell she is!" roared Big Al.

"Seems like a nice enough boy," Lew Krenshaw said. "Reminds me when I was young."

Myrtle Thornton looked at him askance.

"You talk as though you're already in the grave."

"Nawthin' never turned out right fer me," Lew complained. "Life's downright discouraging."

"You've got a lot to be thankful for, seems to me."

Big Al interjected, "Lew's been like this ever since I met 'im. No matter what happens, it ain't enough. If he ever made it to heaven, he'd tell Jesus that it weren't what he'd hoped for."

Big Al noticed the approach of his daughter and Duane Braddock, each carrying plates covered with food. Big Al muttered something unmentionable, while Lew Krenshaw turned toward the couple. He couldn't help comparing Duane to his son, and something told the old man that the Circle K and Bar T would never merge, which provided a new reason for unhappiness. I ain't a-gonna git no grandsons, he thought mournfully.

Duane looked as if he'd rather be in Santa Fe as he sat on a chair beside Phyllis. He kept undressing her in his imagination, but her parents terrified him, and the wizened old man sitting nearby peered at him curiously. Duane figured that her ex-cowboy father knew precisely what was occurring in the deepest convolutions of his billy goat mind.

He tried to eat calmly, but his main ambition was to go to a quiet place with Phyllis Thornton, and remove her clothing. I'll never last till Christmas, he thought. I wonder if there's any way I can get her alone?

Meanwhile, the quantity of whiskey steadily diminished, while dancing became more uninhibited. The men clattered like horses and jumped like rabbits, as the women spun smoothly through the air, their skirts and petticoats rising, affording an occasional glimpse of leg. The afternoon hadn't reached midpoint yet, but a few cowboys already had passed out from injudicious drinking habits.

The cowboys from the Bar T and Circle K kept away from each other, to avoid sudden death. Males outnumbered ladies eight to one, and vied for dance rights, while shy, aging, or philosophical cowboys sat on the sidelines, got drunk, and watched the activities.

Don Jordan came to a stop in front of Duane and said, "Ramrod wants to see you, pronto."

Duane wiped his mouth with his napkin, winked at Phyllis, and said, "Excuse me." Then he followed Jordan across the yard. "What's up?"

"Ramrod didn't tell me, but it sure looks like you're doing all right with the boss's daughter, you lucky son of a bitch."

The ramrod sat in a wagon, his back against the slats, a bottle of whiskey in his hand. "Come on in here, Mister Braddock, and have a seat. I want to talk with you."

Duane climbed into the wagon, sat opposite the ramrod, and waited for his assignment.

"You was a-lookin' a little green around the gills," McGrath said, "so I thought I'd git you away fer a spell. You ain't a-screwin' Miss Phyllis, are you?"

"Hell no," Duane said. "We're just . . ." Duane struggled for a word to describe what he and Phyllis meant to each other.

"Let me tell you about Big Al. He's not as mean as he looks, and his daughter has got him wrapped around her little finger. You shouldn't have nawthin' to worry 'bout, less'n he catches you with yer hand up her dress, afore yer married. You got any preference about whar you want to git buried?"

"You don't have to dig a hole, ramrod. Just leave me for the buzzards."

Duane felt two small coals burning into the side of his head, and noticed Vanessa Fontaine Dawes looking at him. Their eyes met, and Duane flashed on her naked in bed with the Pecos Kid, clawing and biting passionately, but now she sat demurely, fully clothed, a paragon of dignity, fashion, and virtue. He decided that he wanted to be alone, so that he could think things through.

"Got to stretch my legs," he said.

He climbed out of the wagon, then headed for the open range. If the boss's daughter likes you, suddenly people start paying attention. It reminded him of the night he'd shot Saul Klevins. He passed the bunkhouse, and filled his lungs with pure clear air. After twenty yards, he dropped to a cross-legged sitting position on the open range. All I want is a simple, peaceful life. Why does everything happen to me?

He heard a growl behind him, and spun around, reaching for his Colt. It was Sparky pointed to the corner of the bunkhouse, baring his teeth. "Who's there?" Duane asked.

A man with a black hat and no chin stepped into the open embarrassedly. "Just me," said Amos Raybart.

Duane recognized him as a Circle K cowboy. "What can I do for you?"

"Just takin' a walk. Ain't you the feller called Duane Braddock?"

"What if I am?"

"I heered that you lived the monk's life not long ago, and I was a-wonderin' if you ever missed it."

Duane was taken aback by the question.

"Sometimes . . . why do you ask?"

Raybart looked Duane over at close range, looking for a mark of the devil, and instead caught clear sharp eyes that made him turn away. "I'm a religious man, too," he admitted. "D'ya think we could pray together?"

Again, Duane was surprised. "All right," he agreed, closing his eyes, but not all the way.

Raybart clasped his hands together. "Lord, show us righteousness. Give us your strength. Teach us your wisdom."

Raybart droned on, and Duane tried to figure his game. The encounter had been too sudden, and it appeared that Sparky had caught the stranger spying. Finally, Raybart came to the end of his prayer. "Thank you, Jesus, fer all yer many blessin's." He opened his eyes and smiled beatifically.

"What's your name?" Duane asked.

Raybart told him, but it didn't ring bells in Duane's mind. "How come you're talking to me? I thought the Circle K cowboys were mad at the Bar T."

"Has God ever spoken with you?"

Duane blinked in surprise at the latest question. "Sometimes," he confessed. "How about you?"

"He said that I should follow Him unto the ends of the earth."

"Then you should."

Raybart appeared to be undergoing a powerful spiritual experience. His hands trembled and his face drained of color. "Thank you, sir," he replied. "You been very kind."

Tipping his hat and bowing, Raybart backed toward the corner of the bunkhouse. Duane watched his hands, because the man obviously was insane. The Pecos Kid could imagine no other reason for his bizarre and inexplicable conduct.

Raybart walked alongside the bunkhouse, so deep in thought that he barely was aware of what occurred around him. He'd seen a force in Duane's eyes that reminded him of the monastery in the clouds. He's told me what I've gotta do, Raybart realized.

Raybart felt purified as he approached the front of the bunkhouse. I'll take my pay at the end of the month and head for the Guadalupe Mountains. Then I'll follow Jesus to my dying day, for he has forgave me my sins.

A hand reached suddenly out of the shadows, and grabbed him around the neck. "What you think yer doin', asshole?"

Raybart looked fearfully at the sinister features of Jay Krenshaw accompanied by tobacco stench issuing from his rotten teeth. "Just takin' a walk, boss man."

"What'd you and Braddock talk about?"

"We prayed together."

Krenshaw's eyes widened, and he took a step backward. "You what?"

"Prayed together."

"Are you tryin' to shit me?"

"He's a god-fearin' man, and so am I. You may not realize it, but God is a-watchin' every move we make."

Jay Krenshaw had considered Amos Raybart a wicked little man who'd do anything for a dollar, including murder, and the sudden religious talk unnerved him. "Git out of my sight, and don't ever let me see you talking to Braddock again. If you mention a certain trip that you took recently — you'll wake up a-swingin' from a tree."

CHAPTER 11

Dancers hopped about the dance ground, an endless line passed diminishing barbecued animals, and new guests arrived from far-away districts, as the sun sank in a sky mottled with purple, red, and gold.

Big Al's working ranch looked like a carnival, with fiddlers, guitar pickers, and brightly colored ribbons. He felt like a monarch bestowing favors upon his subjects as he blew ash off the end of his cigar. We ought to do this more often, he thought happily.

A Bar T cowboy climbed a ladder and lit the lamp suspended over the steer and pig carcasses as nearby guests gobbled huge quantities of savory meat. One keg of whiskey had been tapped out, and the second already one-quarter gone. Several cowboys were passed out cold, and numerous others staggered about in advanced stages of inebriation, but the overwhelming majority had paced themselves for the long haul.

Duane strolled toward the dance ground, a cigarette dangling out of the corner of his mouth, thumbs hooked in the front pockets of his jeans. His hat sat on the back of his head, and his Colt glowed evilly in the light of an oil lamp lit by cowboys at the entrance to the barn. His eyes roved the riotous scene, and he spotted Phyllis Thornton dancing with an unknown man in a tight-fitting suit. The prettiest girl in the party tried not to look bored, as a line of men awaited their turn with her.

Duane found himself sinking into a vile mood. He wanted to be alone with Phyllis, but instead had to share her with the world. He made his way toward the kegs, filled a glass, and looked for a place to sit down. He found a length of barn and dropped to his heels.

It seemed that every path to happiness was blocked to him. He couldn't have Phyllis, Vanessa didn't want him, and Jay Krenshaw kept stalking through the crowd, tossing hostile glances his way. And then there was the strange cowboy who'd asked to pray with him, and now eyed him thoughtfully from a position near the fire.

The dance came to an end, and a freckle-faced private from the Fourth Cavalry approached Phyllis for the next one. She shook her head, and the corners of his mouth drooped in disappointment. Phyllis headed for the refreshment table, trailed by admirers, and Duane was about to follow, when a pale blue dress caught the corner of his eye. It was Vanessa Fontaine Dawes, moving in the same direction. Duane feared that Phyllis and Vanessa would meet, with the topic of conversation himself. Vanessa had an acid tongue, and Phyllis might push her into a water trough. It appeared that the main event of the evening was about to begin.

The sweating cook sliced off a chunk of meat and dropped it onto Phyllis's plate. Her mouth watered as she collected a mug of lemonade. The dancing had excited an appetite that she could satiate, unlike certain other unfulfilled desires. She sat at a long table, and her male admirers surrounded her, yapping like hound dogs, trying to catch her attention.

They were decent, hard-working men, and she bore them no ill will, but some were too polite and mild-mannered, while others were oafish though well intentioned. She knew that any one would make an acceptable husband, but who wanted an acceptable husband?

Her vision turned to the young man in the black hat with silver conchos, sitting against the barn. Am I a superficial ninny, attracted to his pretty face? she wondered. Will I tire of him after a few years? Or is he the man whom God has sent me to love?

"Mind if I sit down?" asked a female voice above her.

Phyllis was surprised to see Vanessa Fontaine Dawes, the newlywed herself. "If you can find some room," Phyllis replied cautiously.

Vanessa looked at the crowd of young swains sitting around Vanessa. "Gentlemen?"

Embarrassed and awkward, unaccustomed to forceful women, they moved toward the far end of the table. Vanessa sat with her plate of food and picked at a slice of beef. "I guess you know who I am," she began.

"The new schoolmarm," Phyllis replied. "And I understand that you've been married recently."

"As you probably also know, I was scheduled to marry Duane Braddock once. Thank God I didn't, but that doesn't mean that I don't care about him, and don't worry about him. That's why I thought we should have a talk."

Phyllis gazed at blue eyes, stark cheekbones, and golden hair. Vanessa seemed superior in sophistication and maturity, but Phyllis was the daughter of Big Al Thornton. "Duane told me that you broke his heart."

"I didn't mean to, but I'm much older than

he, and my needs are far different from a woman like you. But I'll always love him, in my way. I hope you'll stand by him, because he's not always as strong as he might appear. I loved a man when I was about your age, but he died in the war. I really haven't been right since, and that's why I, a total stranger, am talking to you about intimate matters."

Phyllis was completely taken aback by Vanessa's remarks. No one, not even her mother, had ever talked to her that way, but somehow it had the ring of truth. "We'll have to wait a decent interval," Phyllis explained, "but I don't know if we can last that long. Do you know what I'm talking about?"

Vanessa, the sophisticated woman of the world, merely asked, "But what's the point of waiting? A lot of things can happen between now and Christmas. If I were you, I'd announce my engagement *today*."

Phyllis was aghast at the suggestion. "But I've only known him for a month!"

"I knew my present husband a *week* before I married him, and here we are invited to the finest home in the territory. You'd be surprised how accepting people are, after they get over the initial shock. Personally, I think Duane and you would be a marvelous couple, and your father should consider himself lucky to have such a son-in-law. I advise you to announce your engagement tonight, because, as my husband says, surprise is the most important element of attack."

A fiddler and two guitar pickers started a new tune, prompting young men in the vicinity to gather around Phyllis, clamoring for the next dance. But she was gazing across the courtyard at Duane and had the impression that he was looking at her. Phyllis found Vanessa's logic irresistible. "I'm sorry," she said to the dithering young men, "but I do believe that I've promised the next dance to Duane Braddock."

All eyes were on the beautiful rancher's daughter as she crossed the yard. Duane saw her coming, and all he could do was stand, making a thin smile.

"Care to dance?" she asked.

"People are going to talk."

"I don't care."

She headed for the dance ground as he glanced toward the front lawn. Big Al watched him suspiciously, alongside the lady of the ranch, while Vanessa appeared to be smiling, and Lieutenant Dawes was sitting straighter in his chair.

Duane followed Phyllis toward the dance ground. "What did you talk with Vanessa about?" he asked.

"You."

She took Duane's hand, he held her waist, and they stepped away gracefully. "What did she say?" Duane inquired.

"She thinks that we ought to announce our engagement today, and I agree, because I don't see the point of waiting any longer. Do you?"

"No, but . . ."

She looked into his eyes. "You love me, don't you?"

"Of course, but . . ."

"And you want to marry me, don't you?"

"Sure, but . . ."

She inadvertently on purpose brushed her body against his. "And it's making you a little crazy, isn't it?"

"That's no lie, but . . ."

"Well, we've known each other nearly a month, and a lot of people have got married on much shorter notice, such as your former girlfriend."

"Has she put you up to this?" Duane asked.

"I know what I want, and if you want the same thing, when this dance is over, we'll walk up to my father, and you'll ask for my hand in marriage."

Duane sputtered, "You've got to be loco! Why, there's no telling what he might do!"

"My mother will keep him under control — don't worry about that. What this all boils down to is, do you want to marry me or not?"

"Whatever happened to Christmas?"

"That's when we're getting married."

"But . . ."

"I can't wait much longer than that, Duane. If you know what I mean."

"I can't wait much longer myself," he admitted.

"Well?"

"What's she like?" Lieutenant Dawes asked his wife as she sipped a cup of lemonade beside him.

"She's got a lot to learn."

"Who could teach her better than you?"

She glanced at him sharply. "What's that supposed to mean?"

"You know your way around."

"I'm sure there's much that *you* could teach her, too, but don't get any ideas."

"I have eyes only for you, darling. What did you tell her?"

"Surprise is the most important element of attack."

"Is she going to war, or have you been playing Cupid? I must say, this is a side of you that I haven't seen before. Or are you still in love with Duane, and can't get out of his life?"

She turned to her husband, and her face became demonic in its barely suppressed rage.

"I do think about him, but not in the squalid way that you so crudely suggest."

"If Duane were a little older, and had a better situation, you'd probably be married to him instead of me."

"I told you that I'm sick of your jealousy. Keep talking about him, and I'll leave you."

The newlyweds squabbled like an old married couple that hated each other passionately, while across the yard, Jay Krenshaw sipped whiskey moodily as he watched Duane and Phyllis dance amid swarms of boot-bangers and heel-kickers. Jay was so angry he could scream, but didn't dare misbehave before his father. Holy man, my ass, he muttered darkly. He's just a-tryin' to git into her bloomers, that's all.

The song ended, dancers applauded, and Phyllis took Duane's hand firmly. "Are you ready?"

"If your father shoots me," he replied, "I hope you'll remember me occasionally."

"Don't be such a fraidy-cat," she retorted as she pulled him toward the lawn, where her father sat with Myrtle and Lew Krenshaw. Engulfed by inner turmoil, Duane had a clear perception of impending doom. Big Al would go loco, and reach for his Colt.

"Stop shaking," she said. "I thought you

were supposed to be a hard case from Titus-ville."

The back of his hand brushed her leg, and he remembered the purpose of his mission. "I'd rather walk to California than ask your father for your hand."

"Don't exaggerate," she said with a smile, as she led him like a lamb to the slaughter-house.

Meanwhile, Big Al watched their approach, his eyes knitted with hostility. He noticed that they were holding hands, and didn't like the look of it.

"Here come Phyllis and Duane," Myrtle said. "Don't they look nice together?"

"No," replied Big Al.

His rancor increased as they drew closer, but he knew, deep in his guts, he was defeated before Phyllis opened her mouth. Never had he been able to say no to her, and when she teamed up with his wife, he didn't stand a chance.

"Daddy," she said cheerfully as they came to a stop in front of him. "Everybody's having fun, and Duane and I thought it might be a good time to announce our engagement. You see, we thought we'd get married this Christ-mas."

Big Al's complexion became a peculiar green hue. He turned toward Duane, who looked him in the eye, and said, "I love your daughter, and I'm asking for your permission to marry her."

Big Al had known that the request would come some day, but not so soon, and not from the Pecos Kid. He opened his mouth to speak, but no sound came out. He thought about pulling out his gun, but there were too many witnesses. Before he could find his voice, Myrtle said, "I think that's a marvelous idea! Don't you, Alfred?"

Big Al didn't know what to say. His throat had constricted to where he could barely swallow. Finally, he was able to force out a series of croaks and squeaks that said, "She's too young, and they scarcely know each other. How's he a-goin' to support her?"

"I've got a job," Duane said, "and if you fire me, I'll find another. As long as I've got a roof over my head, your daughter'll have a roof over hers."

"Easy to say," Big Al replied, his voice growing stronger. "The world can be awful mean."

"We could've eloped, but we're trying to do it the right way."

Big Al drew himself slowly to his full six feet and four inches. He leaned toward Duane and said, "You elope with my daughter, and I'll shoot yer ass."

Before Duane could respond, Phyllis stepped in front of him and said, "You shoot Duane, you'll have to shoot me first!"

She said it so emphatically that Big Al realized she was in love with Duane Braddock, and there wasn't much he could do about it. But he couldn't give up easily. He searched his brain for a sensible objection, but his wife's arm wrapped around the back of his waist. "Don't be a stubborn old jackass," she said. "I think Duane would make a fine husband for Phyllis, but if he turns out bad, *then* you can shoot him."

Big Al couldn't help smiling at his wife's remark, because it illustrated his ridiculous behavior. But he couldn't give in too easily. "She's still a child," he uttered.

"Maybe you'd better take a good look at your daughter, Mister Thornton. Girls get married even younger, and you know it."

"He's a drifter, and he don't have a pot to piss in."

"Neither did you when we got married, but we turned out all right. I think that you should say *yes*, because the next man who comes along might not be as nice as Duane."

Big Al had heard stories about other men's daughters running off with drummers, outlaws, and scamps. At least Duane was capable of hard work, according to the ramrod, and he didn't get drunk Saturday nights with the other cowboys. Besides, Christmas was a long way off.

"Please, Daddy," she begged. "I'll never be happy unless you give us your permission."

Big Al wanted to exert his authority, but not over his darling daughter. He felt backed into a corner, no way out. "Wa'al," he said gruffly, "if'n that's what you want, I ain't a-gonna stand in yer way. But I ain't happy about it."

Myrtle dug her elbow into his brisket. "Stop being such a cow turd, and give them your permission."

Big Al looked at Duane and narrowed his eyes. "You ever wrong my daughter, I'll kill you."

The magic word roused old Lew Krenshaw from the torpor where he customarily found himself. "Somebody get kilt?" he asked in his crackling voice.

"Not yet," replied Big Al, looking straight at Duane. "But maybe soon."

Phyllis hugged her father tightly. "Thank you, Daddy. You'll never regret it — I promise."

"I guess it's official," Myrtle replied. "Why don't you make the announcement, darling?"

"What announcement?" asked Big Al.

"The announcement of the engagement — what else?"

"Like hell I will!"

"Who's a-gittin' hitched?" asked befuddled Lew Krenshaw.

Myrtle replied, "Phyllis and Duane."

Lew Krenshaw pondered that statement as Myrtle moved in front of Big Al, placed her fists on her hips, and looked into his eyes. "It's your job, as father of the bride, to make the announcement."

Duane noticed Big Al's discomfort, and decided to let him off the hook. "He doesn't have to. We'll just tell people ourselves."

Big Al realized that he was becoming a fool before his future son-in-law, whom he didn't particularly like. And Christmas was a long way off. "That's all right," he said grandly. "I'll do it. If my daughter is crazy enough to marry a saddle bum, I'm crazy enough to make the announcement." He filled his lungs with air, cupped his hands around his mouth, and hollered, "Gather 'round folks — I wanna say somethin'!"

His old ramrod voice echoed off buildings and drowned out the music. The fiddler and guitarists stopped playing, and everyone turned toward the front lawn, where Big Al placed one arm around his daughter's shoulders, and the other around Duane. "Ladies and gentlemen," he roared, "I've got an important announcement. My daughter, Phyllis Jean, has just got herself engaged to Mister Duane Braddock here, and if he don't treat her right, as God is my witness, I'm a-goin' to *shoot* him!"

The guests didn't know whether to laugh, cheer, or run for cover, because it was the strangest wedding announcement that they'd ever heard, but then Myrtle began clapping her hands, followed in a few moments by Vanessa and Lieutenant Dawes. The Bar T cowboys roared their approval, townspeople and other guests whistled and hooted, as Lew Krenshaw stepped forward to congratulate the bride and groom-to-be.

"I hope yer happy together," he said, his eyes damp with sentiment.

The crowd applauded again, but the cowboys from the Circle K were confused, and Jay had turned pale, his real estate dream dashed, while unrequited love rotted his soul. The gall was especially bitter when Lew Krenshaw shook hands with the groom-to-be. I'll bet my own father wishes Duane Braddock was his son, 'stead of me. If they knew the truth about that little son of a whore, they wouldn't cheer so loud.

Jay felt as though his head would explode. Nothing he did ever turned out right. Sometimes he thought his cowboys were laughing behind his back, and ranch earnings had plummeted ever since he'd taken over as boss. Something was eluding him, but he didn't quite get it, as though certain strands weren't connecting in his so-called mind.

Jay believed that he was being cheated, because Braddock wasn't what everybody thought. He saw his father kiss the bride on the cheek, as the townspeople lined up to congratulate the couple. Jay wished that he could receive everyone's good wishes, instead of their contempt and distaste.

Jay had employees, but not a friend in the world, and could never talk with his father, who appeared not to like him much, even moving into another house so that he didn't have to live with his son. I can't let them do this to me, Jay thought.

One foot moved in front of the other as he headed toward the newly engaged couple. An inner voice told him to stop, keep his mouth shut, and run away, but he felt as if his head steamed inside his hat.

Nobody paid attention to him, except the Circle K cowboys. They formed a disorganized mass behind the rancher's son and followed him toward the front lawn, where other guests crowded around the fortunate couple.

Duane tried to smile meanwhile, shaken to

his boots by a friendly slap on the back. He'd awakened that morning another sleepy face in the bunkhouse, and now was marrying the boss's daughter? His wildest dreams were coming true, and he wanted to fall on his knees and thank God, but men pumped his hand constantly, while women kissed his cheek. The former acolyte didn't know what to make of it, events tumbling too quickly, he felt swept along by the whirlwind.

The lawn and yard filled with rejoicing as the musicians performed a lighthearted wedding serenade. Cowboys and soldiers whom Duane had never met treated him like a long-lost brother, and he was beginning to enjoy himself, when he saw Vanessa approach in the long line of well-wishers.

She held out her hand elegantly. "The best of luck to you, Duane. You couldn't've found a finer girl."

He couldn't understand how she could be so casual, and it made him realize once more that she'd never really loved him. He wanted to rip her clothes off and feel her long, lissome legs wrapped around him, but it was over forever. He tried to think of a clever rejoinder, but nothing came to mind.

Next thing he knew, his hand was grasped by the commanding officer himself, Duane's former rival. "Good luck," said Lieutenant

Dawes, a faint smile on his face. "You'll need it."

Duane wanted to punch him, but Phyllis squeezed his hand reassuringly, and that brought the Pecos Kid back to reality. Lieutenant Dawes took one step to the left and found himself in front of the newest bride-to-be. He shook her hand and had to admit that she was exquisite in the light of coal oil lamps suspended over their heads.

"My very best wishes," he said.

Phyllis looked at his gleaming brass buttons, gold shoulder boards, and wide-brimmed cavalry hat. "I've met your wife, and I consider you a very fortunate man."

Lieutenant Dawes smiled ingratiatingly and was about to say something witty, when he heard footsteps behind him. A crowd of Circle K cowboys were approaching, led by Jay Krenshaw, and the festive atmosphere of the shindig suddenly turned sinister. Lieutenant Dawes stepped out of the way as Jay came to a stop in front of Phyllis. Jay turned down the corners of his mouth and hooked his thumbs in the front pockets of his jeans. "I'd like to congratulate you, ma'am, but don't feel that I can, under the circumstances. You see — I don't think you know who this man is that yer a-marryin'." Jay turned toward Duane. "Should I tell 'er, Pecos, or will you?"

Duane went cold, and his mouth formed a thin indomitable line. Jay felt that his moment of triumph had finally arrived. He pointed toward Duane and said, "This feller here — he ain't the angel what everybody thinks. Duane Braddock is a fast hand what shot five men that I know about, and God only knows how many others!"

The crowd was silent, and not even Big Al knew what to say. Duane felt as if his heart would stop as Phyllis clutched his hand tightly.

"Duane Braddock," Jay continued, "is a killer, but that ain't all I know about him. The rest of us here, no matter who we are, had parents who was married, but Duane Braddock is the bastard son of a dance hall whore and an outlaw named Joe Braddock, who got hung from a tree!"

The words echoed across the yard, bounced off the barn, and ricocheted against the main house. Duane tried to catch his breath as all eyes turned toward him. It was his most hideous secret exposed to the world, and it felt as though the ground opened up, swallowing him and all his dreams.

Jay leaned toward Phyllis, painted a cocky half smile on his face, and said, "If'n you want to marry this li'l white trash bastard, that's yer bizness, ma'am, but don't 'spect me to congratulate you."

Something snapped inside Duane as he charged Jay Krenshaw. Jay was prepared for that eventuality, and threw a vicious left hook at Duane's head coming in. Duane blocked it with his right arm, and shot a stiff left jab to Jay's nose. Jay's head snapped back, and Duane cut loose a lifetime of pent-up embarrassment as he hurled a blizzard of unrelenting punches. Everything connected, and Jay was dazed, reeling, struggling to stay on his feet, while Duane bashed him unmercifully. The cartilage of Jay's nose cracked, his front teeth were knocked loose, and a cut opened over his right eye as he struggled to cover up and get away.

Duane stayed after him, throwing heavy shots with both fists, trying to inflict as much damage as possible. An overhand right sent Jay sprawling against the side of the barn, as Duane moved in for the kill. A tiny part of Duane's mind begged for caution, but Duane had never been so enraged. Duane slammed Jay in the mouth, split his lower lip, and Jay's head bounced off the side of the barn. Duane pushed him backward, whacked him in the liver, and threw a straight right down the middle, flattening what remained of Jay's nose. Jay's head crashed into the barn, bounced, and Duane clocked him with a solid left jab.

Jay was ready to drop, but Duane wouldn't

let him fall. Jay's eyes were bloused, his mouth a bloody mass, and Duane was loading up for another overhand right, when a gang of soldiers and cowboys jumped onto him, to end the gory massacre.

Duane felt their arms clamp over him, but wouldn't give up. He threw one soldier to the ground, elbowed another on the cheek, but then they were all over him, and the weight of their numbers forced him to the ground. They piled on top of him and buried him as he struggled to get loose. He heard women screaming, men shouting, and then the voice of Lieutenant Dawes. "Let him up!"

The soldiers and cowboys removed themselves from the pile as Duane tried to work himself free. Finally the last man climbed off, and Duane saw Lieutenant Dawes pointing his service revolver at him. "You're under arrest!"

Meanwhile, Circle K cowboys gathered around the prostrate form of Jay Krenshaw. "He's still alive," one of them said.

The time had arrived for Big Al to take control of his ranch. He stepped in front of his guests and said, "You can't arrest this man fer fightin'. Why, after the lies that Jay Krenshaw said — what'd you expect him to do?"

A weak voice replied haltingly, "They ain't lies."

Everyone turned toward Jay Krenshaw struggling to regain his feet, assisted by his cowboys. Jay's face was a red mask, he spat out a tooth, blood leaked from his left ear, and he looked as if a stagecoach had run over him.

"Where's Raybart?" he asked.

In the darkness at the fringe of the crowd, a short chinless man said, "Here I am, boss man."

"Tell 'em the truth."

All eyes refocused on Raybart, who felt a strange thrill at being center of attention. He wanted to help Duane Braddock, but had to tell the truth, no matter who got hurt, and where the chips fell. "I went to a Cathlick monastery in the Guadalupe Mountains, where Duane Braddock growed up, and I found out . . ." Raybart's throat went dry, because he saw himself as Judas Iscariot, ". . . that his father was an outlaw, and his mother was a . . . soiled dove, and they wasn't married."

Duane felt naked, vulnerable, and loathsome as he lowered his eyes. The disgrace overwhelmed him, and he felt their glares as a painful force. He had to get away, and almost wished someone would shoot him in the back as he headed toward the bunkhouse. Now everyone knew the unmentionable truth.

He felt sick to his stomach, his beautiful dream exploded in his face. It took an eternity to reach the bunkhouse, and inside, he gathered his paltry belongings, stuffed them into his saddlebags, rolled his blanket, and hiked it to his shoulders. Then he heard a sound, and looked down to see Sparky, who whimpered sadly. "You can come with me," Duane said, "but it's not going to be easy."

Duane opened the door, and Phyllis stood before him, with her parents, while behind them, other party guests congregated expectantly.

"Where are you going?" asked Phyllis.

"Away," he replied laconically, carrying his bedroll toward the corral.

"But I don't want you to leave."

Duane couldn't talk about the most embarrassing fact of his life, so he continued on his way. But then Big Al cut in front of him. "Now hold on, thar. You don't run out on my daughter, 'specially after I made the announcement."

Duane looked him in the eye. "Get out of my way or I'll go right through you."

An expression of tenderness came over Big Al's eyes. "It don't matter where you come from, or who yer daddy was. All God cares about is what you do from now on."

Myrtle Thornton reached toward Duane. "You'll break Phyllis's heart if you leave. You're not the only one whose folks weren't hitched. Sometimes it happens that way, but all a body can do is just keep going."

Duane was flabbergasted by the sudden turn of events. Phyllis wrapped her arms around him and kissed his cheek. "I'll always love you no matter what."

Duane felt her body flush against him, and his resolution wavered. Cowboys and soldiers gathered around, and Duane thought that perhaps they understood what he felt, and some of them had illicit backgrounds, too.

"I'll die if you go away like this," Phyllis said.

Then Lew Krenshaw moved closer, hat in hand, a downcast expression on his face. "I'd like to 'pologize fer what my son done said," he uttered. "He shouldn't've put yer bizness in front of us like that. I hate to say it, 'cause he's my son and all, but mebbe he deserved to git the shit beat out of him. If anybody'd said it to me, I'd do the same damned thang!"

Silence fell over the gathering as Duane held Phyllis in his arms. The warmth of her body filtered through his clothes, and he speculated that perhaps he wasn't as dirty as he'd thought. Just because my mother and father never got married, it doesn't mean that they didn't love each other, and even if they hated each other, what's that got to do with me?

The Bar T ramrod shuffled onto the scene, his hat crooked on his head, gun belt low on his hips. "Where the hell do you think yer a-goin'!" he bellowed. "I don't recall a-firin' you!"

Duane carried his bedroll back toward the bunkhouse, as Big Al shouted, "What happened to the music!"

Jay Krenshaw had the worst headache of his life, and no matter how much he drank, it wouldn't go away. His mouth felt empty, because he'd lost three teeth, and he no longer could breathe through his nose.

He went to bed for several days, refused to bathe or change clothes, and brooded hour after hour. Sometimes he'd pace the floor, imagining how wonderful it would be to bludgeon Duane Braddock to death.

A younger man had beaten the daylights out of him. He couldn't imagine a worse humiliation, and the worst part was that his own father had never returned home. Evidently he was living at the Bar T, sickened by his son's behavior.

Jay felt abandoned by his own father and blamed Duane Braddock. How can Big Al let his daughter marry that weasel? The more he thought about it, the more demoralized he became. And where in hell is Otis Puckett? He prob'ly din't git my letter, and I'll have to find another gunfighter to do my killin'.

Jay spent hours in bed, unable to move. He felt as if a massive weight lay upon him as he drifted in and out of consciousness. He saw himself hacking Duane to pieces with an ax, or shooting out his eyes with a gun, or stabbing him with a Bowie knife. Images of blood and revenge gushed through his mind. No matter what it takes, Duane Braddock is going to die.

Lew Krenshaw slept in the hayloft of the Bar T, although the Thorntons had offered him the guest room in the main building. Every morning he looked out the window at range land extending to the horizon and wondered at the splendor of God's creation.

He took his meals in the main house, and during one breakfast, Big Al turned to him and asked, "What're you gonna do about that rotten son of yer's?"

They were seated at the dining room table, with Phyllis and her mother in the kitchen. Lew Krenshaw shrugged and said, "Damned if I know. He should've died afore he was borned."

"Now, now," Big Al consoled. "That ain't

no way ter talk about yer own flesh and blood."

"I ain't got no use fer a man who carries on like Jay, and I don't care whose son he is."

"But mebbe you and him can have a talk."

"You think I ain't tried? There's somethin' wrong with 'im, always has been, and always will be. Damned if I know whar it comes from."

"If you don't do somethin' about yer ranch, pardner, you ain't a-gonna have nawthin' left," Big Al counseled.

"You're a-gonna give up yer ranch some-day, too, whether you want to or not. There'll be no room fer it in yer grave."

"But I ain't in that grave yet, and I don't want to fade away like some old fart."

"You always was happy 'bout somethin'," Lew recollected, "but my Jenny died when Jay was a baby, and Jay has growed up to be a snake in the grass. I know it's turrible to say, but it's true."

"Mebbe you should have a talk with him. Might be all he needs."

"He ain't innerested in nawthin' 'cept bossin' people, gittin' drunk, and actin' rowdy. I used to try, don't think I din't, but he was stubborn, mean, an' no good practically from the day he was born."

It was late Thursday night, and Fred Gibson stood behind the bar of his new saloon. A few soldiers played cards at one table, a carpenter sprawled at another, and the blacksmith stood at the end of the bar, chatting with a traveling salesman who'd arrived on the stage yesterday.

Gibson poured himself a glass of whiskey, and took a sip off the top. Life was going well, and it appeared that he was on his way to financial security, provided nobody opened a saloon across the street, an unlikely prospect since he owned nearly all of the town. He felt confident that the army post would grow in size, attracting other investors and businessmen to the area. If the railroad constructed a special trunk line to Shelby, he'd be dirty filthy stinking *rich!* I'll build Gertrude a house three stories high, and we'll have servants. He imagined the governor visiting his flower gardens, when suddenly the front door of the saloon opened.

Gibson returned from his reverie. A stranger with narrow shoulders and a potbelly appeared spectrally in black pants, white shirt, and black vest, his hat crooked on the back of his head. The stranger took one look around, then tramped toward the bar.

"What can I do fer you?" Mr. Gibson asked

cheerfully, for everyone new meant additional wealth.

"Whiskey," the man said.

Gibson poured the drink and pushed it forward. The man raised the glass to his chapped lips, leaned back, and drained the glass. Then he placed it on the counter.

"Hit me again."

Gibson refilled the glass. "Ain't seen you afore."

The stranger winked. "You may never see me again."

"Movin' on?"

"I'm a-lookin fer an hombre name of Jay Krenshaw. Know whar he lives?"

"Out at the Circle K." Gibson pointed in a northeasterly direction. "Are you a friend of Jay's?"

The stranger didn't reply. Instead, he raised the second glass of whiskey and knocked it back. He threw some coins onto the counter, then headed for the door. In seconds, he was gone. Mr. Gibson scooped up the coins and tossed them into his coin box.

He felt a chill up his back. There'd been something odd about the stranger, who hadn't introduced himself, or said what he wanted to see Jay Krenshaw about. Gibson lived in fear of outlaws. There was no bank to lock his money in, and it was hidden beneath the floorboards of his bedroom. I mustn't take counsel of my fears, the shopkeeper reminded himself. I'm sure he's just another harmless stranger passing through, on his way to God Knows Where.

Vanessa Fontaine sat in the combination parlor and dining room of her new home, which had been built by soldiers in their usual slapdash manner. The furniture consisted of a few pieces crafted by the same soldier carpenters, and the table leaned in one direction, the chairs in another, while the bed was lopsided, and the ceiling leaked when it rained.

But Vanessa was trying to make the best of it, although her husband had been on a scout for the past four days, and she wondered whether he'd return in one piece. She felt vaguely dissatisfied as she looked around her ramshackle home. It was the sort of hasty structure that her father's slaves had lived in, but at least her financial problems were over. Never again need she worry about becoming a prostitute, and if Comanches killed Lieutenant Dawes, she'd receive a small widow's allowance, and perhaps even an inheritance.

She could go for a walk, except there was nothing to see. If she roamed onto the sage, a Comanche might grab her. There was no library and she had nothing to read. She'd quit her schoolmarm job because she couldn't manage unruly children who'd rather run and jump than learn to read.

Sometimes she experienced pleasant memories of her singing career, traveling from town to town, singing old Confederate Civil War songs for veterans of that massive conflict. It had given her a strange satisfaction, and she'd loved their enthusiastic applause, but the work was unsteady, and her finances fluctuated radically. She'd arrived in Titusville practically destitute, and if it hadn't been for a stroke of luck, she might've ended in the cribs.

At least I'm safe from that, she thought. There are worse things than being an officer's wife. When she felt most despairing, she recalled a certain young man. She couldn't help wondering if he still thought of the woman with a cashbox where her heart was supposed to be.

"Time to get up."

Duane Braddock opened his eyes. He lay on the ground near the campfire on a stretch of open range. The face of Ferguson hovered above him.

"I'm awake," Duane said.

Ferguson headed for his bedroll, while Duane pulled on his boots. Then he stood and strapped on his Colt as his teeth chattered in the cool night air. He pulled on an old red sweater, looked around, and saw no Comanches sneaking up on him. He sat on a rock near the dying embers of the fire and rolled a cigarette in the darkness.

Men slept around him like caterpillars in cocoons, and he was their eyes and ears for two hours. If the ramrod caught anybody napping on guard, it meant immediate dismissal. Duane was scheduled to marry the boss's daughter, but determined to pull his weight along with the others.

He shuffled toward the remuda, to make certain no Comanches were stealing horses. Then he examined the chuck wagon, to assure that no Comanche was setting it on fire. Finally he returned to the men sleeping around the fire pit to check whether a Comanche was slitting anybody's throat.

Duane returned to the rock and felt fading warmth in the seat of his pants. The sky blazed with stars, the moon a gleaming scimitar floating through wisps of clouds. He absentmindedly flexed the knuckles of his right hand, and winced at the pain. The recently deceased Clyde Butterfield had warned about fistfights, because they produced bruised knuckles, which impeded the classic draw. Duane hoped his hand would heal by the weekend, because the Bar T cowboys were throwing a party in his honor at Gibson's General Store, to celebrate his engagement in appropriate cowboy fashion.

Duane had gone from rank tenderfoot to king of the hill in only a month. Everyone deferred to the future son of the boss, and even McGrath had become more conciliatory. They knew that Duane would give the orders someday, and nobody was anxious to get fired.

My future looks wonderful, Duane considered. It just goes to show you that if you lead a decent Christian life, all good things will come to you.

The same silver scimitar hung over the chimney of the Circle K ranch as Otis Puckett climbed down from his saddle. He looked around to make sure no one was creeping up on him, then headed for the front porch, where a guard arose from a chair, rifle in hand.

Before the guard could reach full height, a startling phenomenon took place. One moment a fat man walked toward him, and an instant later the guard found himself looking down the barrel of a Colt.

"Drop it," Puckett said.

The rifle fell to the floorboards, and the

cowboy raised his hands. Puckett stepped forward, his toes pointed outward like a duck's. "I'm here to see Jay Krenshaw."

"Foller me." The cowboy led Puckett into the house and pointed to a door. "In there."

The cowboy retreated as Puckett knocked, but there was no answer. He knocked again, waited a few moments, and then opened the door. A dark figure lay on the bed, wrapped in blankets. Puckett lit a lamp, and couldn't help grinning. Jay Krenshaw was fast asleep, sucking his thumb like a baby.

Puckett wondered if he himself did anything strange while he was asleep. He took out his leather tobacco bag, rolled a cigarette, and scraped a match on the floor. The man on the bed didn't stir. It was the first time Puckett had seen a grown man suck his thumb, but Puckett had worked for many different clients throughout his career, and once had been hired by a woman.

He puffed the cigarette lazily, content that his long journey was finally over. He was ready for a bath, a hot meal, and then get on with the job. The sooner he finished, the sooner he'd be with Rosita and her smooth golden body that thrilled and delighted him continually.

"Who's there?" The figure stirred on the

bed, and his hand reached beneath the pillow for his Colt.

Puckett drew his gun and pressed the cold metal barrel to Jay's head. "Don't move," he uttered.

Jay Krenshaw thought the Pecos Kid had finally got him, except the voice didn't sound like the Kid's. Jay turned and was surprised to see a man who looked like Humpty Dumpty in a cowboy hat. Jay wanted to laugh, except Humpty Dumpty was aiming a gun at his head. "Who're you?" Jay asked.

"Din't you send fer me, Mister Krenshaw?"

A smile creased Jay's face as the truth dawned upon him. "I thought you'd got lost!"

Puckett spun the cylinder of his Colt with the side of his thumb, then dropped the weapon into its holster. "Who do you want dead, and where can I find 'im?"

"His name's Braddock, and they calls him the Pecos Kid. Ever hear of the name?"

"They've got a Kid fer every corner of Texas — I can't keep up with 'em all. What's he done?"

"He shot Saul Klevins."

Puckett's ears perked up. "What else you know about Mister Pecos?"

"His father was an outlaw named Joe Braddock, and his mother was a whore, but they never got married." Jay gazed into

Puckett's little pig eyes. "I want you to kill him."

Puckett examined the split lip, broken nose, and toothless mouth before him. "Looks like he beat the shit out of you."

Jay glanced away. "He hit me when I weren't lookin'."

"That's why yer supposed to keep yer eyes open. Where is he now?"

"He works at the Bar T. They're a-throwin' a party fer him in town on Saturday night, and that might be the best time to nail 'im."

"Don't know if I want to wait 'till Saturday night. I got a wife and family to go home to."

"If you ride out to the Bar T, you'll have to take on the bunkhouse."

"What's the party fer?"

"He's a-gittin' married."

Puckett puffed his cigarette as he gazed into Krenshaw's puffy and blackened eyes. "That's one wedding that'll never take place."

Big Al struggled to breathe. He felt as if a giant were sitting on his chest, as he opened his eyes. He gasped, coughed, and finally the air came through. He took a deep breath, sat up in bed, and reached for a glass of water.

"Are you all right?" Myrtle asked sleepily.

"Natcherly," he replied reassuringly.

But he wasn't all right. Often he awoke in

the middle of the night, unable to breathe, with pains in his chest. And he knew that one night the air wouldn't come, and he'd die. It was as though Death were heralding his arrival.

Big Al rolled out of bed, threw on his shaggy Buffalo robe, and sat in the chair by the window. The horizon was a faint scrawl in the moonlight, while the heavens sparkled with millions of stars. He felt ancient, and knew that his days were numbered.

Big Al had few regrets. He'd been blessed with a good wife, a beautiful daughter, and the Bar T Ranch. His property would pass to Phyllis someday, and then to Phyllis's heirs, until the end of time.

Big Al preferred to take the long view, because short term considerations were gruesome. He'd get progressively weaker, and shortness of breath would become more prevalent. One day he'd keel over like a sack of potatoes, and then the worms would get him.

Sometimes he thought the Apaches had the right idea. When their people got old, they were left alone with a leather bag full of water, and a few handfuls of food. He'd rather die alone on a forgotten desert than have people staring curiously at his final creaking debilitations. But if I had to play the same hand over,

I'd throw down the cards exactly the same way.

The words were brave, but Big Al felt the icy breath of Death upon him. It made him shiver, but he didn't stop to think that maybe Death was searching for somebody else.

Otis Puckett lit the lamp in the guest room, revealing a bed and chair. Exhausted, he sat on the bed and pulled off his boots. His confidence was challenged by news that he'd have to fight a fast hand, instead of the usual easy opponent. He resolved to start practicing in earnest tomorrow morning. He didn't want to take the chances of not seeing Rosita and little Julio ever again.

Puckett knew that even the fastest gunfighter was slow if he'd drunk too much, and maybe that's what did in Saul Klevins, or maybe he'd been sick, or perhaps he'd just been with a woman, and was weakened. Puckett would let no whiskey pass his lips until after he killed Duane Braddock. Neither would he sleep with a woman, or expose himself to cold drafts. He wanted to be in perfect condition for the fast hand from the Bar T, who was scheduled to marry the boss's daughter. Am I going to ruin his plans, Puckett thought sardonically.

He pulled out his Colt .44, and it boasted

well-worn ivory grips. He'd purchased it in St. Louis when he'd been fifty pounds lighter, and fifteen years younger, at the beginning of his gunfighting career. Since then he'd traveled back and forth across the frontier, killing for dollars.

He plotted his career like any banker or government functionary, and expected a big boost after he shot the man who'd outdrawn Saul Klevins. People would pass the word along, and more work would come his way. Saturday night, the job will be done, Puckett told himself. I'll have my money, while Duane Braddock can visit his father in the next world.

Phyllis dreamed about making love with Duane Braddock. She was sprawled belly down on her bed, hugging her pillow as if it were flesh and blood. Duane writhed beneath her ministrations, a half smile on his face, his body perfectly formed, a healthy fragrance arising from his chest, reminding her of morning on the sage. "Oh, my darling," she whispered. "I love you so much!"

Duane became splattered with blood, and she screamed, awakening herself. She pulled back, opened her eyes, and the mangled pillow lay beneath her, her body covered with perspiration, and she was filled with a terrible foreboding.

Her door flung open, and her mother entered the bedroom, her long pigtail trailing behind her. "Are you all right?"

"I had a bad dream," Phyllis said weakly. "I saw Duane get killed."

Myrtle sat beside her daughter and wrapped her arm over her shoulders. "Don't worry about Duane," she soothed. "He's perfectly capable of taking care of himself."

"But somebody might shoot him in the back," Phyllis whimpered, "or he could get into an accident."

"It might be raining pink frogs in Kansas, and the moon might be made of green cheese. We can't lead our lives on *might* and *if* and *maybe*. Duane is a strong young man, and soon you'll be married to him. Now go to sleep, because we all have work to do."

Myrtle kissed her daughter on the forehead, then departed. Phyllis dropped to her damp sheets and pulled the covers over her. Despite what her mother said, the queasy feeling remained, and would continue to haunt her in the days to come.

CHAPTER 13

Jay Krenshaw had seen fast hands in his day, but nothing like Otis Puckett. The gunfighter drew so quickly, Krenshaw couldn't perceive the individual hand movements. It reminded him of the sudden lunge of a rattler, or the kick of a mustang. It seemed as if no man could move that quickly, particularly with so much fat around his middle.

Jay lounged against a cottonwood tree, watching Otis Puckett practice. Bottles and cans were lined on a plank behind the kitchen, and Puckett sent glass and tin flying through the sky.

Puckett worked systematically, with no trick moves or flashy conceits. All he did was draw and fire with incredible speed, never missing. Krenshaw didn't dare open his mouth to break the master's concentration. You git what you pay fer, Krenshaw thought happily, and I paid fer the best.

Jay had taken a bath, shaved, and changed his clothing. He felt as if his life were turning around, because soon he'd wreak vengeance against Duane Braddock, and everybody would know that they'd better watch out for Jay Krenshaw. *And maybe little Phyllis will see me in a new light. I'll end up with that gal yet, if'n I play my cards right.*

Suddenly Puckett spun around and aimed his gun at the corner of the toolshed. "Who's there?"

A figure emerged, with a sheepish expression and no discernable chin. "I was just a-wonderin' what all the shootin' was about," said Amos Raybart.

Puckett turned toward Jay. "Get him out of here."

Krenshaw arose, hiked up his gun belt, and strolled toward Raybart, who smiled nervously. "You heard what he said. Get the hell out've here. And by the way, why ain't you with the others?"

"The ramrod told me to fix the stovepipe. I was jest a-gittin' started, when I heard the shootin'. Thought it might be Comanches a-raidin' the horses."

"Go back to the stove," Krenshaw growled. "And keep yer mouth shut about what you seen here."

"Yessir," replied Raybart. He scooted

away, acting the fool, but knew that he'd just seen something significant. Ordinary cowboys don't draw that fast, he told himself. I'll bet Jay hired him to kill Duane Braddock!

Raybart sat at the table inside the bunkhouse, listening to steady gunfire, and wanted to warn Duane, but Jay would fire him, and Puckett might even kill him. Yet he couldn't let the former acolyte walk into a gunfight with a professional.

Raybart puffed a cigarette nervously and looked out the window at the clear blue sky. Maybe I should let God take care of it. If He wants Duane to die, it's His business, not mine. Raybart fretted, as in the distance he could hear the thunder of the gunfighter's Colt.

"What d'ya wanna kill him for?" Puckett asked as he and Krenshaw were having dinner in the main house that afternoon.

Krenshaw looked up from his big bowl of Son of a Bitch Stew, consisting of the brains, heart, kidneys, liver, marrow gut, and sweetbreads of a steer. The question was so preposterous, Jay couldn't think of anything to say.

"I hope you don't mind me a-askin'," Puckett said, "but sometimes I git curious. Why don't you just fergit about 'im, and go on with yer bizness?"

"The li'l bastard beat the shit out of me

when I wasn't a-lookin'. You ain't a-backin' out've the deal, are you?"

"Don't git me wrong, Mister Krenshaw," Puckett replied. "When I show up in town, somebody's a-goin' to die."

The cavalry detachment returned to Shelby that evening, and Lieutenant Dawes headed for his home immediately after dismissing the formation. He found his wife dropped to one knee before the stove, examining something that smelled slightly burned. "My God — what are you doing?" he asked.

"I'm learning to cook."

He took her in his dusty arms and pressed his dried lips against hers. She felt warmed by the touch of his beard, while his massive physicality turned her on.

"I thought you hated to cook," he said. "What happened?"

"I needed something to do, otherwise I'll go loco."

"I know the feeling," he admitted, as he kissed her nose. "You've been on my mind constantly while I've been on patrol. You look lovely as always."

"There's no one to talk with when you're not here, and I have difficulty sleeping. I hope we'll be able to move to Fort Richardson soon."

"Unfortunately, we're stuck here for the time being, and we've got to make the best of it. The worst thing about these small, out-of-the-way towns is that nothing exciting ever happens."

CHAPTER 14

On Saturday afternoon, the Bar T cowboys returned to the ranch, herded their horses into the corral, stowed gear, and began preparing for Saturday night. Since it was Duane's party, he got to use the bathtub first. Then he shaved, put on a clean pair of black jeans, black shirt, and green bandanna. He planted his black hat firmly on his head, and headed toward the main house, while the others took their turns in the bathtub.

Duane looked forward to the party, although he knew that it invariably would turn into the usual drunken brawl, with cowboys vomiting over themselves, and probably a few fights. He worked the joints of his right hand gingerly, because the pain hadn't gone entirely. Duane swore that he wasn't getting into any more fistfights, no matter what the provocation.

He approached the front door of the main

ranch building, soon to become his residence. Cowboy carpenters had been laboring on a new addition, where he and Phyllis would sleep in a big brass bed, if it ever arrived from Chicago. He came to the front door, knocked three times, and the moment his knuckle parted company with the door, it opened. Phyllis stood before him, a big smile on her face. "Why, it's Duane," she said, as if expecting someone else. "Has something happened?"

"Let's take a walk."

He took her hand, an acceptable familiarity now that they were officially engaged. Side by side they advanced onto the sage, their arms and legs touching, sending thrills from body to body.

"What's bothering you?" she asked.

He pinched his lips together, then said, "I can't stop thinking about you. If we don't . . . pretty soon, I think I'll die."

"I haven't slept a wink since you've been gone," she confessed. "I've never been so sick in my life."

"Maybe I can ask McGrath to put me in a line shack, but I don't think it'd help. The thought of you gets me going, like now."

They stopped, turned, and faced each other only inches apart. "Maybe we should just do it and get it over with," she said wearily.

"Where do you think we can go?"

"Meet me in the hayloft after you get back from town."

They gazed into each other's eyes, and both realized that they'd come to the ultimate decision. "I feel better already," he said.

"I hope you're not going to get too drunk tonight."

"I'm practically a married man, and it's time for me to grow up."

"I hope you won't lose your temper with somebody. We don't want any more fights."

"I'm not looking for trouble," Duane replied, "and if trouble comes looking for me, I'll just walk the other way."

At the Circle K, cowboys and their horses stood in front of the main house, waiting for Jay Krenshaw and Otis Puckett to come out. They smoked cigarettes in the gathering twilight, mumbling about gunfighters, shootouts, and bloodshed. On a decently managed ranch, they would've been good cowboys, but Jay Krenshaw was disorganized and capricious, and they'd become a lazy bunch with no purpose to their lives. If the job weren't so easy, they would've left long ago.

The front door of the house opened, and two men stepped onto the veranda. One was tall, the other short, round, and funny looking, but nobody dared laugh. Without a word, Krenshaw and Puckett walked toward their horses and mounted up. They wheeled the horses toward Shelby, and the cowboys followed dutifully.

Some cowboys wanted to see Duane Braddock die, because they liked blood, but a few hoped he'd win, since they favored the underdog. Amos Raybart carried a message scrawled on a scrap of paper, which he hoped to slip to Duane Braddock:

Fat man been hired to kill you. Git the hell outer here fast as you kin.

a friend

The cowboys from the Bar T climbed into their saddles and were about to ride off, when a small rotund creature with a black eye appeared before them, his tail wagging excitedly as he let out a strangled yelp.

McGrath pulled back on his reins. "What the hell do you want!" he roared. "You don't think yer a-comin' to town with us, do you?"

Uncle Ray replied, out of the corner of his mouth, "Reckon he wants to go to the party, too."

McGrath wagged his gnarled sausagelike finger at the mongrel. "You can come, long as you stay out've trouble."

Sparky barked in agreement, McGrath put the spurs to his horse's flanks, and the Bar T crew headed toward Shelby. They passed the main house, and Duane saw light in the parlor, where Phyllis and her parents were spending a quiet evening with Lew Krenshaw, permanent resident of the barn.

Duane rode in the midst of the cowboys, not on the periphery as when he'd been tenderfoot. Not only had they accepted him, they also treated him like the boss's son, which sometimes made him feel a freak, but at least he didn't have to worry about rattlesnakes in his bed anymore. Sparky and the cowboys advanced onto the open range as Duane meditated upon his future prospects. I'm going to own this ranch someday, so I can't be a drunken fool anymore. If a man can't manage himself, how can he expect to manage others?

Lieutenant Clayton Dawes and his wife, the former Vanessa Fontaine of Charleston, South Carolina, sat in their parlor and looked at each other blankly. They were finished with supper, a soldier had washed their pots, pans, and dishes, and now they were alone.

"What do we do now?" she asked, a trace of boredom in her voice.

"I'm conversant on many topics. Take your pick."

"What do most officers' wives do in circumstances like this."

"They have children."

Vanessa raised her eyebrows. "Don't get any ideas, please."

"I suppose I should've asked before I married you, but my mind was on other things. Don't you like children?"

"Of course I like children. Do you think I'm a monster? But I don't think I'm in any condition to have a child. I mean, what if I need a doctor?"

"If you became pregnant, then I suppose I'd have to let you live at Fort Richardson, near the saw-bones."

Vanessa reflected upon his response. "It doesn't solve the problem of what to do right now."

"We could go to bed," he offered.

"It's too early."

"Not for me."

"All you ever think of is procreation and food. Then you ride off for four days, and I'm left alone with nothing to do. You have a career, and I have this broken-down shack. Somehow it doesn't seem fair."

He leaned toward her and looked into her eyes. "My dear, there are many days when I wish I could live your life, sitting here in this cozy little home, without worrying about water, heat, and five hundred Comanches sneaking up on me. Perhaps you should count your blessings."

She became exasperated. "I know I sound like a spoiled child, but I can't help it if I have an active mind. I need something to entertain me."

"I'll teach you how to play poker." He strolled in his big cavalry boots to the bedroom, where he removed a worn deck of cards from his saddlebags. Then he returned to the table.

"What'll we play for?" she asked.

"It wouldn't make sense for us to gamble for money, because whether I won or lost, it all comes from the same place." He snapped his fingers as if he'd just had a great idea. "I know — we can play Strip Poker."

She wrinkled her pretty nose. "What's that?"

"When one of us loses a game, that person has to remove an article of clothing. The person who has no more clothing left is the loser."

"It sounds like an awfully stupid game," she said, "and I'm sure I'll regret it for the rest of my life, but I'm so bored — go ahead and deal."

At the other end of town, the cowboys from

the Circle K were arriving, led by Jay Krenshaw and Otis Puckett. They rode down the main street and came to a stop in front of Gibson's General Store. Only a few horses were tied to the rail, and none carried the Bar T brand.

"They ain't here yet," Jay said.

Puckett climbed down from his horse, threw the reins over the rail, and headed for the door. A cowboy opened it, and Puckett entered the saloon. Straight ahead was the bar, with two bartenders grinning at him. "Howdy," one said.

Puckett's belly hung over his belt, his shirt was unevenly tucked, and he looked like a slob, but there was a mean gleam in his eye as he climbed onto a stool. "Coffee."

The bartender poured a steaming cup and pushed it toward Puckett. The gunfighter raised it to his lips as the other cowboys crowded around the bar. Jay Krenshaw sat at the far end, where he'd be out of the line of fire.

Puckett had shot men in houses, hotels, saloons, and once he'd even ventilated a gentleman's head during a solemn church service. But most of the time it was a saloon, not very different from the one he was in. Just another night's work, he tried to convince himself.

But he knew it was a lie. Tonight he'd be

facing another fast hand, and one younger than he. Puckett knew that he was losing his powers gradually, but the Kid would improve for another several years. Puckett couldn't take the Kid lightly, since he'd out-drawn Saul Klevins. The gunfighter spat into the brass cuspidor. I've practiced all week, and still as good as ever.

Some Circle K cowboys sat at tables, while others drank at the bar. It wasn't their typical Saturday night in Shelby, and they were jumpy, ill at ease, and fearful, because flying bullets sometimes struck the wrong cowboy. They had no personal stake in the outcome, and hoped it would end quickly.

Raybart sat with his glass of whiskey in the darkest corner. He didn't want to be Peter, who denied Christ three times on that tragic night of nights. Raybart's hand fingered the note in his pocket. How can I give it to 'im without a-gittin' caught?

At the end of the bar, Jay Krenshaw savored his glass of whiskey. His nose might never be straight, and chewing would be a problem for the rest of his life, but at last his hour of vengeance was at hand. He yearned to see Duane Braddock lying dead on the floor, so that he could laugh at him.

Mr. Gibson entered the saloon from the corridor in back, and was struck by a sense of foreboding. Instead of the usual drunken merriment, his saloon had the atmosphere of a wake. Maybe I need some musicians, or a dancing girl.

His ambition was a hotel, saloon, and gambling hall towering into the sky like a mountain, with bright lights, and throngs of well-dressed couples strolling about with drinks in their hands. Maybe someday, he thought. John Jacob Astor started with a few beaver skins, and became the richest man in New York.

The cowboys, bartenders, and hired gun sat with their dreams and demons, waiting for *it* to happen, only the entrepreneur hadn't a clue about what *it* was. A few men played cards, but it was difficult to concentrate on the game. Other cowboys were afraid to talk, because they didn't want to disturb the fat man at the bar.

They continually glanced at him, because it wasn't every day that they saw a famous fast hand. It was difficult for them to believe that such an odd-looking person could be a killer. His legs were short, and he had virtually no shoulders as though he'd never worked in his life. Yet they'd seen him practicing behind the main house, and no one dared antagonize such blinding speed.

They waited and sipped whiskey in the silence; even the bartenders felt obliged to keep their mouths shut. Damnation and the faint trace of brimstone filled the air as the minutes ticked away in the cuckoo clock above the bar. Puckett was beginning to feel the strain. He wanted a stiff shot of whiskey, but had to remain steady if he was going to shoot The Pecos Kid.

"Somebody's comin'," said Reade. He looked out the window, and his voice fell in disappointment. "It's soldiers."

The men in blue, off duty at last, piled into the saloon and assaulted the bar. Puckett arose from his stool and meandered to a table against the left wall, where he sat alone, pleased that his audience was growing. He'd give the soldiers something to remember for the rest of their lives.

A tiny worm of doubt continued to plague him, because the Pecos Kid had shot Saul Klevins. Was it beginner's luck, or raw talent? Maybe Saul Klevins had been a fraud, and really didn't have a fast hand. There were so many variables, Puckett was getting a headache. *I wish he'd show up, so I can get this mess over with.*

At first he thought it was blood rushing past his ears, but then became aware of hoofbeats on the street outside. Reade dashed to the window, and his face brightened. "It's the Bar T!"

All eyes turned to Puckett, for the time had come to earn his money. He leaned against the wall, lowered his hat over his eyes, and watched the door. Reade was supposed to point out which one was the Pecos Kid, and then the fun would start.

They heard cowboys in front of the saloon, and the jangling of spurs. Horses snorted, a man laughed, and somebody shouted, "Whoopee!" The Bar T had arrived for their big bachelor party, but it was going to be a funeral.

The door was thrown open, and a cowboy appeared, followed by others. The men from the Bar T swaggered into the saloon, and Puckett scanned them quickly, trying to pick out the Pecos Kid. His eyes fell on a glittering silver concho hatband, and the youthful handsome face beneath it. A chill came over Puckett as Reade indicated him clandestinely. The Pecos Kid vaguely resembled the Angel of Death whom Puckett had seen in his dreams.

He noted the Kid's relaxed manner as he made his way to the bar. The Kid had wide shoulders and a narrow waist, exactly the opposite of Puckett, and the gunfighter felt a twinge of envy. I'll bet Rosita would fall for him, if she ever saw him, but she never will, and neither will anybody else after tonight.

A Bar T cowboy shouted, "Here's to Duane and Miss Phyllis!"

They touched Duane's glass, then bolted down the whiskey, but Puckett noticed that the Pecos Kid only took a sip. A terrific commotion occurred at the bar as cowboys slapped Duane on the back, shook his hand, and wished him well. Even Sparky was elated, jumping around and snapping his jaws in acknowledgment of his boss's great good fortune.

At the far end of the bar, Jay Krenshaw nearly choked on bitter rage. To see his enemy receiving accolades was almost too much to bear. Jay wished he were the object of such adulation, respect, and comradely love. But he was despised even by his father, and men followed his orders for the money, like whores.

Against the back wall, Raybart arose from his chair. The time had come to make his move, and he didn't dare waste another moment. He pulled the slip of paper out of his pocket, held it tight in his fist, and strolled toward the bar as if to refill his glass.

He entered the cluster of cheering Bar T cowboys, and it reminded him of Jerusalem when Christ arrived on the back of a donkey, the throngs throwing palm leaves, and shouting *Hosanna in the highest!* He lurched drunkenly toward Duane, bumped against him, and placed the slip of paper into his hand. "Sorry," he burped, and then leaned against the bar. "Whiskey!"

Raybart didn't dare turn around, so he couldn't see the paper fall to the floor. Duane bent over to pick it up, for he'd felt it press urgently into his palm. He raised himself to his full height, and read the scrawled warning:

> *Fat man been hired to kill you. Git the hell outer here fast as you kin.*
>
> *a friend*

Just when everything had been going so well, he had to receive such a warning. Cowboys continued to congratulate him, and he mumbled his thanks as he scrutinized the usual crowd of cowboys and soldiers. He glanced at Jay Krenshaw at the end of the bar and noticed the position of his right hand.

Duane continued to scan faces, but nothing seemed threatening. He was looking for a big, fat man, not a short, roly-poly fellow sitting at a table in the darkness. He believed that he could handle Krenshaw, and the Bar T cowboys would back him if anyone else tried to jump in. Maybe it's a joke, and I can't just walk out of here in the middle of the party. McGrath and the others'll think I've gone loco. So he raised his glass, and decided to stay awhile.

"I always hoped Miss Phyllis'd notice me someday," said Don Jordan as he slammed his palm on Duane's shoulder, "but how could I guess that she'd fall in love with *you!*"

The good-natured banter went back and forth as bartenders filled glasses. No one from the Bar T noticed that the Circle K cowboys were unusually subdued, and an overweight stranger was arising from his table against the left wall.

Otis Puckett had studied his opponent carefully, and knew what he was up against. But an experienced fast hand could defeat a flash in the pan any day, he told himself. He crossed the aisle and plunged into the array of tables, on his way to the bar. No one noticed him, until he approached the Bar T cowboys congregated around the Pecos Kid. They wouldn't move out of Puckett's way, so the gunfighter grabbed one by the scruff of his neck, and pushed him to the side.

The cowboy lost his balance and crashed into the nearby wall, suddenly electrifying the saloon. Men arose from tables, and a few Bar T cowboys went for their guns, but Punkett's hand dropped, and a split second later he was aiming his Colt toward them.

It was silent in the saloon, and everyone

heard a drop of water fall from the counter to the floor. All eyes ogled the fat cowboy, who said, "I'm here for Duane Braddock."

Duane had seen the draw, and now understood the import of the note. He wished he'd taken the advice, but too late now. All he could do was reply, "I guess that's me."

"My name's Otis Puckett. I'm a-goin' to shoot you, so say yer prayers."

"Whoa!" said a new voice. It was McGrath stepping forward, a friendly grin on his weatherbeaten visage. "Mister Puckett — I saw you at work some years ago in El Paso, but this boy ain't done nawthin' to you, and we're a-celebratin' his weddin' engagement. Why don't you have a drink with us, and cool off?"

"Out of the way," Puckett replied, "because lead's a-gonna fly in about a minute." The hired killer faced Duane. "I got no time to play with you, boy. Make your move."

"But . . . why do you want to kill me?" Duane asked, mystified.

"Business," spat Puckett.

Duane turned toward the end of the bar, and saw Jay Krenshaw with a faint grin covering his toothless mouth. Cold malevolence passed over Duane as the pieces came together in his mind. He broke into a cold sweat and hoped someone would stop the nightmare, but it didn't appear so. He'd plummeted from the pinnacle of life to the depths of hell in seconds. "Would you mind if I have another whiskey?" he asked. "You're really taking me by surprise."

"I ain't got time. Make yer move, or I'll make mine."

Duane spread his legs and dropped into his gunfighter's crouch. Powerful chemicals from glands working overtime dumped into his bloodstream, and his heart beat furiously. It was a showdown to the death, out of the blue, and he tried to remember everything that his mentor, Clyde Butterfield, had taught him. Then he gritted his teeth, measured his opponent, and reached for his Colt.

Observers afterward would argue over what happened next. Some thought Duane drew first, others Puckett, but all agreed that a dog had growled in the vicinity of Puckett's boots just as Puckett went for his gun. The professional killer was distracted for a moment, but then whipped out his Colt, took aim at the center of Duane's chest, and felt his head crack apart.

Somehow Duane fired the first shot, and it landed in the middle of Puckett's forehead. Puckett's eyes stared glassily as he limped from side to side, blood pumping out the hole. The famous fast hand dropped to his knees, took one last look at the man who'd ended his career, and pitched onto his face.

Gunsmoke filled the small, enclosed space, and every cowboy's ears rang. Duane turned, aiming his gun at Jay Krenshaw, who was in the act of drawing, his intention a fast shot in Duane's back. Jay's fingers hung in the air above his gun, an expression of horror forming over his face. Somehow, against all the odds, Duane Braddock had shot Otis Puckett! Jay didn't know what to make of it. It looked like he'd come to the end of his road.

But Duane found that he couldn't shoot a man in cold blood. "I'll give you a chance," he said. "Go ahead and draw."

"Not me," Jay replied in a shaky voice. "Yer too fast."

"You hired him to kill me, you sneaky son of a bitch!"

Jay pointed at the dead body of the fat gunfighter. "I never seed him afore in my life."

"Not true!" hollered Raybart, who pointed accusingly at Jay. "He's had Puckett at the ranch all week, and Puckett's was a-practicin' fer a-shootin' you!"

"Keep yer mouth shut!" screamed Krenshaw.

But Raybart had a strange holy gleam in his eye. "Today God has triumphed over the

Devil, my brethren! See it, and believe!"

"You little fuck!"

Krenshaw drew his Colt and fired at Raybart. The saloon echoed with the shot, the air became dense with gunsmoke, and Raybart collapsed onto the floor, a beatific smile on his face. "My Lord," he whispered, "I see you . . . waiting . . ."

Raybart went slack as his spirit departed. Duane wondered what his strange game had been as Krenshaw slowly holstered his gun. "I ain't a-gonna draw on you, Kid. If yer too fast fer Otis Puckett, yer too fast fer me."

Duane realized once again that he couldn't shoot anybody in cold blood, but still wanted revenge. So he holstered his gun, turned his back to Jay, and reached for his glass, hoping that Jay would attempt a dirty trick.

Something rustled behind him, like a sleeve moving up a man's arm when he reaches for his gun. Duane spun, yanked his Colt, and saw Krenshaw in the middle of his draw. Duane pulled his trigger, the gun fired, and Jay Krenshaw was drilled through the chest. Jay's gun fired at the floorboards, sending splinters whizzing through the air, then he sagged downward, his eyes glazing over; the gun dropped from his hand. He fell in a clump and lay still in a widening pool of blood.

Duane reached for his glass with his left hand, while the gun in his right emitted a wisp of smoke. He shook all over as he raised the glass; a few drops spilled onto his shirt. Everyone was looking at him as he struggled to calm down. He'd just shot two men in less time than it takes to smoke a cigarette.

Something rustled near his feet, and he looked at Sparky, his faithful dog. Duane patted Sparky's head. "Thanks, pardner. When I move into the main house, so do you."

The front door was thrown open, and Lieutenant Dawes stood there, his tunic half unbuttoned, hat crooked on the back of his head. He'd dressed hastily, and had an angry expression in his eyes as he stepped into the saloon, service revolver in hand. "What the hell's going on here?"

Sergeant Mahoney saluted and gave his report. "There was a shootin', sir. That man," he pointed to Puckett, "braced Mister Braddock, but Mister Braddock won the draw. Then Mister Krenshaw shot that cowboy" — he pointed at Raybart — "and after that, he tried to shoot Mister Braddock in the back, but Braddock fired first."

Lieutenant Dawes took in the bloody scene, trying to understand how such incredible mayhem could occur a short distance from where he'd been engaged in a transcendent act with his wife. Then his eyes fell on Duane leaning one elbow on the bar, sipping a glass of whiskey.

Dawes was in an extremely filthy mood, due to the interruption. It had been, without question, the most passionate instant of his life, and Duane Braddock had wiped it away with the pull of a trigger. Before the West Pointer could stop himself, the words were out of his mouth, "You're under arrest! Drop that gun, or I'll shoot you where you stand!"

Duane contemplated a quick draw, but Lieutenant Dawes aimed his service revolver steadily, and Duane figured that a man couldn't become an officer unless he knew how to shoot straight. "Krenshaw hired this professional gunfighter to kill me," he explained. "Then Krenshaw tried to shoot me in the back. You're going to arrest me for that?"

"You're goddamned right. Sergeant Mahoney — take his gun."

Mahoney wasn't sure Duane would give it up easily. It was a tense moment, then the Bar T ramrod spoke, his hands spread in supplication. "But he was only defendin' hisself. You cain't arrest a man fer that in Texas!"

Before Lieutenant Dawes could open his mouth, somebody shouted, "That's a lie!" It was Reade, still earning his pay. "Braddock suckered Jay into the fight, so's he could kill him!"

A hubbub filled the saloon as both bunkhouses moved into battle positions. A gun fired suddenly, and a bullet burrowed into the ceiling. "Hold it right there!" hollered Dawes, with an irresistible argument in his right hand. "Take these men's weapons," he said to Sergeant Mahoney.

"You ain't a-gittin' my gun!" said Uncle Ray, whipping it out quickly, for he'd shot a few people, too, in his long and checkered career.

"Mine neither!" added Ross, hauling iron.

Guns were drawn all across the saloon, and Duane wasn't about to get left out. He stood with his back to the bar, gun in hand, ready for anything. Dawes looked at the sea of weapons and realized that the situation had deteriorated considerably since his arrival. "A crime has been committed here," he said levelly, "and I'm the lawfully constituted authority. If you civilians don't start obeying my commands, I'll have to treat you like Comanches. Sergeant Mahoney — tell the men to open fire at the civilian nearest him on my command."

The cowboys became uncertain as soldiers readied their rifles. McGrath spread his great arms once more and smiled ingratiatingly.

"Yer a-makin' a mountain out of a molehill, sir. No jury'll convict that man fer defendin' his life."

"The jury can do what they like, but right now he's under arrest for murder, and I'm taking him away. He'll come peacefully, or he'll come feet first, but as long as there's the Fourth Cavalry — he's coming."

Duane could shoot Lieutenant Dawes, plus a few innocent bluecoats, but after that they'd get him, and maybe some of his friends would be killed. "I know why you're doing this," Duane said, narrowing his eyes at Dawes. "Once your wife was my woman, and it pisses you off!"

Lieutenant Dawes faced the greatest temptation of his life, but he was a fiercely disciplined man. "Sergeant Mahoney, I believe I just gave you an order."

"Yes, sir." Sergeant Mahoney advanced toward Duane, service revolver in his right hand, and left hand open. "Hand it over," he said to Duane, "or yer a dead son of a bitch."

Duane passed the Colt handle first, Sergeant Mahoney accepted it, turned toward Lieutenant Dawes, and said, "His weapon is secured, sir."

"Take him to the camp, tie him up, and post a guard. And if he tries to escape, do *not* aim over his head, and do *not* aim at his legs. You will aim at the center of the prisoner's back, and *bring him down!*"

Lieutenant Dawes felt exhausted as he hung his hat near the door of his home.

"What happened?" asked Vanessa, waiting in the parlor. "Did anybody get hurt?"

Lieutenant Dawes poured whiskey into a glass, then sat on the makeshift sofa, its green lumber creaking as his weight settled. "Two civilians dead, and guess who pulled the trigger?"

Her face drained of color. "Duane?"

"Evidently Jay Krenshaw hired somebody to kill him, but your boy got the drop on him. Then he turned around and shot Krenshaw for good measure. The Pecos Kid is having himself a helluva night, but I charged him with murder, and that ought to calm him down for a while."

"But," Vanessa protested, "it sounds like he was only protecting himself."

"I have reason to believe that he killed

Krenshaw in cold blood, but made it look like a shootout so that he could plead self-defense. You weren't there, you haven't seen a damned thing, but you've already decided that he's innocent. Very interesting, the way you always defend that reckless little killer."

"That's not why you arrested him," she replied in a deadly voice. "You can fool others, but I know you too well. You arrested him out of ordinary disgusting human jealousy."

"It may please your vanity to think that, but I arrested him fundamentally because he shot two men. And speaking of vanity, would you care to explain why a woman your age might run off with a desperado like that? Were you trying to convince yourself that you were still young, or were you so jaded that you needed a killer to make you feel alive?"

His words hit her like a slap in the face, and she lost her Charleston composure. "You damned Yankee!" she screamed. "I've had just about enough of your bullshit! When the next stagecoach comes, I'm going to be on it! Until then, I'll thank you to stay out of this house!"

Duane held his hands over his head as soldiers marched him through the encampment. They came to a wagon loaded with supplies, a canvas roof stretched overhead. "Sit in front of that wheel," Sergeant Mahoney ordered.

"You're not going to tie me down, are you, Sarge?" Duane asked in disbelief.

"I said sit in front of the wheel."

Duane panicked and dashed toward the open sage, but a trooper jumped in front of him, blocking his path. Duane tried to wrestle the rifle from the trooper's hands, but then received another rifle butt upside his head. His vision blurred, he lost his balance, and felt himself being dragged to the wheel. The soldiers tied his hands to the spokes, then wrapped rope around his ankles and bound them together tightly.

"That ought to hold the li'l fucker fer a while," Sergeant Mahoney said. "Private Jansen, you let 'im git away, you'll serve his time."

"He ain't goin' nowheres," replied the guard.

Duane's head felt whacked in two as he watched the soldiers march away. Private Jansen sat nearby, cradled the rifle in his arms, and said, "I wouldn't try nothin' if'n I was you. I'd blow yer fuckin' brains out, rather'n serve yer time."

Sweat poured from Duane's face, like Christ in the Garden of Olives. Never in his life had he been tied down, and he felt like shrieking. He felt crushed, suffocated, and his body broke into a million itches that he couldn't scratch. They'd tied his hands too securely, and his fingertips proceeded to go numb.

He wished he were back at the bunkhouse, entwined in his blankets and dreams of Phyllis Thornton. This is what can happen to a cowboy who goes to town on a Saturday night. God only knows how I'll get out of this one, and they might even hang me!

Phyllis sat at the hayloft window, watching for Duane. She thought he'd be back by now, and wondered if he'd forgotten her during his party in Shelby.

She'd put on her cowboy outfit and snuck out of the house like a Comanche, eluding the guard. Then she slipped into the barn, climbed the ladder to the hayloft, and had been waiting impatiently ever since. She couldn't wait to see him, but no matter how hard she searched, she couldn't detect his silver conchos flashing in the moonlight. More time elapsed, and she began to fidget.

She wondered if the Comanches had got him, or if he'd been in a fight with another cowboy. Maybe he's forgotten all about me, she speculated. He's probably got his arms around some Mexican girl, or maybe he's passed out drunk in a corner, with a cuspidor for his pillow. If he doesn't show up, I'll break off the damned engagement. I couldn't marry a man who could *forget* about me.

She heard faint rumblings in the distance and thought it rolling thunder, but then gradually it became a large number of horses coming fast. She knew that strangers in the night meant trouble and feared that something had happened to Duane. She ran across the hayloft and descended the ladder swiftly.

Meanwhile, on the front porch, the cowboy on guard also heard hoofbeats. He charged into the house and knocked loudly on Big Al's door. "Riders a-comin'!"

Big Al reached underneath his pillow, drew out his Colt, jumped toward the window, and looked outside. Hoofbeats pounded closer, and he wondered if they were Comanches. Myrtle put on her robe and took down the shotgun from the wall. Big Al jumped into his boots, dropped his hat on his head, sailed through the door, and joined the cowboy guard on the front porch.

Riders came into view, and Big Al let out a sigh of relief. It was his own cowboy crew, and McGrath rode in front like a calvary colonel. He drew back his reins as he came abreast of the house, his leg was over the saddle before his horse came to a halt, and he dropped to the ground. His men followed him up the lawn to where Big Al and Myrtle stood on the porch.

"Duane's been arrested by the army," McGrath reported. "Jay Krenshaw hired somebody to shoot Duane, but Duane outdrew the son of a bitch. Then Jay tried to shoot Duane in the back, but Duane plugged him first. Next thing we knew, Lieutenant Dawes arrested Duane for murder, and he's in the army camp, tied to a wagon like a dog!"

Big Al didn't have to think about it. "Have one of them cowboys saddle my horse!"

Myrtle asked her husband, "Where the hell do you think you're going!"

"We're a-gonna turn Duane loose!"

"Get ready to fight the Fourth Cavalry, because that's what it'll take. The best thing would be for us to talk to that lieutenant *reasonably* first thing in the morning. You can't jail a man because he defended himself, and if the lieutenant is too dumb to see that, we'll hire the best lawyer we can find. But if you ride to that army post in the middle of the night, there'll be a massacre."

Big Al rubbed his cheek thoughtfully. "Mebbe we'd better think this through, but I'll tell you this: Just as sure as I'm a-standin' here — when I get through with that fancy-pants lieutenant, he'll be a-walkin' a post in *Alaska!*"

Duane slept fitfully, tied to the wagon wheel. His bones and muscles ached, but he could do nothing to ease the pain. There were moments when he awakened suddenly and nearly panicked. It was terrifying to be helpless and unable to move in a land of snakes, scorpions, and Comanches.

He hung from the wagon wheel, and found himself detesting the lieutenant who'd arrested him. *If I ever get my hands on him, God help him.* He saw something move, and the guard aimed his rifle in the direction of the sound. "Halt! Who goes there!"

Sparky came into view, chin low to the ground, wagging his tail sadly. He walked past the guard, came to a stop in front of Duane, and gazed into his eyes.

"I wish you knew how to untie knots," Duane said.

But I don't, Sparky's eyes seemed to say.

The dog lay beside Duane and placed his chin on Duane's leg. *I'll get out of this mess sooner or later,* Duane thought optimistically. *They can't hold me for defending myself.* He tried to sleep, but couldn't find a comfortable spot on the wagon wheel; his spine felt as if tiny pins were sticking into it. Night breezes fluttered the canvas of tents, and he heard a man and woman arguing somewhere in the distance, but figured it was a bad dream as he drifted in and out of slumber.

Vanessa and Lieutenant Dawes faced each other across the dining room table, and they'd been going at it for hours, hurling insult after recrimination, clawing into each other's most sensitive spots.

"I never realized," Vanessa said, "how petty you could be! I thought you were a gentlemen, but you're a horrible person!"

"You think you're so beautiful," he retorted, "that I'd arrest somebody because of you? How little you understand me, but what else could I expect from an adventuress who ran off with an eighteen-year-old killer!"

"He's *not* a killer, and I wish you'd stop saying that! It's not his fault that he stands out in a crowd, and everybody wants to shoot him. Is he supposed to cooperate with them?"

"If he'd been five feet tall, and his nose had been three inches longer, you would never have looked at him twice. It's his pretty face that attracts you, just as my steady army paycheck lured you into our so-called marriage. Have you ever thought of doing it for love, Vanessa?"

She threw a pot at him, which he caught in midair, but he wasn't fast enough to prevent a dish from breaking against the wall over his head. Cowering, blocking airborne plates and other kitchen utensils, all he could do was conduct a strategic retreat, and file for divorce. They'd laugh at him at the Officers' Club, but it was better than being drummed out of the army for murdering his wife.

"I regret the day I ever set eyes on you!" he shouted as he headed for the door. "You're nothing but a high-classed slut!"

"Weakling!" she shrieked. "Coward! Jealous bird-brained idiot!"

But he was already out the door, headed for the army post, his stomach like a den of angry rattlesnakes. Behind him, he could hear more china and crockery bursting against the walls of his former home. Lieutenant Dawes shook with rage, most of it directed toward himself. Why did I marry that crazy woman? I didn't even know her! This is why people are supposed to have long engagements, so they can get to know each other. I was lonely and desperate, and now I'm worse off than before.

He came to the long row of tents, grumbling about women. They all pretend to be great ladies, but when nobody is looking, they sleep with filthy bums. You can't trust them, and they're all crazy. He approached the wagon where the prisoner was held, and the guard jumped to his feet. "Halt — who goes there!"

Lieutenant Dawes identified himself, and the guard permitted him to pass. Duane opened his eyes sleepily, and Sparky raised his chin as the Lieutenant kneeled before his prisoner.

"You've got people fooled," Lieutenant Dawes said, "but you're just a slimy little killer, and the sooner you hang, the better the world will be. I wish you'd try to escape, so that I can shoot you."

"It was self-defense, and you know it," Duane replied through his teeth. "You're exceeding your authority."

"I'll leave it to the judge to decide, and I hope that he hangs you, you little son of a bitch."

Duane made a tight little smile. "Next time you see Vanessa, say hello for me."

Lieutenant Dawes wanted to draw his service revolver and put one between Duane's eyes, but instead mumbled something incoherent, and headed for his command post tent, where he sat upon the cot and stared at the darkness. I got married to escape this goddamned lonely life, but now I'm lonelier than ever, thanks to that murderous little varmint. If he thinks he's getting off easily, he's in for a surprise. So far he's killed two men, ruined my marriage, and undermined my career. I hope the judge takes his own sweet time to dispose of the case, and the Pecos Kid rots on that wagon wheel.

Or maybe I should simply shoot him and say that he tried to escape.

On a barren far-off range, two horses galloped through the night, kicking clods of dirt behind them. One of the animals, a chestnut stallion, was riderless, while Phyllis Thornton sat low on the other, working with the motions of the horse's great musculature. She wore her cowboy outfit and a Mexican poncho that concealed a gun belt with one Colt in the holster and another jammed into the waist. Her saddlebags contained more guns and ammunition, and a Henry rifle rattled in its scabbard attached to the saddle.

The two horses were the best that her father owned, and she'd stolen them along with food, money, and additional clothes. She was on her way to Shelby, to free Duane from the Fourth Cavalry. She couldn't let Duane spend the next few weeks tied to a wagon wheel, while waiting for the slow wheels of injustice to turn.

The horses' hooves thundered against the ground as they raced toward Shelby. Phyllis believed that she didn't have a moment to lose, because for all she knew, a Circle K cowboy might be sneaking up on Duane that very moment to put a bullet into his skull. Somehow she had to turn him loose, no matter what the price. He was her first love, and she had to stand by her man.

She knew that her future had taken a dramatic new direction when she'd stolen the horses and guns, but she couldn't sleep knowing Duane was a prisoner of the Fourth Cavalry. The legal system might spit him into a jailhouse, or onto a gallows.

She felt as if he were part of her, and anything that he suffered, she suffered. We'll go to Mexico, where nobody knows us, and we'll come back after the lawyers settle the mess. Lights flickered in the distance as she approached her rendezvous with destiny. Something told her that she was being vainglorious, but a strange insistent madness drove her onward.

A knife was sheathed in her right cowboy boot, and she had enough ammunition to wage a small war. Maybe she'd get shot, possibly she'd be arrested, but she had to try. She was at the age where she didn't worry about unpleasant consequences, as if her youth and sense of right and wrong could defeat anything.

She drew closer to town, and uttered a prayer as the windstream creased the brim of her white cowboy hat. Lord, if you can't help

Duane Braddock now, just don't help the Fourth Calvary.

She slowed the horses on the main street of Shelby, and they snorted, shaking their great heads as they made their way toward the army encampment. They passed Gibson's General Store and she looked through the window at soldiers gathered around the bar, while others were passed out at a table. She found a hitching rail near the encampment, dismounted, and tethered the horses. Then she took a drink of water from her canteen, checked the guns, and removed a chunk of meat and loaf of bread from one of the saddlebags. She didn't bother loosening the cinches beneath the saddles, because she intended to be back shortly, with Duane. Here goes, she thought optimistically as she headed toward the army encampment.

She'd never lied on a grand scale before, and hoped she could bring it off now. She'd noticed that men often became nervous around her, and hoped to use it to her advantage. She needed Duane with an almost engulfing physical passion. She straightened her spine, sucked in her tummy, and stepped forward with her cowboy hat slanted low over her eyes. Ahead of her, the sentry stood with his rifle at high port arms. "Halt — who goes there!"

"My name's Phyllis Thornton," she said sweetly, making a big Texas smile. "I've brought Duane Braddock some food." She held up the chunk of meat and loaf of bread.

"Wa'al, I don't know," the trooper stuttered, "it's late at night . . . the lieutenant gave orders. Mebbe you should come back in the mornin' and ask the lieutenant."

"But I just want to give him some food. Wouldn't you be hungry if you were tied to a wagon wheel?" She reached into her pocket, pulled out a five dollar coin, and held it out to him. "Next time you come to town, have a drink on me."

The trooper earned thirteen dollars per month, and the temptation was too great. He snatched the coin from her hand. "Don't make no trubble, 'cause I'd shoot you just like I'd shoot a man."

Phyllis heard men snoring in their tents as she made her way toward the wagon indicated by the guard. It loomed out of the darkness, and she perceived Duane tied to the wheel with his arms outstretched.

The second guard spun around. "Halt — who goes there!"

"Howdy," Phyllis replied, noticing Duane stirring against the wheel, while Sparky looked at her suspiciously. "I'm here to bring the prisoner some food."

"Now?" the guard asked querulously. "Are you loco?"

"People get hungry at night, too, you know." She held up the beef and bread. "Want some?"

Duane stared at her, wondering if he were hallucinating. He tried to move, but the rope held him tightly to the wheel.

The soldier growled, "I think you'd better get out of here, or I'll call the sergeant of the guard."

"Where's he at?" she asked, looking around the encampment.

The soldier pointed his rifle toward another group of tents. "Thataway."

Phyllis pulled out her Colt while his attention was distracted. He heard the click of her hammer being thumbed back, and turned to see a gun barrel pointed at his nose.

"Lay your rifle gently on the ground," she said, "and if you try something dumb, I won't hesitate to shoot. Look into my eyes, and you'll see that I'm capable of it."

The soldier peered into those gleaming orbs and saw reckless abandon shining brightly. "You won't get away with this," he said. "Lieutenant Dawes will chase you all the way to Mexico."

"Untie Mister Braddock, or I'll shoot you where you stand." She closed one eye, aimed down the barrel at his nose, and her knuckle whitened around the trigger.

"Yes, ma'am."

The soldier kneeled behind Duane and untangled the knots; circulation returned to Duane's fingers.

"You took a helluva chance," Duane told her, unlimbering his joints.

"They're not keeping you tied up as long as I'm alive," she replied, passing him a Colt.

He disarmed the guard and tied him to the wheel. "Don't make a sound," Duane warned him, "or she'll shoot, and I do believe that she's crazy enough to do it."

Phyllis knelt beside him, cut a length of cloth from the soldier's trousers, and tied a gag around his mouth. The soldier protested, but only faint gurgling sounds came out.

"I've got horses near the general store," Phyllis said.

They ducked into the shadows, ran across the sage, and reentered town through a back alley. Halfway down it, Duane placed his hand on her shoulder. "I don't know if we're going to get away with this," Duane said, "but if not . . ."

He took her in his arms and felt her body tightly against him as his lips searched for hers. Her fingernails dug into his back, their tongues touched tenderly, and Duane felt a

326

rush of lust. He wanted to kiss her naked breast, but there'd be time for that later, he hoped. He pushed her away, but she clung to him, unwilling to let go.

"Let's get out of this town," he uttered, "and don't stop for anything."

He took her hand and led her toward the street. With his back to the wall, he looked both ways, then nodded. They rushed across the open space, untied the horses, and she jumped onto Suzie's back, while he took the chestnut stallion. They wheeled the horses in the middle of the street, applied spurs, and the animals broke into a gallop, thundering out of town, heading toward the gardens of Mexico.

CHAPTER 16

Myrtle rushed into the kitchen and shouted: "She's gone!"

Big Al looked up from the thick slice of bacon that he was slicing. It was dawn at the Bar T, and the ranch just coming to life. "Are you sure she's not wandering around someplace?"

"I looked everywhere, and the cowboys told me that two horses are missing from the corral!"

Big Al leaned back in his chair, and it didn't take long to figure out which direction she went. "I'll tell McGrath to saddle the horses. We're going to town."

"I hope that the Comanches didn't get her," Myrtle replied, wringing her hands. "My little baby — gone."

"Looks like she ain't a little baby anymore," Big Al said ruefully as he headed for the door.

★ ★ ★

"Sir?"

Lieutenant Dawes lay on his cot fully clothed, with his boots off. The faint glow of dawn came to him from the crack of the tent. "What is it?"

Sergeant Mahoney stood at attention, knees quivering with the cold. "Prisoner has escaped, sir. Miss Thornton showed up in the middle of the night and got the drop on the guard."

Lieutenant Dawes was astounded at the news, and at first couldn't speak. Then he recovered his voice, and ordered, "Round up the scouts, and have the men prepare for a long pursuit."

Sergeant Mahoney ran from the tent, leaving Lieutenant Dawes alone. The West Pointer sat on his cot, rolled a cigarette, and puffed thoughtfully. Probably the Comanches will get them.

He looked at himself in the mirror, straightened his yellow bandanna, and strolled out of the tent. A scene of furious activity greeted his eyes as soldiers prepared for the pursuit. It'd take at least an hour before they were ready, so Lieutenant Dawes headed toward town.

He felt as if an enormous weight had been removed from his shoulders. Now he didn't have to worry about the Pecos Kid, and the matter would resolve itself without embarrassment to his career. In a few months, everybody would forget the Pecos Kid. He'll get what he deserves someday, the little bastard.

He arrived at his former house and entered the bedroom. Still dark, he could perceive Vanessa's languorous form beneath the covers. He sat on the edge of the bed, and said, "Guess what?"

She opened eyes still red with crying. "What are *you* doing here?" she asked sleepily. "I thought I told you to go away."

"Duane Braddock is on the loose. Seems that Phyllis Thornton busted him out of the encampment last night."

Vanessa sat bolt upright in bed and smiled. "Really?"

"They're probably headed for Mexico — crazy goddamned kids. They'll end in the bellies of buzzards, if they're not careful."

"You'd like that, I'll bet," she said sarcastically. "And by the way, do I have to write to Colonel MacKenzie to keep you away?"

"I've been up all night," he said, "and I wanted to tell you that if I'm jealous of Duane Braddock, it's only because of you."

"Don't blame it on me," she replied, wagging her long index finger from side to side. "I haven't even spoken with him since the shindig, but you're a fool, and that's the source of our difficulties."

"I can't bear to think of you with somebody else. It's even making me physically ill. You're right — we should get a divorce. Perhaps I can slip Parson Jones a few dollars and tell him to forget that he ever married us."

"If that's the way you feel about it . . ."

She looked at his noble profile as he headed toward the door, and for the first time felt sympathetic toward him, instead of Duane. He'd said that love for her had made him jealous, and what was so wrong with that? "Wait a minute!" she called.

He turned slowly and looked at her sternly. "What is it this time?"

"If you weren't so thickheaded, I believe that we could be happy together."

"Unfortunately, I've been trained to examine facts objectively. When my wife continually tells me how wonderful Duane Braddock is, it makes me wonder why I married her."

"Perhaps I'm not always as considerate as I should be, but when you constantly belittle my former boyfriend, you also belittle me. He wasn't *that* bad."

There was silence as they gazed at each other in the increasing dawn light. Then he said, with a lump in his throat, "Do you think you could forgive me, and let me come back?"

"I don't enjoy sleeping alone either," she

said wearily. "Perhaps we could forgive each other?"

Dawn broke over the mountains, revealing a coyote sitting at the mouth of her cave. She scanned terrain intently, twitching her nose, looking for an old mule deer, or maybe a wayward rabbit. Her sharp eyes picked up objects in motion as she focused intently on two riders moving swiftly across the basin below. The coyote snarled in surprise at the unusual spectacle, for riders seldom came to this lonely end of Texas.

Then the coyote noticed a small dog following the riders. It was white, with black spots and much meat on his bones, but moving too quickly, and the coyote didn't feel like speeding first thing in the morning. The riders and dog swerved around a stand of cottonwood trees and continued down an arroyo.

Duane Braddock, Phyllis Thornton, and Sparky were running for their lives. They approached a trail that bisected their path, and Duane raised his hand. Phyllis slowed beside him, and Suzie raised her front hooves in the air, anxious to keep going.

"Why are we stopping?" Phyllis asked, her face covered with perspiration as Suzie danced around Duane's chestnut stallion.

Duane pulled his horse backward, until he was alongside Phyllis. Both animals felt wild, free, and eager to run. Saliva dripped from their lips, and their great eyes gleamed in the light of morning. Duane, too, was covered with sweat, and a stubble of beard made his features shadowy and sinister. "It's not too late for you to turn back," he said. "I'm sure that your father can get the law off your back, but if you come with me, there'll be Comanches and Apaches all the way to Mexico, plus bears, wild dogs, rattlesnakes, and scorpions. It's real easy to die on the desert, understand?"

Her cheeks were blotched with exertion, and she was covered with alkali dust. "If you can do it — I can do it."

He pointed his finger at her. "This is your last chance. From now on, we're on the dodge together. The law might get us, or we could run out of water. The injuns could stake me to an anthill, and turn you into a slave, after every warrior in the tribe has spent a night with you. We might even get hung by a posse."

She pulled out her Colt and grinned. "They'll never take me alive."

He laughed, but there was no time for mutual adoration. He wheeled his horse onto the trail leading to Mexico and kicked his spurs.

The animal leapt forward, Phyllis followed him, their mounts raced desperately across the plain, followed by Sparky and rays of morning sunlight glinting off Duane's silver concho hatband.

The coyote licked her chops hungrily as she watched them merge with the horizon, and then they disappeared.